Jimmy Boyle was born in 1944 and raised in Glasgow's notorious Gorbals area. His early years were spent in the grip of the Gorbals' culture and he embarked on a life of crime, eventually being sentenced to life in prison at the age of twenty-three for a murder he did not commit. The brutality of the prison regime is graphically described in his two autobiographies, *A Sense of Freedom*, which was also made into a film, and *The Pain of Confinement*. Since his release in 1982 Jimmy Boyle has founded and worked for Gateway Exchange, a centre to help young people at risk. He is also a playwright and renowned sculptor. He married Sarah Trevelyan in 1980 and they have two children.

Jimmy Boyle

Hero of the Underworld

A catalogue record for this book is available from
the British Library on request

The right of Jimmy Boyle to be identified as the author
of this work has been asserted by him in accordance with
the Copyright, Designs and Patents Act 1988

Copyright © Jimmy Boyle 1999

First published in 1999 by Serpent's Tail,
4 Blackstock Mews, London N4

Website: www.serpentstail.com

Phototypeset in Plantin by Intype London Ltd
Printed in Great Britain by Mackays of Chatham plc

10 9 8 7 6 5 4 3 2 1

Contents

A forethought   1
The Institution   3
The Abattoir   31
The Mortician   123
The Underworld   185
The Epilogue   209

A forethought . . .

In trying to describe the vacuum of my solitude, I can only compare its monotony to the constant drip of tap-water from the nearby sink. Thereafter, being a totally subjective experience, it defied description. What I became aware of after a while, however, was the way in which the aloneness allowed me time for profound thought; to think deeply about life and death, to probe and question the meaning of existence. These periods were so engrossing, that large blocks of time, including the dripping tap, vanished as though into a black hole in space. It was almost as if everything physical and material melted, momentarily, into some mysterious dimension, which then carried me off to a spiritual refuge, where my soul found succour. I often wondered, though I have no evidence to substantiate it, if this was nature's way of intervening, to ensure the survival of the human spirit. If so, why me, and did it do me any favours? I say this, for when re-emerging from this black hole, I seemed to be even more conscious of the brutality of my physical surroundings. Try as I might to get back to this mysterious refuge, I couldn't. I was often puzzled and frustrated by this, particularly as it compounded the powerlessness I felt in being held captive.

Although now, at this rather distant and reflective point of the experience, I can recall it in a less personal way, it did in reality have another side. In being a monastic type of existence, it was a piece of concentrated life, free from ordinary, day-to-day activity and distraction. And yet, its daily harshness brought me face to face with the cruelty of my guards, and the institutions which they served. Such was the severity of mistreatment and abuse handed out inside these places, that all of us were driven to the edge of the abyss, searching for a place of safety. During this search, some preferred to jump over the edge rather than endure more of what was on offer.

The Institution

The structure of the place, brick on brick, had monotony
built into its foundations. Clearly the architect was so badly
affected by the reality of his design, that a facile attempt
at camouflage by painting the metal bars failed miserably.
Indeed, their garish colour served only to reinforce the
totality of my confinement. Souls trapped in these circumstances suck every gasp of air allowed to circulate,
imagining that each gulp will secure inner freedom. The
imagination of each of us incarcerated, is the life-raft of
our very existence; it is this that protects me from the
reality of my surroundings. These walls and bars enclose
me with a tenacity that, at times, almost drives me crazy.
My relationship with them is similar to that of a parting
couple, still swirling in the lava of a volcanic fling: one
wants desperately to leave, while the other intensely refuses.
I pace this small square shouting, 'FUCK OFF!' It echoes
back. Echoes! Now there's a word to sum it all up. Every
part of my present life is dominated by echoes from the
past; thoughts, memories, and dreams. They are my sustenance, the only thing that remains uncontaminated and
that is truly mine. What a rare possession to have in this
place which dominates and controls every aspect of my
life. Here boredom is a disease that fragments one's will;
eventually it crushes the spirit. I've known giants to weep
in the face of this continuous void. Muscular morons with

hate in their veins who have challenged the system with such brute force, that it has taken an army of guards to get them into the sweat box. Despite this awesome strength, I have listened to them wilt and crack in this vacuum. Fear permeates this enclosed space, as we all lie in isolation, locked into small concrete boxes; someone sits, another curls up on the floor, yet more of us pace these tiny areas, lost in our thoughts.

At least once a month, someone is driven to that point of despair from which there is no return. It is as though the Grim Reaper, having selected that person, has suddenly scythed all hope from him. I can see in my mind's eye my neighbour pacing the concrete floor furiously. The low hum of his gibberish chants increase in volume throughout the day, long into the night. All of us, at some time or another, talk to ourselves. This is different. Soon his repetitive incantations so fill our ears to bursting point that there is loathing when he has endured one more day. I personally get furious when insanity lingers; my fear is that it could become infectious. When madness finally throttles the life out of him, it takes the form of highly erratic sounds; inaudible at first, almost as though it is burrowing deeper and deeper into his mind before reaching that final gasp, and you need only hear that gasp once to know exactly what it is. There is no escaping its presence as it shudders through thick walls to tell us that death has come. I exhilarate, just for a second, at the conclusion of another round. These are the heady days of my existence; the moments when life and death stand side by side. So intense, so concentrated is it that I feel as though I'm giving my brains a blow job then milking every little speck of come. This moment, mysteriously elongated, whacks me with a kaleidoscope of dreams and fantasies that spew like vomit to reveal images so revolting that they would melt your eyeballs. It's a roller-coaster ride where moods swirl a dance that takes me to new highs, and inevitably, to unimaginable depths. I am on the move and bewildered by it. This high velocity trip is crash-helmet material, pulling flesh taut, stretching first in one direction, before tugging in another. No sooner started than it ends. Always the ending is the same, me flat on the floor torn between a headful of dreams and heartful of pain. This aloneness is frightening, occasionally exciting, but oft-times frustrating. Best described, my gnawing sore is my present reality. All the more so with the knowledge that one more of our number now lies still and cold on the concrete floor in the nearby cage. Another heartbeat silenced forever.

Take this guy in the sweat box next to me; the only sound worth listening to is his bowel movement. He can blow his gas as sweet as Satchmo. That is, until the smell hits me. Then all I want to do is feed him a suppository full of Semtex. A giant of a man, he has yards of chest; an arsehole as big as Calcutta that smells every bit as bad. His inflated body weight is down to his being pumped full of Largactil over the years. That, however, is not an uncommon occurrence here.

I first set eyes on him in the long ward some time ago. On another occasion, when walking into the toilet recess, I found him sitting in front of an unconscious Guard, casually humming to himself 'These boots are made for walking . . .' Undoing the Guard's boots, he peeled off one sock first and then the other. Lifting the right foot he began by biting off one toe before moving on to another. The sound of cracking bone and wrenching grizzle combined with sounds from his trumpeting arsehole was music to my ears. I looked on, mesmerised. Here then was a phenomenon worthy of consideration, a contradiction in terms.

A triumph of willpower over anti-psychotic drugs. Drugs whose sole purpose was to fragment the thought processes. Yet here before my very eyes was the personification of concentration. Having reached toe number three, the Guard surfaced from deep comatose to scream in agony. The rest is history. The one lasting thought I had from this, admittedly a bit academic, was a curious fascination for the varying levels of unconsciousness we are capable of reaching. Why did that Guard suddenly become conscious after the third toe had gone?

The screws in here, mind you, they prefer to be referred to by the genteel title of Nurse, use instances like this to tell the world that we are all the same. And boy, do I get miffed. But who gives a shit? To them I am just a turd. When a lad misbehaves, like the Toe Cruncher, they parade it to the fucking world for two good reasons. One they use it to hike up their salaries and two, to make life more of a misery for us in here. No one ever asks us about them, and boy! could I tell a few tales. Chief Nurse Gorky, for instance, stands around the dormitory. The minute I see him do this I swallow a handful of laxatives, the super blasting, purgative type that take immediate effect. I simply haul the bed sheets around my neck, trapping the smell of warm shit. By the time lights-out comes round I'm as deadly as a skunk's nest. This, then, is my own invention; a modern-day chastity belt. Particularly when Gorky starts his rounds, prowling from bed to bed shagging the arse off heavily sedated patients. Sometimes doing three a night. Fuck knows what he got up to on the female side. More than once he's crept up on me, that cider-fuelled breath of his panting in my ear, 'Okay hot arse I'm a-coming in,' he'd say, sliding under the sheets. First time I used the laxative he rammed his hand under the sheets to grope my arse and grabbed a handful of the smelliest shit you could imagine. Particularly as we'd had ratatouille for tea that night. Gave it a fine texture it did. Did he or did he not bellow like a walrus? So loud was it he awakened old Nembutal Nick, whose nightly dosage of drugs is served to him by the shovelful. 'I've slept through six fires and eight suicides without ever waking,' he groaned next day. Mind you, this undercover tactic of mine came as a result of hard experience. As hard as you can get. Second night in the place and there he was piling his meat dagger into me; poor me bleeding and howling like a stuck pig. No sooner was he out than Fat Head was plugging away louder than a road driller. Stormy nights are not for me, I reckoned, so from that minute on I became the keenest laxative hoarder since Joe Walsh, the champion dabbity collector. Places like this attract these people like flies. It's almost as though it's a CV requirement for entry: 'No previous buggery record, no job. Next please!' The lechers on the staff, you can spot them a mile off. Forever scratching their balls, or eyeballing arses, taking every opportunity to rub against us.

As for the doctors, well, Snider had the distinction of being the first female to head such an institution, and it just so happened, she was the fucking worst. Rumour had it she got commission from the pharmaceuticals for giving out drugs. Her answer to everyone's problem was 'Give him a shot.' Often described as a woman of many talents, she was known to us on the inside as Mrs Hyde and on the outside as the renowned and respected Dr Jekyll; one face for their world, and another for ours. Snider came into her own on those infrequent days when The Watchdog Committee did their walkabout inspections. They'd speak to one or two residents in the day-room or dormitory asking about the level of treatment meted out by the staff. Little did they know Snider had beaten them to it by coming round earlier pumping us full of drugs. She wielded that needle like no one else on earth. If she'd played darts she'd be a world champion. As a result the Committee would see an assortment of loony tune characters whose faces were filled with blissful melancholy.

I broke the rules of course. It was one of those rare occasions when Snider failed to give me a shot. Cunningly positioning myself, so they'd pass close to me, I intervened.

'Excuse me, can I make a complaint?' I asked solicitously.

It stopped them dead in their tracks. Gorky and Fat Head following up the rear turned purple with rage. Snider, in lily-white coat, looked at me benignly. 'Ah, Ferguson, what's on your mind today then?' she asked.

The Watchdog Chairman turned to me. 'Okay, let's have it,' he demanded menacingly.

What a question, where do I start? 'It would be better if I could speak to the Committee in private, if you don't mind,' I suggested, looking at Fat Head and Gorky, both of whom were now trembling with fury. The benign look had fallen from Snider's face and had been replaced with one resembling that of a dangerous viper.

'Righto, in here,' said the Chairman, pushing me into the tiny staff room; plumping himself on the edge of the desk while his two colleagues stood against the closed door. Behind the Watchdog Chairman was a large observation window showing the faces of Snider, Fat Head and Gorky; over their shoulders peered the residents who, even in their condition, knew something momentous was taking place. They looked on expectantly like a group of glass-eyed penguins. I could actually see in them the faintest glimmer of hope. It's stupid, it's down-right naïve I know, but in that briefest of moments I felt heroic.

Before I could begin, the Chairman cautioned me by

saying, 'Ferguson, it's my duty to warn you that any complaints you may make must be proven, otherwise we will charge you for making false allegations. I've been coming to The Institution for a number of years, during that time there have been no complaints, indeed I've never seen a more contented bunch of residents since Dr Snider took over. Now young man, get on with it.'

I gulped. 'Well, mmm, Mr Gorky's been biffing us residents for a start,' I muttered hesitantly.

'What! You mean assaulting people? Chief Nurse Gorky?' He put his face close to mine.

'No, I mean. Well, that as well, but shagging us too.'

Leaping from the desk, he pushed aside his colleagues and opened the door. 'Dr Snider, this resident is sick beyond imagination. I will not listen to him for one moment longer.' He shook his head furiously as he stormed out of the day-room.

'I'm sorry sir, I should've warned you that Ferguson has a delusory complex but we'll increase his dosage,' said Snider, giving the nod. And I was hauled away by Gorky and Fat Head to the sweat box where I've been for eleven years now. Not that I'm complaining; being the sort of person I am, I always salvage the good from the bad. Here, the rules of the game change. No need for laxatives, or any of that nonsense.

Fat Head's with me at this moment; he's one of those guys with masses of lard in his head, and it shows. Strikes me that if he was decapitated, the blubber in his cranium would see the Eskimos through a decade of winters. It's all those years of being ordered around, never having to think for himself. I'm sure they have to wind him up every morning, he is the perfect toy guard. It comes as no surprise that he and Gorky are bosom pals. Each day at food-time one or other takes the trouble to give me a lunchtime surprise. Yesterday, the green pea soup had a sour cidery taste as a result of Gorky relieving himself in it. Today old Fat Head shows some artistic merit, green phlegm decorates the top of my dessert. Having shoved the plastic tray and spoon across the floor he slammed the door, a twisted smile on his lips. His eyeball now peers through the spyhole so let's tease him a bit. I let my spoon skirt around the edges, toying with the green lump. I bet the bastards are masturbating to this. The tightrope syndrome is ever present; by acknowledging their mind games I fall prey to them. Each encounter of this nature is designed to wear me down. Not a grand conspiracy of evildoers, but more a case of bored morons whiling away their equally monotonous days by breaking the spirits of their charges. The best that could be said for them both is that underneath all their nasty facade they're probably two nice chaps. Trouble is, it would take a team of coal-hungry miners a lifetime to find them. We could have an amicable time if only they didn't try to pull out the worst in me. I know that for them it's a matter of pride to have every single one of us exactly where, and in what condition, they want us. This place is full of faces congealed in deadpan, staring out of their boxes; witless in their zombified state. Amid this I struggle to keep my head.

Look what happened to Handgrenade Austin for bombing his lethal fists into other people's faces, grinding them to a pulp. Gorky and Fat Head, ably assisted by the voluptuous Ms Snider, set to work imploding chemical cocktails to defuse the power of his blows. Late at night he'd lie rollicking on the floor shouting, 'My arse is like a fucking pin cushion!' It wasn't so much that they succeeded, it was the fact that they rendered him blind in the process. The sound of Handgrenade as he shuffles along the corridor terrifies me. Over and over he shouts to no one in particular, 'They've turned the lights out.'

Rumour had it that Snider, as a student, was a great admirer of the late Dr Walter Freeman, well-known lobotomist. It was said that she bid in auction for his leucotomes, the knives especially designed for the operation. Apparently the blade often broke and got lost in the patient's brain, sometimes being successfully located and extracted with a fair dollop of brain tissue. Someone whispered that Handgrenade was given a lobotomy by Snider with these very same knives. Trouble is, in here it's impossible to tell fact from fiction. Quite often that which is consigned to the latter turns out to be the former. I'm sure the tell-tale sign of drill holes on his forehead would confirm or deny the rumour, but here in the sweat box the faces of others are rarely seen. Oh sweet Jesus, may the winds of change storm through the gates and set me free! I am slightly out of touch with the ways of the world, partly disorientated, almost alienated. I shouldn't let small things like this get to me, gotta keep a sense of perspective, remembering always to look at the whole picture, keeping it there in front of me in cinemascope, thinking, visualising, conceptualising. Trying like fuck to keep faith in human nature. Each time I tell myself this, something else comes along to challenge it. And yet, sitting here, I munch and crunch my food, chew it, swallow it, digest it, manure it, and then sewer it. Down there it stinks of it. Meanwhile Fat Head's saucer eye monitors my movements and I urge myself to play to the crowd. Raising an imaginary glass to the Dionysian God of wine, women and song, I try hard not to vomit as I centre his gob on my spoon. Shaking its jelly composition, I lift it slowly to my lips, tilt it into my mouth and begin munching it scrumptiously. His eye is birling with joy, popping with ecstasy and I can just imagine him

masturbating behind the door. I show no hint of distaste.
Damn these bastards to hell. Internally I reel and fall, yet
I show no emotion, and by doing so reduce the extent of
his victory. In this way I eke out fragments of rebellion to
nourish my soul and spirit.

But there is a price to pay, in that I become a divided
self. Whilst the facade portrays a bland emotionless
exterior, the knockabout emotions run rampant inside. I
am alone and vulnerable through making immense efforts
to heave myself out of this abyss. Seeking that point of
relief where all of it ceases to exist; the bricks, the bars,
the walls, the darkness. Away from this nightmare. I desire
that moment when, as in a clandestine love affair, the
elusive mistress appears before me, naked. Body to body,
skin-tight; pubic hairs entangled as we lick, suck and fuck.
She reaches deep inside me to caress my pain, and in one
moment end these years of agony. Long dead emotions
resurrected; a twitching groin bringing fire and life to my
penis, now standing proud, despite the years of celibacy.
My aeons of solitude are broken by her gentle voice: 'I'll
wander around the thunder and lightning in your skies . . .
I'm glad, ever so glad that I didn't create your unkind
universe.' I swim liberating strokes across the lake, a clear
blue water, calmness without any impending storm, and
here I lose myself to the grip of my hand. The strangulated
grip that masturbates as its one-eyed purple head peers up
at me. I lose the moment, letting my gaze shift to the eye
of Fat Head still staring; and change tack while lying on
my back. I punch the bulbous head like a boxer in training
working on a punch-bag, first with a left then a right
followed by a series of sharp uppercuts; all the while
shouting incoherently, telling the fat bastard it's a wank to
the death. His against mine. With this momentary lapse I
lose the place completely.

I knew all of this was doing me no good whatsoever but shit, I got a kick out of Fat Head's eyeball spinning like a peery. Finally, in that triumphant moment, when everything focuses, bringing it to a head, I jumped to my feet and spat, his spit into his eye. Until then, I had always considered myself a bad shot. But this, the thickest gob on earth, landed bang on target. I stood frozen to the spot, observing my accuracy. Not one tiny spray escaped the direct hit. All of it gravitated to its natural home. Although time seemed to have stood still, I was shaken from this day-dream by the rumble of footsteps in the corridor, but even this impending danger couldn't detract from the glory I felt. In their own way, perverse though it may seem, they were giving me my award.

The steel door opened to reveal a cluster of angry faces. I smiled wistfully at them. Fat Head, banging his baton off the steel door, pushed his way to the front.

I couldn't resist saying, 'You must admit, it was a crackin' shot.' This only increased the intensity of the blows from their batons, one or two of which splintered on impact. Curling myself into a ball I had a peculiar thought, of how my old friend Tinarse was fond of saying that every Guard he knew was a frustrated orchestra conductor, that each loved wielding his baton. I guess he had a point, but as someone constantly on the receiving end, even my vivid imagination nose-dived at the thought of appreciating their Bludgeon Symphony.

Once they were back outside with the door slammed secure behind them, I unfolded to inspect the damage. Hmmm, could be worse, a few lumps here, a welt of blue bruising there, but all in all, I'd be fine. Periodically, different eyes appear at the spy-hole. They are not without a tinge of remorse or misgiving. Primarily their concern is one of self-preservation. If a resident dies after attending a

Bludgeon Symphony then it becomes rather messy. The Guards, not known for their mental quick-footedness, are tested to the utmost by concocting a story which – and this is the hard part – they have to co-ordinate and remember. There was one previous occasion, some years ago, when they brutalised one particular resident to death, passing it off as self-inflicted wounds. The coroner, fortunately for them, was a pillar of society, and as it so happens, bridge partner to Dr Snider, and he did accept the possibility of the chap having inflicted thirty-two lesions on his own head while indulging in some bizarre sexual practice. The latter remark made as a result of a baton found protruding from the dead man's anus. Still, stranger and worse things have happened here. 'When is a concentration camp not a concentration camp?' one drugged patient asked another. Shaking his head the other replied 'Dunno.' His pal answered, 'When it's in this country.'

Incarceration of an unlimited period is tantamount to being overwhelmed by a tidal wave of time that diminishes by the second. Time indeed, hangs heavy. Yesterday Gorky hung a clock outside the doors. Peering through the pin-sized holes in the metal ventilator, I watched Fat Head hold the ladder while Gorky wobbled aloft. Now there was a sight to behold, such tenderness, such care for each other! Hmmm, true love, I guess.

'Is it straight?' asked Gorky.

'Fall,' I urge.

'No, turn it to your right, just a touch,' replied Fat Head.

'Fall,' I pleaded.

'A teeny bit more,' instructed Fat Head. The big man by now wobbling like a Jumbo on a tightrope.

'Please, please, please fall, just for me,' I implore in a quiet whisper. Lo and behold he does. This, I thought, is the stuff that satisfaction is made of. He suspended himself in mid-air, just for me I'm sure, before plunging. He lay there, face down, groaning with what I can only gleefully describe as acute pain of the severest kind. These are the moments when one's imagination runs amok. Did I see splintered bones protruding from each arm and leg, was that his head lopped off? Oh deary, deary me. No matter, flying to my feet I danced a barefoot jig in silent celebration. Contained inside me was this pleasure bursting to be seen and heard. Oh, what a mighty struggle I had keeping it in! Why should I share it with anyone, when there is so little to go round? The pair retreated, leaving behind an echo of groans. I peered into the corridor; a desolate ladder lay prostrate, abandoned on the floor. This, I tell myself, is my monument, my secret weapon – mind over matter.

Ah, but what new sound is this that permeates our small, intimate world? If I angle my eye to the lowest hole I can see the shiny white, impassive face of a huge clock, its penetrating tick matching its doom-laden tock. Now there is an instrument of torture if ever I saw one. Someone nearby sobs loudly. Unlike them I am something of a long-distance runner. Chest puffed in defiance I yell 'Hero!' Again and again. Another neighbour whines in anguish. The clock ignores each and every cry. 'Hero!' I shout aloud, hoping to drown the cries of my neighbour. This new challenge uplifts me to the extent that I float around the small space on my toes, shadow-boxing. My nostrils expel sharp bursts of air with each jab. 'Hero!' I shout again. I will fight it, I will fight it. All the way I will fight it! On the other hand, like a kid, I cannot escape the novelty of the clock; kneeling down I observe the time, '8.30 – hmmm, day or night?'

Salacious Sam was the first to go. Exactly eight days after its installation the noises began. 'Tick, tock, tick, tock . . . .' he shouted, imitating the instrument. After some hours he changed rhythm. 'Tock . . . . . . tock . . . . . . tock . . . . . .' Ah, he's conquered the clock language problem, has he? This continued for five days, and it was only then that my exasperation began to fray at the edges. 'Shut fucking up, you loony!' I cried. It always gets me like this at the beginning. It's almost as though I'm breaking through the wall to gather my second wind. His manic, gibberish sounds intensified, then came the wrench and tear of bed sheets. Oh, it's getting close, ever so close. If he kills himself before lunch there is a generous twist to the tale – they share his food between the rest of us.

'Have a thought for us,' I whisper to myself.

Quiet footsteps move along the corridors. Obviously the Guards have come to witness the grand finale. Sure enough, that well-known gasp is followed by the whiff of dead shit.

'That was quick,' said Gorky to someone.

Poor old Sam, never known for his speed, he made short work of that lot. Didn't have a lot to say at the best of times. Rumour had it his mother caught him reading porno magazines, and so he killed her, cutting the body into tiny pieces. Imagine fingering inside of your mum, from whence you came! Poor Sam, who were you anyway, what did you look like, and where did you come from? Six years he's been my neighbour and I couldn't as fuck tell whether he was white, black, yellow or just plain pink. Each of us is a mere shadow in the lives of our neighbours. Morsels of information picked up along the way allowed me to put together a small cameo of him. Most of it conjured from my imagination to give his shadowy presence an identity, but now he's gone, obliterated by rampant insanity, so who gives a fuck?

Shortly afterwards Fat Head gave me two helpings of

dessert, each decorated with a gob. Closing the door he shuffled away.

These monstrous moments are balanced by newsreeled memories from the past zooming through my head. The hop, skip and jumps on to the knee of my mother. Her gentle nuzzles and nudges; me folded securely into her bosom. Those early years edge forward. Hamstrung by blushes I falter, smiling coyly. 'Twinkle, twinkle little star, how I wonder what you are . . .' Peels of laughter and applause follow as her hands run through my hair. That flick of the fingers, so gentle and reassuring, always there, even when falling from the kitchen table. Her fearful look as she runs forward to scoop me up, planting kisses while cradling me to her. As the doctor tends my scuffs and scrapes, Mum shushes my fear into retreat. Laughter, fun and long hazy days spent in her presence.

CRASH! interrupts the resounding echo of a trolley being pushed along the corridor.

Coaxing my mouth open she examines my teeth. 'Have you cleaned them properly?'

THUD! as the sound of Sam's coffin falls to the floor.

'That's a good boy, straight to bed now.' I run from her, throwing myself under the blankets, pretending invisibility.

'Cut the fucking knot . . . oh, don't worry, he'll never feel a thing,' shouts Gorky.

Pulling me by the ankles from beneath the covers, her fingers tickle my thighs. 'Don't, don't, don't' I shriek as she pulls me on to her knee.

SMACK! Sam's skull hits the concrete floor. 'Like breaking a coconut,' laughs Fat Head.

Tucking the blanket warmly around my chin, she begins to read in her soft, warm tones: 'Once upon a time there was a wicked witch . . .'

Grunts come from the nearby cell, 'Bastard weighs a

ton.' More grunts. 'Told you we feed the cunts too well.'
SLAM! the lid closes on the coffin. 'Did you read'm his
last rites?' shouts a voice in jest as the squeaky trolley is
wheeled along the corridor. Fuckers, they do that deliberately, just to frighten us. 'Sam, Sam,' I sigh. You're better
off out of it. Who's next? I wonder. The remainder of us,
sitting alone in confinement, pay homage to the dead. That
great equaliser has now settled over these sweat boxes.
'Pray silence for me,' it commands. And we obey. None of
us, just yet, are thrusting ourselves into death's fold.

Even those few madmen, wretched with torment, crawl
into a corner, where they peer dolefully into space. The
silence is deafening, save for the guards whistling a jolly
tune while brushing away what remains of Sam.

Within the hour the sound of goose-steps rattles down
the corridor bringing Sam's successor. An inexhaustible
procession of us come and go. This new blood breaks the
silence, taking Sam from our midst. The newcomer brings
with him a repertoire of sound and movement. A rapid
mover, he scurries across the small space. His footsteps
pad lightly on the concrete, is he a fleet-footed biggie or a
small, reedy lightweight? That's the thing about this
animal-like existence; I find that years of living this way
brings to the fore senses that one normally wouldn't use.
For instance, no matter how hard the Guards may try to
hide their presence, I can always tell they're there. If they
smoke, the smell of tobacco in their pocket gives them
away but, more often than not, it's the shoe polish. I can
whiff it a mile away, that and the after-shave. Sometimes
they slip off their shoes before creeping along the corridor.
They beat their batons off the metal doors, striking fear
and shock into the unsuspecting resident. Every novice gets
caught, but those of us who stay the course are on constant
alert. Come to think of it, there's only two of us who've

never been caught unawares, me and Handgrenade – and look at him. The rest? Well, they've gone the way of Sam, or been trundled off to the Refractory, back of beyond. It's notorious as the place of no return and, once you're there, they've won, it's the equivalent of a Lifetime Fruitcake Award. No question about it. Only a few have managed to get out of there but rumour has it none of them were ever the full shilling again.

My keepers want me in there but one has to admire, even in adversity, their cool, calculated way of going about it. I guess they rarely meet anyone with my tenacity, so it introduces a new pace to the usual domino-like collapse of my predecessors and contemporaries. I think they admire me for this, though none of them show it. Or maybe they do in some perverse way that has, until now, escaped me. Let's see, a blunt needle up the bum, a gob of spit whose dollops of verdigris are so intense, or a pulsating whack from a baton. Trouble is, no one knows what they're thinking, and I guess that goes for them with me. Thank God. They're under the impression that, because I'm here in solitary, I long for the company of other human beings, namely them. Ha, if only they knew, that I much prefer my own company to theirs. If I could devise a system where only a small slot allowed my food in here without seeing them . . . Anything, rather than having to see them three times a day. They take great delight in confusing me. Sometimes putting a lunch meal in at breakfast, or vice versa, knowing that in here there is no such thing as daylight or darkness. For my part, who gives a shit? Food is merely sustenance. Others, however, fall for it. They get themselves worked up into a full-blooded argument with the Guards, not realising that this is what they want. Any old excuse to slap on the specially designed strait-jacket with a hole in the bottom so that old Gorky can give them a meat injection. 'A wee bit of rumpy pumpy will sort you out lad,' he was fond of saying.

It's funny how things happen but, somewhere between my singing a happy song and pissing into my chamber pot from a distance, a whole change in the monotonous routine occurred. If I believed in Him I'd call it a miracle but, as someone who has learned to believe more in myself, I'd consider it a just reward for endurance. No word was spoken, there never is. It all began with the intimidating scrape of the door opening. If it were at all possible, and I guess this was my first hint of it, I perceived Fat Head and Gorky as having a more sombre aura. I was marched along dim, brick-lined corridors, amazed that after all these years I was outside my small space. The vastness was incomprehensible and all the while my tormentors tugged me in this or that direction, as door after door was locked and unlocked. Eventually I was pulled to a halt before a massive vault-like contraption. It took two of them to undo the locks before pulling it open. Inside, barely a yard away, was another door, smaller in stature, but formidable none-theless.

'They say a break's as good as a holiday,' said Gorky, a broad smile creasing his face. 'Well, have a good one in our newly designed Silent Cell.' Undoing the lock he pushed me forward. Here, I thought, is where they'll give me it good and proper. Inside, the walls were painted white, as was the door, which was slammed shut.

Once the large outer door was closed, an eerie silence descended. I circled the place, much larger than my last one, with trepid circumspection. What on earth are they up to now, I wondered. Although fearful of their motives and intentions, I was excited by the challenge, thrilled the stakes were upped. Within a few minutes I grasped that nowhere would I be more alone than here. In Sam's last moments, I wondered, as he was tying the knot around his neck, did he at least take some comfort from the knowledge that we kindred souls were nearby? If so, I reckoned that, should my mind snap here, in this silent place, no one would be the wiser.

In varying shapes and permutations, these thoughts occupied me for hours on end until I was shaken from them by the outer door being unlocked. It was as though I was incarcerated in some sort of time capsule for, as the doors opened, stale air was sucked out as fresh air whooshed in. Fat Head, uttering not one word, entered holding a tubular metal chair on which was draped a suit of civilian clothing. Waow, civvie threads! Placing it inside the cell he then threw a brightly polished pair of brown shoes on to the floor. This was a new one on me. Now, I don't, and never have, underestimated the enemy but this did take the biscuit. What on earth was going on? Lifting the clothing I searched the pockets. Nothing. A faint recollection beckoned from somewhere in the back of my mind. No, it was nothing to do with the smell of mothballs. Holding the jacket to me I could see it was much too small.

'Put them on,' said a voice.

I could see Gorky's lips oozing through the spy-hole, giving a good impression that he was a talking door. I had been so carried away by all of this, I hadn't heard them begin to open the cell. Yes, yes, now I remembered these threads from so many years ago. They conjured up memories long forgotten, like when Fat Head had two chins instead of five. When Gorky shagged two people a night instead of four. When Snider possibly, though most unlikely, gave residents placebos. The suit felt as tight as a corset. Drugs had bloated my body. Wearing it was the

funniest thing though. Only yesterday Sam's skull had
cracked off the concrete floor and today I was dressed up
to the nines, dilly-dallying around the silent cell. Without
much ado, however, I was extracted from the place hand-
cuffed and towed by my guards along a succession of
corridors. This, the most tumultuous day in years, left me
feeling like a carbuncle about to be lopped off. Drawing to
a halt I stood between two locked doors, in a no man's
land, as though between heaven and hell. A group of
Guards surrounded me, their faces frozen with contempt,
their eyes, opaque and lifeless. These men had forsaken
their humanity to The Institution. I wanted them to understand that all those years of being suffocated to their bosom
meant nothing. Oh fuck, it was bad, it was ugly and often
downright murderous. But, and will some bastard please
hear this, it was part of my life. Good, bad and indifferent,
I lived with you bastards, I wanted to scream. Instead we
looked at each other stonily; none of us capable of brea-
ching our trenches, sadly none of us knew how to.

'John Alexander Ferguson . . .'

'Hero.'

'What did you say?' asked Gorky.

'Hero, my name's Hero.'

'Your name is John Alexander FUCKING Ferguson,'
shouted Gorky.

'I DON'T WANT IT!' I screamed back louder.

'Right loony, for some fucking reason, the Secretary of
State has authorised your discharge. I will read out to you
your discharge instructions under Section 127. You will
report to your supervisor immediately at the time and place
in this order form. The sum of money given to you by the
gate officer will provide sufficient funds for you to reach
your destination. Is that clear?'

'If you don't, you'll come straight back to us,' mimicked Fat Head.

'Then the fun will start, eh nutcase?' smirked Gorky.

Not so much as a goodbye or a good luck before being deposited on the outside. What a strange world. Salacious Sam hadn't been buried, yet here I was standing on the street out-fucking-side! Handgrenade would be shuffling around in his cell not knowing I was here fingering some grubby notes in my pocket.

Barely one step into freedom and my feet, like lead, anchored me to the ground, leaving me in a state of paralysis. I stared transfixed as people and traffic passed me by. An onslaught of sights and sound, a scramble of movement, an acceleration of everything denied to me these past twelve years. It was now here before me. I just couldn't believe the speed with which it all happened.

A bus stopped, letting people off. They chatted away to each other, unaware, in fact oblivious to the fact that I, me, Hero was back amongst them. The strange thing was that I felt I stood out like a sore thumb. That man there, look at him boarding the bus while reading a paper. How can he do that? See that young boy weaving his cycle through the stalled traffic? Oh, my God! That man standing on the top floor window sill cleaning the windows. He's standing there without holding on! This is the most disturbing spectacle I'm ever likely to see.

Already, the moral fibre that held me together in there was frantically groping for new bearings. The wide open space before me filled with everyday activity was so menacing that I wanted to knock the door down to get back inside. Instead, I shit myself. There was nothing I could do, it simply ran out of me like water. I became so preoccupied with this embarrassing predicament that everything else receded. Legs apart I waddled my first few steps of freedom. All the glorious dreams I had had about this moment suddenly lost their glow. Taking an old newspaper from a yellow litter bin, I slid into a nearby cul-de-sac to clean myself. 'How could this happen, what's fucking wrong with me?' I muttered to myself. Turning my breeks inside out, I scraped them as near to clean as possible.

My supervisor had the demeanour of an SS guard; lean and hungry, his steely eyes glared suspiciously from behind granny specs. Everything about him, from his slick hair to his leather shoes, was from an era long since gone. It was almost as though the one thing we had in common was being locked away in a place where time stood still. Taking out a calculator he ordered me to empty my pockets and hand over the bus stub that I clutched like grim death. Separating the coins, he counted them with the expertise of a banker. What did I buy, how long did the journey take, what route? The interrogation was thorough and precise. During the questioning, I plucked a piece of grit from between my teeth, spitting it out only to see it land on his shirt sleeve. He stepped back speechless, examining it with a look of incredulity that couldn't comprehend what I had done.

'Imbecile,' he muttered, moving swiftly into the nearby toilet.

On emerging he stared contemptuously at me. 'Right Ferguson . . .'

I coughed. 'My name's Hero, if you don't mind,' I said.

'What . . . not according to these papers, this is my bible, and yours don't forget, so quit the impertinence and listen to these instructions. As part of your release programme you'll report to me once a month. Your accommodation will be with a Mr Rafferty, who is very supportive of people released from The Institution. Others have taken advantage of Mr Rafferty's generosity in the past; therefore, I'm warning you to be on your best behaviour. You will start work in the Abattoir tomorrow morning at 5.30 a.m. I warn you, Ferguson, that any breach of your supervision will see you back inside.' Handing me twenty-seven quid, he dismissed me with the efficiency of an ejector seat. As I paused to take a deep breath outside his office, an old lady standing beside me scurried off hissing, 'I don't know how you can stand it.'

True, the smell was pretty off-putting. Across the street a large SALE sign drew my attention. A pair of clean pants would herald a new beginning. A shady-looking salesman wearing a shark grin beckoned me forward. He refused to let me try on the new pants. Putting the breeks in a bag he took the ten-pound note by the corner, spraying it with air freshener before placing it in the till. I stood, hand outstretched, awaiting my change. Banging the money drawer closed he gave me a dead-eyed stare that lasted all of two minutes. Reluctantly, with my supervisor's words still ringing in my ears, I withdrew.

I rushed into a nearby public toilet and pulled off my trousers to clean the stain between my legs. While doing so a scream filled the air. Turning round I looked into the face of a distraught woman emerging from a cubicle.

'You dirty pervert, get out of here or I'll get the police to you,' she screamed.

Fuck, a women's bog. Panicking, I ran into the street before realising I had no trousers on. The woman followed me, blasting a barrage of vitriol as I stood, back to the wall, with the new pants covering my front. Oh fuck, what happens if I get arrested for indecency? Passers-by craning their necks in my direction burst out laughing as I struggled to get my trousers on. That done, I hared off down the street.

The cutting edge of everyday life was rapidly slicing away the pleasure of my freedom. Already I was suffering from over-exposure. Moving into a dark recess off the busy street I sat in a corner whispering, 'Why, oh why doesn't someone help me with all of this? Just for a wee bit, to see me on my way.' It was difficult to understand what was happening. Everything was all of a jumble. Try as I might to get a grip on things, whatever I put my hands to went wrong. I was lost, literally lost, with no idea of where I was going, or how to get to my destination. At this moment my eyes felt as though they were being sucked into my brain, the ache of tiredness riddled my body. Tears streamed down my face, my body shuddered and I was on the verge of collapse. The steel corset that had held me together in The Institution finally burst wide open. Once again, I lost control. I shit myself.

Mr Rafferty, by any standards, was huge. Being quite tall myself, it was unusual for me to look up to someone. Not only to him, but also to his sidekick, Sally. Both could become tourist attractions if they stood still long enough. Their spick and span appearance had a distinct anti-environmental feel; they obviously used aerosol after-shave like machine guns. Far from being the benevolent landlord described by my supervisor, Slates Rafferty, the property tycoon, rapped me on the head with a huge key, warning me that if I fucked around I'd be evicted with my legs broken. Sally and Slates obviously worked in close harmony for, while he warned me, Sally ripped the pocket from my new trousers before counting the total.

'He's only got seventeen quid,' he informed his boss.

'Where's the rest, big spender?' asked Slates.

'I bought a pair of trousers,' I replied.

Both of them swatched down at my soiled pants shaking their heads in disbelief. Slates thumped me on the head with the key. 'Don't fuck around, arsehole. The key deposit is twenty quid so you're off to a bad start being in debt to me.' He went on to explain that Sally would collect my wages from the abattoir every week, deducting my rent and any extras. Any misdemeanours or hanky panky would be reported to my supervisor. All in all it seemed that these guys had it all sewn up. No messing with these two. Mr Nice Guys they weren't. Two painful lumps on my head bore witness to that.

Still, even this couldn't detract from the joy I felt at having the key to my own door. A small brass Yale key. Well used, its number was 2253681. 'Two, two, five, three, six, eight, one,' I whispered. On the way upstairs I sang the key numbers to the tune of 'She'll be coming round the mountains when she comes . . .' The door was coloured dark brown with an oblong gap pretending to be a letterbox. Putting the key in the door was a proud moment for me. Gently I pushed it open, listening to its loud creak. Pulling it closed I repeated the action just to experience it once more. The dark cramped entrance hall had a musty smell, a lead gas pipe hanging off the wall. The flat itself was a mess, the sort of place that even cockroaches would be afraid to invade. That explained where I fitted in the pecking order. The bed, for some unknown reason, was high off the ground but I couldn't give a toss. Lying on the floor next to the bed was a pair of blood encrusted trousers. I couldn't be arsed to give any thought to this and clambered into bed to instantly fall asleep.

My dreams exploded with a velocity that would've fired an astronaut into space. Fat Head sat on me, as Gorky picked his nose, the contents of which he subsequently rubbed on the back of my head while raping me. Once he'd withdrawn, Snider used my arse as a dartboard while the Guards roared 'Bull's Eye!' Then I was tying a bed sheet around my neck, tying it so hard to ensure immediate death. What an ironic twist of fate to have endured all that only to be driven to suicide on my very first day of freedom. Standing on a shaky chair I jumped off with a vengeance, and next I sat bolt upright. Sitting staring at me was a knobbly midget in blood drenched clothes, his forehead projecting in a massive bulge that looked like a roo bar.

'What are you doing here?' asked the midget.

Wha . . . who . . . who're you?' I asked.

'This is my house, and bed,' he replied.

'No, it's mine, ask Mr Rafferty,' I protested.

'Big sly bastard,' uttered the midget, more to himself than me. 'That's my love life fucked now.'

'What d'you mean?' I asked.

'Debbie, my bird, that's what I mean,' he replied in exasperation.

'Does she live with you?'

'Sometimes.'

'I can always do a vanishing act when she's around,' I volunteered, feeling sorry for him.

'It's not that easy. Debbie's as shy as fuck. She'll think you're hanging around snooping or something. What a bastard! I paid those fuckers big bucks to be on my own as well.' Jumping from the bed on to the floor he looked tiny.

'I don't understand how this has happened,' I murmured.

'Aw, it's Slates and Sally. They collect ex-inmates like postage stamps. The Social Security guarantees them loadsa dosh, no questions asked. They're wide boys, know that nobody gives a shit about us, and we all fear being put back inside. They'll exploit it. Now they have two rents for the one pokey dive. Don't be surprised if they turn this cupboard into a sardine can,' warned the midget. 'Oh, my name's Bonecrusher by the way,' he said, waving.

I lifted a hand in acknowledgement saying, 'Mine's Hero.'

Giving a casual but severe nod to my lower part he advised, 'I think, Hero, you'd do us both a favour by heading for the toilet, seeing as we both share the same bed.'

The Abattoir

Each morning Bonecrusher opened his eyes dead on five. It never failed to amaze me how he'd then tumble sleepily out of bed mumbling, 'I'll saw those legs short today if it's the last thing I do.' He never got round to it.

'Why is the bed so high anyway?' I enquired that first day. 'They used to rent the place to Goliath,' he muttered cynically.

Being winter there was no hint of light these early mornings so, on hitting the floor, we headed straight for our clothes. Bonecrusher's, caked in blood, almost stood to attention for him to jump into. Bonecrusher was devoid of inhibitions. He'd spend ages peering at his huge forehead in the mirror, pulling hair over it as a camouflage. Posing from one profile to another, he'd meticulously scoop handfuls of old-fashioned pluko (the 'long hold' variety), and clump the hair strands on to his forehead like a set of rat's tails.

'If only I had a decent patch of hair to cover it,' he frequently sighed. 'My one attempt at sorting it was a disaster.' He explained how he had spent days on end standing outside the wigmaker's shop, trying to build up the nerve to go in. Always he bottled out at the last minute. A warm smile covered his face as he told me how he met his only friend, Mohair Sam, the wigmaker. Seeing him standing there one day, Sam beckoned, asking his assistance to help shift a filing cabinet. While doing so Sam made him an offer he couldn't refuse.

'Would you like me to carpet your top floor?' he asked. Bonecrusher went all coy.

'I'll do a good job for you at a reasonable price. Go on, I like a challenge.'

Bonecrusher took to the sittings like a duck to water. Sam went to great lengths in choosing the hair and the style Bonecrusher should have. It was all going swimmingly and, during this period, they became friends. Sam revealed himself as being an inveterate bed-wetter, or as suffering from urinal incontinence, he said, giving it its Sunday name. Winking at me knowingly Bonecrusher nodded. 'You being a number two man.'

I groaned, 'Oh fuck.' Sam had been to acupuncturists, hypnotists and every other fakir on God's earth, all to no avail. 'Where is he now, I mean did he find a cure?' I asked.

'Hold your horses, just give me a minute to finish. Well, the upshot of it all was, I told him, turn this to your advantage as I've always found a lot of good information in porn magazines, they've been a great help to me. So, he stuck an advertisement into *Forum*: "Sexy female sailor sought – must endure nights of high tides and heavy gales." Sure enough along came a buxom blonde wearing oilskins, resulting in them launching into some far-off pisseroo, where tidal waves of it must've drowned Sam. There I was with half a wig to my name, never seeing hide nor hair of him again. The bastard, just did a bunk.' Reaching into the top drawer he hauled it out, placing it flat on his head to prove the point.

The morning was cold and windy as we approached the Abattoir. The joys of freedom still had me enraptured, as

Bonecrusher held the half-wig, stroking it fondly, dreaming no doubt of what it could have been. For some reason he stuck it on his head as we entered the Abattoir, a gesture that bordered on reckless. The meat packers, seeing it, broke into loud taunts. They whistled, jeered and mocked him, before finally snatching it from his head and throwing the wig from one to another till finally it fell into the pig pen. Before you could say 'bacon rasher' it was gobbled up by an enormous sow.

The place was full of giants; tall, often gross men wearing heavy duty aprons, hair as thick as gorse, covering arms that swung knives and cleavers with surgeon-like precision. Animal carcasses twisted, turned and slit in one fluent motion. Heads and hooves fell disinterestedly to the floor. One group of men, the elite Chief Killers, neither grunted nor groaned with exertion; instead they smiled and chatted jocularly while tearing hide from cattle and ears from the heads of sows. This factory of death and destruction, its sole purpose to put meat on plates. It was apparent, from their size, that the Killers ate heartily from the bodies they butchered. Pig Thompson, once seen, could never be forgotten. Mountainously grotesque, he stopped me dead in my tracks. This must surely be the world's eighth wonder. His movements, on foot, were so cumbersome it probably took his bulk all of ten minutes to turn ninety degrees. This most certainly belied the swiftness of his arms. Seeing my fixed stare, he pulled a boning knife from his apron while simultaneously snatching a sad-eyed sheep and decapitating it the way one would slice through butter. He grabbed a pewter jug, held it towards the thrashing body, letting blood pour into it. Leaning against his bench, he drank heartily from the cup. Seeing me watching him, wide-eyed, he grabbed me by the scruff of the neck and poured the remaining hot, sickly liquid down my throat.

Holding me like a wet rag, he laughed then let me drop. The headless sheep still thrashed its blood on to the floor.

The Abattoir was filled with the atmosphere of impending death. Pigs that were normally playful squealed balefully; the bellowing noise from the cattle now sounded mournful. The penned animals could not escape seeing their immediate future, no crystal ball gazing was needed here as trolley after trolley laden with rows of bloody carcasses whizzed past them.

Bonecrusher and I stopped to look at a solitary bull awaiting his death; his defiance conceded nothing to the deadly circumstance in which he now found himself. His power was awesome. Head held high, his hoof prodded the cobblestones underfoot. Bonecrusher walked determinedly to the metal pen, peering through at it.

'They're gonna prod and push you into that door; lock you in so tight that you cannot move. Pig Thompson knows you're here. He'll use you to get a laugh out of the others just as he does me.' The midget became carried away gripping tight the steel parapet, his knuckles turning white. 'Look out for the mean sod. Arms like tree trunks, he'll have a metal jug in one hand, a sharp knife in the other. Straight into your neck it'll go. He'll fill his jug as your life ebbs away, then you'll fade into oblivion while he glugs it down his throat, and his fellow sycophants, like hyenas, will laugh. They're the worst, weak as piss, they're no better than the sheep they put down. Those shiny eyes of yours will pop with fear. Beauties like you only come along once in a blue moon. You'll fill the aisles, you will. At the end of it, you'll have found your true destination. Summed up, as a steak on somebody's plate.'

The bull broke the spell by rattling its horns off the metal rail and both of us jumped back startled.

'Dumb fucking animal!' shouted Bonecrusher.

'What did it do to deserve that?' I asked.

'Thinks it's a smartarse. All that posing and snorting counts for nothing here.'

'Are you jealous of that bull?'

'Me, jealous of a fucking animal, you must be joking,' he sniped, a bit too defensively.

What a strange character, I thought, quite sensible one minute and nutty the next. It was clear to me immediately that he had an obsession with sex, cracking open his fly before breakfast and whisking out his cock to challenge me to a 'whose is the biggest' duel. Later he advised me to read a porn magazine cutting on the toilet wall that told how some beautiful women are turned on by midgets. This was a source of great pride to him.

'Has it worked for you yet?'

'Speak to Debbie,' he boasted.

'When will I meet her?'

'Depends.'

'She sounds great, you're so lucky having a woman,' I said, feeling envious.

'Well, it's a case of keeping them in their place. The best thing about Debs, apart from her amazing body, that is, is that she knows how to keep her mouth shut. She doesn't annoy me by prattling on, and does everything I want her to in bed without a word of complaint. Now that's the sort of woman you need, Hero.'

'Does she have any pals?' I asked eagerly.

'Keeps herself to herself does my Debs,' he smirked.

It was funny listening to him go on about Debbie. Considering how weird he was to look at, I found it difficult to imagine him with a woman. Truth be told, I did feel a bit jealous but, on the other hand, he was so pig-ugly that he made me look like a film star. If he could dig up a woman then so could I, I thought. The one thing that sent shivers up my spine was the faded circular scars on either side of his head. Tell-tale signs of a lobotomy, but he certainly didn't show the symptoms of a lethargic, almost zombified patient. Not this one, that's for sure.

Our howff was the Offal Room, which we entered by descending a wide, concrete ramp that led deep into the bowels of the Abattoir basement. A large rectangular room, it was filled with six huge, metal containers, each divided by a narrow passageway, barely wide enough to allow our trolleys through. In the centre was a small square where two butcher's benches squatted, scarred by years of slaughter. Some natural light was shed through a series of windows that levelled on to the pavement outside. Bonecrusher, easing himself into waders, muttered 'Tank day.' I followed suit.

Clambering into one container, he plunged thigh-deep into thick red sludge. 'See what strokes they've been pulling today,' he mumbled.

'Who do you mean?' I asked.

'Them up there, the comedians.' Plunging his arm into the liquid he extracted bloody lumps of offal. 'There, I knew it, what arseholes they are.'

I felt my stomach begin to flip.

'They've mixed the hearts in with fucking lungs again. I've told them a million times but the lazy bastards tip everything into the first tank they come to. Right then, you jump into that one there'n see if they've mixed them up,' he ordered.

'How do I tell the difference?' I blurted.

'Oh fuck, c'mere and I'll show you.' Since he had done the job for two years, Bonecrusher knew everything there was to know. Having given me a rapid introduction to animal innards, he accurately tossed the trespassing hearts or lungs or whatever to their rightful tanks. I, meantime, found myself slithering in a fankle of intestines. Roy Rogers and his lasso came to mind, as I curled heavy strands of the stuff round my right arm. He didn't learn this way I bet. Once they were looped, I tied it all lariat-style, before returning it to the sludge.

I could, I thought, with a little practice, lasso the head of Pig Thompson, scaling his body to pitch camp on his back. He'd never in a month of Sundays know I was there. If he accidentally, or deliberately for that matter, sat on Bonecrusher, the little tike would be lost forever between the jaws of his arse. Imagine being suffocated by a cluster of Pig's piles, now there's a spine-chilling thought.

'Where's the piles . . . sorry, I mean the kidneys?' I asked.

'The one beneath the windows,' he replied.

At lunchtime as we sat on our benches I was amazed when Bonecrusher drew out a huge femur from the bone bunker. Placing it flat on the bench, he held its knobbly ends and brought his forehead down on it with a mighty crack, smashing it in two. 'There,' he said.

'That was fucking impressive . . . where did you learn that?'

'From my head,' he replied, heaving himself on to the bench, where he dipped his forefinger into the broken ends, scooping out marrow which he then sucked.

'Ugh!' I said with a shudder.

'Your problem is that you don't know what's good for you. That sandwich, what's on it?' he enquired.

'Bacon.' I parted the bread to let him see.

'That is shit, a bit of pig's bum, that's what that is. Take this marrow,' he said, scooping out a piece. 'This is pure unadulterated goodness, it's what keeps the body structure solid, just like my forehead. This as well,' he continued, leaning down to lift what looked like an enormous jar of pickles. Putting a hand in, he plucked one out and popped it into his mouth. It made a loud crunch. 'These are an elixir if ever there was one.'

Holding out the jar he offered me one. I examined it carefully. 'What is it?' I queried.

'There you go, Doubting Thomas. It's my kind of pickle,' he proudly proclaimed.

Sniffing it, I detected a strong vinegary scent. 'Not had a pickle in donkey's years,' I said excitedly, putting it into my mouth. I crunched it and discovered a nasty, bitter taste. 'Christ! that's vile!' I yelled, spitting it on to the floor. 'They're not pickled onions!' I gagged.

He laughed gleefully while popping another into his mouth. 'Never said they were. Pickled pig's balls, that's what they are. My own invention and cracking stuff too,' he raved, crunching his teeth through it. 'Soon they'll be exporting them all the way to Switzerland, where they'll pay a fortune for them. They'll be selling them to old bastards like Mick Jagger, who jag monkey glands into themselves to stay young; these are good for your dick size. Just the job for Debbie I reckon, six months of these'll see me with a cock to rival Leroy Delroy,' he said, grabbing his crotch.

'Who?' I asked.

'You know, that spade in my porn magazines, Black Paradise.'

The wee man lived in a world of his own that was dominated by pricks and hair. The longer I was with him the more eager I was to meet Debbie. She had to be a deaf and blind nympho to put up with him. He was loony tunes writ large. How the fuck he managed to get out of The Institution in the first place puzzled me. Don't get me wrong, no one should be in there, but this wee guy was something else.

★

The cow looked up at me accusingly, the tongue hanging listlessly to the side, as I pushed a trolley full of heads to the tongue extraction bench. C.P. Horn, the youngest Killer in the Abattoir, stooped over as I passed. He had, they say, the instincts of a hitman and looked the part, being tall, dark and handsome, his eyes hooded and lifeless, his lips a deadly slash that had rarely seen a smile. His long thin fingers curled inside the mouth of a dead head that he tossed effortlessly on to my trolley. A young man of nineteen, he'd reputedly drunk five pewters of blood, one after the other, at his initiation ceremony. Just one short of the legendary Pig. Unlike the others, C.P. had style. Above his bench burnt into the woodwork were the words: 'I Killed Cock Robin', as well as a magnetised steel rack holding a row of shiny knives and cleavers with personalised handles. On a shelf nearby sat an old Bush radio, spewing out a succession of pop songs. The managing director would occasionally escort a group of trainee butchers around the place. Although butchery was long considered the last male bastion, some young women were now entering the trade. Occasionally a female group would be given a guided tour, and Bonecrusher would call me to his lookout point on top of the huge freezers. The group, with their white coats and tiny white hats, would move from one department to another. Whenever they reached C.P. Horn, the women members of the group would linger dewy-eyed at his bench. They would sway to the music, admiring the way in which he dissected carcasses. Occasionally one would be bold enough to reach out a hand gripping the animal's ears while he, with one swift blow, sliced it off. Although he performed this without acknowledging her assistance, it obviously enthralled the woman who, just as quickly, stashed the animal ear into her pocket as a memento.

'What a lucky bastard,' Bonecrusher would sigh. 'He's a

smoothy if ever there was one. Loves himself to death he does.' To the right of the knife rack was a mirror with a comb tied to it. Others in the Killer section had to wear white cloth hygiene caps, but not C.P. When he wasn't chopping up a dead animal he was staring into the mirror, combing back his slick black hair.

The Abattoir and my living with Bonecrusher took some getting used to. Still I couldn't get The Institution out of my system, constantly thinking that I'd wake up some morning to find that my being outside was all a dream. Even during the day, in solitary moments, I would find myself so overwhelmed and disorientated that I'd be lifted into some strange space that left me confused as to what was and wasn't real. For instance, one morning, sitting having a shit, in the proper place for a change, I began tearing some paper to wipe myself when suddenly the face of Snider peered up at me. It was a medical journal with an interview with her as its main feature article.

In days gone by the very mention of the old Criminal Lunatic Departments (CLDs) was enough to send shivers down anyone's spine. Such places were notorious for their dark dungeons, with lunatics fettered in chains, a place where they would be locked away without hope of redemption. Nowadays, treatment in such places is dispensed with a new rehabilitative ethos that assists patient recovery, allowing more of them to re-join normal society. This outstanding success must surely be attributed to the miracle of modern drugs and a dedicated staff who dispense such medication. Here in Europe, the biggest of these is The Institution, which has had at its helm for the past fifteen years Dr Olive Snider.

It described Dr Snider as being an early admirer of the Freeman-Watts standard lobotomy operation, which she had revived, performing it while the patient was under local anaesthetic. She detailed how the handdrilled holes on either side of the head would be widened manually by breaking away bits of skull, how she would then insert the blunt instrument, swinging it in an arc, thus destroying the targeted nerve matter. Finally, she emphasised her patients' total co-operation by getting them to sing or talk while she performed the operation.

Reading this brought my head to bursting point. 'You lying two-faced bitch.' Getting her photo square on to my palm, I gave my arse a good wiping. All of this was getting too much for me, and not at all helped by Bonecrusher kicking on the door.

'Are you in there, Hero? C'mere and have one of these treats for lunch.'

The midget startled me from a confusing jumble of thoughts, like peering through a mortician's kaleidoscope filled with every conceivable part of the animal body either sawn or hacked apart.

'I'll be there in a minute,' I shouted angrily, suddenly drawn back to the present. When I opened the door he stood there holding a fish-tank filled with eyeballs removed from bulls, sheep, cows, pigs and every other poor creature brought into this death factory. I shuddered at this nightmare image, bound to haunt me.

'Keep this to yourself, you can scramble these like eggs, you know. They're so crispy they just melt in your mouth. I'll do a couple for your breakfast tomorrow.'

Bonecrusher didn't possess a consistent logic, in the way in which he thought, or acted, but there again, who amongst us is such a rare jewel? Time and again, as we sat at lunch or lay in bed, he'd return to the subject of sex.

'Have you ever had a woman?' he asked.

'Never,' I replied sheepishly.

'Every night I banged a different one till I met Debbie, but now I keep it just for her.'

I felt a twinge of jealousy.

'What about a tit Hero, have you ever felt one?'

'Never,' I repeated, sighing deeply.

'Debbie has crackers,' he whispered tantalisingly.

'When are you seeing her again, so I can get a swatch at her?'

'Depends; she's a bit down at the moment but anyway, as I said, she doesn't have a lot to say at the best of times. I've got to keep her in her place, just to let her know I'm not dependent on her.'

Some nights he would simply turn over and chug away at himself. This was a well-known pastime for those of us from The Institution, many never having had the real thing. There was no secret about it. Anyway, that would've been difficult in the open wards. Beds creaked rhythmically, climaxing groans telling the tale. Masturbation in the wards was considered healthy, not that everyone could achieve a boner. No, that was a luxury the drugs obliterated. Quite often a guy would thrash away at his limp flesh with a vengeance, needing treatment for friction burns. What a pathetic bunch, what a jamboree of misfits!

The recollection of such misery was frequently to surface in me, especially on nights when Bonecrusher was giving himself a hand job. I remember lying in bed with these scars etched in my memory, catapulting themselves forward, numbing me into a condition that borders on catatonic. Lifeless, helpless, powerless. Prostrate in bed, or crouched on the toilet seat for that matter, I relive the agony. This condition, in rendering me helpless, epitomises what my life is like; this suffocating blackness, that smothers me in its embrace. It's that ever-present touch of

death that, like a sponge, has soaked up the lives of Salacious Sam and others who have died in The Institution.
What have I done to deserve this? Why me? Why can't I,
like the midget, lie playing with myself, as though all else
in the feeling arena had been lobotomised? Or is this
midget putting on a good act? Maybe he just can't express
it. Perhaps it's been pummelled so deep into him that he
has nothing left to say. Fuck it, I received from those kinky
bastards what I did, and I was an ordinary punter. Imagine
what they'd do to a deformed dwarf. Squashed by tyranny,
impaled, night after night by Gorky. All of us, cast into a
living inferno, created by lesser men than Dante, far
removed from the tender pages of literature.

I remember lying in bed beside him in the dark one
bitter, cold night.

'What got to you most in there?' I asked.

There was a long silence. 'Everything from the minute
to the colossal,' he replied angrily.

'But something must've really got to you?' I persisted.

Another deathly silence ensued till, finally, he sat
upright, 'It's okay for you to probe me, isn't it? What about
yourself, eh, what did you hate most? Two can play this
game, the great, grand inquisitor, tell me all your fucking
problems so that I can screw you up some more. Sit down
in the chair and feel at ease while I lock the straps and
shock your system to the fucking core. Hold still while I
cut a wee hole in the side of your head. It's okay, it won't
hurt. No, no, only take a minute, then you'll be as right as
rain. Another fucking pseudo psychiatrist bent on
extracting any fragment of sanity that remains.' He was
screaming, leaning his massive forehead against mine,
grinding it painfully. 'Well, don't fucking worry, I've got it
locked away where you'll never reach, ever!'

He pulled his head back, his eyes showing fear and

confusion, it was almost as though he was about to butt me, giving me the bone treatment, when suddenly he became passive and lay back. At that moment I felt a tremendous pang of empathy. I might be bleeding from what had happened in there, but this poor bastard was haemorrhaging. Somewhere inside him was a small tightly contained box, holding in all those dark secrets of what he had to endure. Seeing him like this brought home to me that, despite what we experienced inside, there is no relief out here, we are simply enslaved by it. Therein lies our hell.

Hell, I was always told, was where you went for doing bad things. I can remember going to confession on a Friday night. 'Bless me Father for I have sinned . . .' Reminded me of a teacher's blackboard and how you could wipe it clean with a duster. That's what the priest did to me when I told him about my sins. He wiped clean my sinned soul. Mind you it was hard to keep it that way, especially till Mass on Sunday morning. One swear-word and suddenly a black stroke would stain that clean soul. There I was on a Sunday kneeling on the pew next to my Maw as Christ himself was about to enter the tabernacle. Every time the priest announced this, me and the other kids would crane our necks wondering if he would reveal himself. He never did. Mind you, it's just as well because there I was, with my black sins looking from Maw to the tabernacle, in a state of indecision. I always worked on the premise that he wasn't in there and, anyway, my Maw would belt me on the lug for being a sinner. In my own pragmatic way I decided that Jesus could catch up with me when I died, so off I'd trot to the altar to swallow his body and blood. He seemed to understand, otherwise he'd have struck me dead. These sins were tiny though; whatever I may have done they were never bad bad. Not like what the good people, so so-called good people, have done to me. I guess that's what I've learned most of all, what keeps me sane is that I'm not bad, that I am okay . . . I'm a good person. That much they can never take away.

I turn to look at the midget. 'Was it sore?' I asked, nodding to his forehead.

He stared blankly in my direction for a long time before replying. 'It wasn't the pain, that had nothing, or very little, to do with it. They kept taking me back when it didn't work. The last one was "ice-pick" lobotomy, d'you know what that is?'

'No, I don't.'

'Well, first they give electric shock treatment as an anaesthetic before drawing the upper eye-lid away to expose the tear duct. The sharp point of the ice-pick is placed in here before being hammered into the brain and, presto, it's all over. No one knows what the fuck they are doing. I guess this big numb skull of mine saved my bacon. When I see what it did to others, I know I got off pretty easy.'

Slates Rafferty was notorious in the district as someone not to be messed with but, most of all, feared. Born with a strong predatory instinct, he was quick to get his act together; a rare combination of having brains to match his brawn. It all began, so the legend goes, when he acquired one flat which he rented out, cramming in tenants to a degree that made sardine packers look humane. His income guaranteed by social security payments, he soon purchased another flat, which then led to others. He is now firmly established as the biggest slum landlord in the city. In the eyes of everyone, Slates has made it. Having been quick to recognise that people in desperate circumstances will agree to desperate solutions, he reaped the benefits. Being street-wise, he had the knack of making the tenants (most of whom lived off the State and despised authority) think they were fucking the system. In conspiring between them to defraud Social Security, the tenants, without much thought, accepted Slates taking eight pounds for every two that went to them. He had structured the fraud in such a way that, should it ever be discovered, then the tenant, not Slates, would be in deep trouble. All his flats bordered on the derelict; a slap of plaster here, a coat of paint there, hiding a multitude of sins. The environmental health or safety regulatory bodies could have him any day. But in these recessionary days, with the building industry crippled, homelessness was a sensitive political issue for all parties, and so they turned a blind eye to the likes of Slates.

This morning, standing on the pavement, Slates glowered in the direction of Bonecrusher who was about to walk away from him. 'How dare he question my decision to let you two share a bed. Fuckin little midget wants me to cash out on another bed for you, what the fuck does he think I am, a millionaire?' he screamed angrily.

'Ungrateful little bastard,' spat Sally.

I slinked past them to catch up with the midget who was pretty pissed off.

'Rotten bastards won't get us another bed,' he growled, 'and that ugly pal of his will get cut down to size one of these days.' In a louder voice he shouted at Sally: 'You're a big lump of wood.'

Sally, catching some of it, rushed across. 'What did you say . . . who's a lump of wood?' He towered over Bonecrusher menacingly.

'What is that you're saying?' asked the midget, pretending deafness.

'Who did you say is a fucking lump of wood?' he repeated. Bonecrusher, quick as a flash, replied 'Pinocchio, that's who.' Turning, he walked away, his small but powerful body strutting along in a blaze of fury. 'I hate big people!'

'Bonecrusher,' I said, trying to cheer him up, 'that's like saying you hate the world.'

'Okay then, I hate the world,' he said. I laughed and he eventually joined in. 'But they are a pair of arseholes,' he said.

It was incomprehensible to me as to why such an awesome figure as Slates needed a minder. But then, no one could understand why both squeezed into, and scooted around in, a small mini when, size apart, Slates was worth a fortune. Both men, it was said, had been friends from childhood. Sally received his nickname after ploughing through a platoon of Salvation Army personnel while they played Christmas carols on the street. Big lads that they were, and with oodles of cash, rumour had it they were as tight as a duck's arse. It was pretty obvious, the way they had things sewn up, that they didn't need to buy anything. Word going around had it that Slates had a fortune stashed away.

The stairway where Bonecrusher and I lived had four floors, each with three flats. Most of the occupants had, at one time or another, been in The Institution or the local prison, another of Slates' guaranteed incomes. Although I had only been here a short period, I had personally witnessed two callous and cruel evictions, carried out by Sally. In one, a woman and two young children were heaved bodily into the street. The other was the brutal bludgeoning of a simple man. Those of us considered stable tenants were given these examples as a lesson to be learned for stepping out of line.

It was on this stairway that I met and fell in love. She was a prostitute, known locally as The Black Widow, who worked the notorious Shore area of the nearby docklands. I was returning from work one night, caked in hard blood, when she descended that stair, passing us like a scented shadow in the night. It was as though I had been struck by lightning as I stood on the stairway, gasping for breath. I turned to the wall drenched in embarrassment as a faint smile crossed her lips. Her perfume, potent and cloying, remained with me for some time afterwards.

'Who the fuck was that?' I asked.

'That was death on two legs, give her a wide berth,' replied Bonecrusher.

'But who is she . . . where does she stay?' I asked.

'That was The Black Widow, a brass nail who sleeps all day in the flat right above us. A cow, that's what she is. Sells herself to half the fleet. Not like my Debbie who keeps herself just for me. Go near The Widow and your dick'll fall off, that's for sure. Even the seagulls at the Shore will tell you that.'

Disregarding his warning, I waited, and began to follow her to work: As luck would have it, on one particular night, the ice between us was broken. I stood in the shadows watching as she kneaded her buttocks with the palms of her hands, causing her taut leather skirt to edge up her thighs. Her pale face, with its hardened beauty, peered into the darkness towards me. She had just been fucked up the arse by an Egyptian. Throwing her, face down, on to a pile of grain sacks in one of the large sheds, he pushed her skirt over her arse. I watched and attempted masturbation, as his big hairy thighs clasped at her while he rammed his dick in the whole length. She seemed to enjoy it. What finally brought us together was the sound of voices raised in anger nearby. Within seconds, a violent fracas between some guys led to one of them being left unconscious on the ground of the quay. The Black Widow emerged from the shadows; swooping like a vulture, she raced over to pick the body clean. Scanning the dark shadows while stuffing the loot into her bag, she caught sight of me. Approaching cautiously she caught sight of my exposed dick.

'You wanker!' she said. Confidently eyeballing me, she muttered, 'You live up my stair, you and that midget.'

Flustered and confused, I nodded.

Squeezing her body against mine, she gently held my cock. 'What did you see big boy, eh,' she whispered.

'Nothing, nothing at all,' I replied. Holding up a silver bracelet taken from the body, she dangled it. 'Take it as a present from me, go on,' she urged, squeezing my prick. Hurriedly I snapped it on to my wrist. A hurricane whipped through my body, reducing me to a quaking mass. All the while she expertly stroked my penis. I could smell her raw, untamed sexuality. 'What's your name?' she asked.

I could hardly speak. 'Hero,' I mumbled shyly. 'Hero, Hero, I love your name, Hero,' she whispered seductively. In all my past dreams and desires, in those moments of pure, unadulterated fantasy, when locked in my sweat box, it was never, ever, this good. This was the magic moment, when all that one has desired becomes reality. That unpredictable introduction that holds itself forever in your heart. And then it happened. I shit myself. It simply passed through my gates before I could do a thing. Here I was with this ravishing woman clinging; and me, with a half-second notice of advancing stench to play with, trying desperately to come up with a diversion. She, my saviour, provided it. 'I think we've stood on something, let's move from here.'

I ran off into the darkness, left her in my wake. I stumbled into one of the warehouses and climbed on to a mountain of sacks. All I could do was curl up in shame.

'What is the matter with me, why does this happen.' She was so beautiful, so beautiful that I could never in a month of Sundays have believed she would acknowledge my existence, and yet she had. I had totally and utterly blown it, in the worst possible way. What was I to do? I mean, it wasn't as though I was still taking laxatives by the handful. All I wanted was the hessian sacks I was lying on to swallow me up. 'So embarrassing, so fucking embarrassing. What would she think of me?'

Daybreak wakened the pigeons nesting in the shed. Reeking of hessian and shit, I walked uneasily in soiled pants along the wharfside feeling as useless as a crumpled cigarette packet. Eve's Bar still heaved with the voices of drunken sailors. Peering in the window through the haze of blue smoke, I could see sailors singing, their bodies swaying as though they were still at sea. I caught sight of The Widow standing beside a woman of stunning beauty, both of them the life and soul of the party, horny hands reaching out to grope them at every twist and turn. My heart sank deeper into despair. I replayed her amorousness; her whispering my name: 'Hero, I like your name'; the touch of her body close to me, the gentle play of her hand as she tried to do a Lazarus on my cock. And yet, here, caked between my legs lay my shame. How could I have done this? Like a skunk, I slunk through the deserted streets to the flat. Every so often I'd lift my arm to look at the damaged bracelet she'd given me.

Bonecrusher was snoring like a grizzly bear, thank fuck, as it deadened the noise of me cleaning myself. Traces of hysteria had me fidgeting nervously. Pulses tugged my eyelid, giving off a nervous tic. I kept reassuring myself that it was alright, it was all contained within me. 'Keep quiet,' I whispered, 'and no one will notice.' I kept reminding myself of all that I had felt while in The

Institution; but curiously, and this was as hard as fuck to admit, a part of me longed to be back there. I cried. This was not a simple release of the ducts, it was a torrent of tears accompanied by a sound that was prehistoric. Peering out of the toilet, I was relieved Bonecrusher hadn't awakened, so crept on tiptoes, fumbling through the darkness, towards the bed. Having cautiously moved to my side, I reached across to pull some blankets from him. At that point my new bracelet caught on something. Oh fuck, I thought, wrenching it free, resulting in a terrifying BANG! Followed by a continuous rasping sound.

'Debbie, Debbie, for fuck's sake,' cried Bonecrusher hysterically.

Hurriedly switching the light on, I fell back astonished at the sight of two female legs deflating before my very eyes.

'You stupid bastard,' screamed the midget torturously.

'That's Debbie?' I pointed dumbfoundedly. 'Your girlfriend!' I repeated in disbelief, as the last rasp of air escaped from the blown-up doll. All that remained intact was her pretty little plastic head, its oral orifice still open and inviting, staring sweetly at the ceiling.

'What a fucking liberty, could you not watch what you were doing! You've done her proper you have,' sighed Bonecrusher looking down at the doll.

'Oh fuck, don't remind me, I've let so many women down tonight.' I held my head in despair.

Having carefully folded Debbie up, he put her gently into the bottom drawer. 'What did I tell you, not one word of complaint, even when she's at her lowest,' he said admiringly.

We lay silently in the dark. Before falling asleep I tried to make a conciliatory gesture. 'Bonecrusher,' I said, 'I am sorry. Tomorrow I'll buy you a puncture outfit.' He didn't reply.

Bonecrusher had obviously taken the huff with me as he ploughed through the early morning slush in silence; not that we rabbited ten to the dozen anyway. I now understood his problem about Debbie, him not getting it off with me around, I mean. It would've been a bit iffy me sitting there while he huffed and puffed while blowing her up. It's not as though he could take her into the backcourt and have a knee-banger. It started to occur to me that maybe he was jealous of me. Maybe it was down to my fancying The Widow. I also wondered if he read more into my late night, early morning wanderings down at the Shore. Boy, if I could dump some of this misery I was now feeling on to him, he'd know all about it. If only he knew the truth . . .

C.P. Horn had taken a liking to me. This came in the form of an approach from Dead Eye, his lackey, who told me that his boss wanted me to tend his bench. This meant I took my trolley to him more often to clear away the animal remains. He made it clear that Horn had no time for the dwarf. Anyway, I decided not to tell Bonecrusher about this in case I hurt his feelings. This invitation sent me rushing from one Killer's bench to another to get to Horn's, where I'd stand, eager as a puppy looking for the slightest recognition. Instead, the monotonous crackle and squelch of dismembering bones, the wrench and tear of gristle and hide, was my only reward. Both men worked incessantly, not a word escaping their lips. Dead Eye, a sickly white film covering the left socket had just that, a dead eye. While working studiously on a carcass his head would automatically look up, the large right eye rotating almost periscopically, to take in the other Killers before finally resting on his boss. Each of the top Killers had a gopher but Dead Eye seemed to have the edge; a thin gangling man, his arms speedily scooped up all manner of animal debris before dropping it into my trolley. The only concession made to me was when Dead Eye would tap me on the shoulder, indicating the trolley was full.

Almost as though it had some magnetic hold on me, I found myself constantly drawn back to the magnificent bull in the pen. It had been held here for an unusually long time, considering the conveyer belt process of killing that went on daily around it. Five days now, and still no sign of his spirit diminishing. The fearsome reputations bulls have, and particularly my own fear of him, ebbed the more I returned to see him. Sometimes, when wheeling my trolley past the pen I'd toss in a carrot, or snatch some hay from a nearby bundle and feed him. The bags of animal food nearby were a barrier, allowing me to sneak in unseen to observe and speak to him.

'You really like him, don't you?' whispered Bonecrusher, sliding alongside me.

'I think he's brilliant.' The bull stood facing us, the ring in his nose glistening. 'Watch this,' I said, holding out a carrot. The beast stretched his snout towards me hesitatingly, then shook his head with a snort.

'It may bite your fucking hand off. It's not a big daft cow you know,' warned Bonecrusher.

I held the carrot steady till eventually the bull came forward, snipping off the end with his teeth. Soon, he had eaten the whole carrot. 'Right, give me a shot,' said Bonecrusher excitedly. We alternated feeding him, which brought him physically closer, and made him more trusting. Both of us left work that night elated at the progress we had made with the animal. Being almost midnight the streets were quiet except for the clatter of our boots on the pavement.

'Mind you,' said Bonecrusher, 'He'll soon be in the knacker's yard.'

Early morning at the Abattoir brought the usual fleet of refrigerated trucks, each reversing on to the ramp nearest the freezers, holding row after row of carcasses. The labourers would wheel the corpses suspended on hooks speedily from one to the other. It was usually a friendly affair with banter flying in all directions. As each freezer was emptied, Bonecrusher and I would clear it out in preparation for the day's slaughter. So cold were they that we'd rush out every few minutes to blow on to our numbed fingers.

'C'mon you two, get moving!' the foreman would shout.

On Friday mornings – pay-day – the voices were always light-hearted, for the others that is. We were left out, for more reasons than one. Slates and Sally always appeared bang on time, with smiles and greetings for everyone else. They would begin wheeling and dealing the minute the pay packets were given out. Slates, who collected ours, would approach while ripping them open, handing us each a fiver.

'Don't spend it all in one shop boys,' he'd say.

Bonecrusher, much more upfront than me, would always scowl at him. I would merely shrug. What was the point; there was nothing we could do about it. The back of their mini would be opened just prior to them leaving, timed for me to arrive with a trolley crammed with parcels filled with the choicest prime cuts.

'Put a plastic bag down you fucking idiot, you'll get blood all over the carpet,' snarled Slates.

'Taking any bets?' shouted the foreman as they were leaving.

Slates screeched to a halt. 'What do you mean? On what?'

'The Aberdeen Angus, it's the best we've had in twenty years. It's pedigree stretches from here to eternity.'

Sally poked his big head through the window. 'Fat lotta good that'll do it now,' he belched, bringing laughter all round.

But Slates reversed back. 'What's the score then?'

'We're holding him to raise the restaurant price. The offers are flooding in. Then there's a race between you-know-who as to who does the killing.'

Slates and Sally looked at each other, recognising there could be money in it for them. 'This is big stuff then eh, between them,' said Slates nodding in the direction of the Killers.

The foreman leaned forward. 'The biggest, and probably the meanest.'

Slates rubbed his hands together gleefully. 'When are they under starter's orders then?'

The foreman shook his head ruefully. 'The bosses aren't saying yet. They're more into getting the hype going to set the highest price, but it shouldn't be too long as the Food Inspector doesn't like things to be too obvious.'

Slates slapped him on the back. 'That's the least of their worries, they'll just up his back-hander.' They all laughed aloud. Slates called from the departing car. 'Mind, keep me in touch.'

I raced into the nearby freezer to inform Bonecrusher of what I'd just heard.

'Oh, fuck, who needs these bastards any meaner than they are? Better keep our heads down or wear crash-helmets,' he warned.

This was the least of my worries as I'd grown fond of the bull and felt sick at his impending slaughter. My obsessive nature found me rushing out to buy a packet of sugar lumps for him. It took a fair lump off my fiver. Still, he lapped them up. Whenever strangers went near the pen, he reared and flashed his fiery temper sending them back apace. In a perverse way, he was attracting a following, some of whom were there to tease and annoy him, others, like me, to look on in admiration. The more people put bets on, the more popular the bull became. Unfortunately his life was peripheral to the clash of the Titans – Pig Thompson and C.P. Horn. Although the other Killers were currently in the race it was already a foregone conclusion that the real contest was between these two. Whilst it was not the done thing for the punters to hang around the benches of the two main contestants, it was okay to do so with the bull.

The atmosphere within the Abattoir was unusually tense. Grabbing my trolley, I headed straight for C.P.'s bench where, lo and behold, he gave me a smile that vanished as quickly as it had appeared. Later that morning when going through the main slaughterhouse, the enormous arms of Pig Thompson hauled me clean off the floor, pinning me against his chest. Two Killers approached carrying the newly slaughtered head of a pig. Forcing it on my head, they screwed it down so that it covered my own to shoulder level, then tied it under my armpits with wire. Blindly I scampered away to the collective squeal of 'Honk, honk, honk.' Try as I might I couldn't dislodge it, as they prodded me along, till suddenly there was an abrupt change in temperature. A door slammed behind me. I was in the freezer. I wrenched the head, by pulling it by the ears, till finally the wire cut through the pig flesh, freeing me. It was then I realised that the door couldn't open from the inside. Banging my boots off the door, I screamed at the top of my voice, 'Let me out, let me out! I'll freeze to death.' No one answered. The small blue light gave the freezer a strange atmosphere, particularly with the rows of carcasses hanging still, and silent. I could feel myself freezing and began moving rapidly to keep warm. Surely to fuck they weren't going to leave me here. 'Somebody open the door for Christ's sake!' I screamed again. My saviour came in the form of Bonecrusher who, on releasing me, helped me down to the Offal Room.

'You're worse than a loose cannon, Hero,' he said.

'What did I do, why did they do that?' I asked.

First, you don't have to do anything, but the fact is, you did, by favouring C.P.'

I was bewildered. 'But I went to all the others too.'

'Spending more time with one Killer on prize bull week is fatal, as you now know to your cost.' He pointed to a large blackboard showing the names of each Killer. 'They'll turn a blind eye to it at the best of times but, when that blackboard comes out, no preferential treatment will be tolerated. Losers are always looking for someone to hang their failure on. Think yourself lucky, they got to you before they got under starter's orders.' He jumped on to his bench and crunched a pig's ball.

'I'm fucking sick of this place,' I said, exasperated.

'Huh, you're sick of it. How long is it now, let me see. Seven weeks! I've had two solid years of these bastards ruling my life and there's fuck all I can do about it.'

Both of us sat for some time in silence.

'Is it the bull then?' I enquired.

'It sure is. The highest slaughter rate of the week gets to kill him. So the knives are sharpened, the tempers frayed, and may the best man win. Everybody, including me, will have a bet on it, so there's a pile as big and heavy as the bull itself at stake.'

I had grown to really like the beast, more so now, when I knew the sort of people competing to kill him. 'Who're you betting on?' I asked.

'There's only one man in the race and that's Pig. C.P. can't match his timing or experience, not yet anyway.'

'I don't know how you can do it,' I said, stroking the half-filled bag of sugar lumps.

'To make money, that's how.'

'Blood money, that's what it is.'

'As long as I can spend it, that's all that matters to me,' he shrugged, patting down his rat-tail fringe.

'Surely other things must matter to you as well?' I asked.

'Don't be daft, of course they do. A hair cream for growing hair or a pill to make dicks big for starters.'

Thereafter, I ducked and dived, trying to evade my goddess but knowing instinctively that the law of averages was stacked against me. Inevitably, soon after, I came across both The Widow and her female friend from Eve's Bar at the top of the stairs in all their glory. I was still wearing my work clothes.

'Hello stranger,' she cooed.

I gulped nervously.

'So this is the one?' said her mate in a strong husky voice. 'Come on up,' The Widow beckoned. I accepted the invitation, entering her flat. It was elegantly furnished with lots of pink and white. The carpet had a pile with the bounce of a trampoline. I couldn't believe our decrepit hovel was directly below this.

'Gloria, this is Hero.' Taking this introduction as her cue, Gloria, saturated in a knock-out perfume, approached and ran her hand down my jersey.

'Hero, now there's a name that sets me on fire,' she said, leaning forward with a mock whisper that The Widow could hear. 'I'll suck your toes for sixty quid, big man.'

Following suit The Widow approached, 'I'll shave your pubes for forty.' Pushing Gloria aside, The Widow put her face close to mine. 'I'll tongue your arsehole clean for thirty.'

The mixture of tease and heady perfume made me dizzy, but still they continued with Gloria grabbing my arm.

'I'll nose-ride you for fifteen.'

Pulling from the other side The Widow muttered, 'I saw you first, so let me chew your balls for nothing.'

This exchange machine-gunned me into stepping back and falling over the couch to the floor behind. The Widow recognised my confusion and helped me on to an armchair.

'Hey, are you okay?' she asked, staring into my face, her eyes exuding concern. I nodded. 'We were only joking, Hmm, d'you want to go?' she nodded to the toilet. I slid in, locking the door behind me.

Sitting there it felt as though my insides had fled from me. I thought of The Widow's concerned look and wondered how she knew this was building up in me. Even I had missed it, being too taken up by what they were doing, to register that the shit was going to fly from me. This woman was definitely for me, she was so on the ball. Back on their spotless couch I sat nervously conscious of my blood-stained clothes.

'Here's some tea,' said Gloria, handing me a mug.

'How long were you in there?' asked The Widow.

'Oh, about three minutes,' I replied.

'Not that, silly, The Institution,' she said, smiling.

Gloria went to the toilet, leaving the door open. I watched as she stood over the bowl, hiked up her skirt, pulled out a penis and pissed. My eyes bulged with shock. I couldn't believe this beautiful woman was actually a man. I turned to look warily at The Widow.

'It's okay, don't worry, I have to sit,' she smiled reassuringly.

'Did you know my brothers, Knucklehead and Lockjaw?' she asked.

'Are they your brothers?' I was in awe. Both of them had legendary status in The Institution.

'Yeah, but Knucklehead never made it, the Refractory finished him off.' There was a tinge of sadness in her voice. 'As a family we're very close, and it's a recipe for disaster in that place. One couldn't see the other treated badly without doing something about it . . .'

I could see the pain in her face as she talked.

' . . . It knocked Lockjaw crazy when they finally gave it to his brother. He's never been the same since. He heard it all, the batons whacking off his head, right down to his last muffled groan. He took everything they could throw at him. They knew that if they didn't finish him, he would come back with a vengeance that would've been too unbearable for them to contemplate . . .'

Listening to her, seeing the anguish on her face as she spoke, brought home to me how wonderful it must have been for the brother to have someone outside to care in the way that she did.

' . . . The patients thought they then would've gone on to Lockjaw but they didn't. I suppose two brothers in the one day would have been over the top, even for that mob. The coroner's report said Knucklehead died while being restrained – he was in a straitjacket!'

I nodded. 'It happens all the time.'

'In the end, the only consolation was Lockjaw being released after the Cassels Inquiry.'

'The what?'

She nodded. 'Didn't you know about it? It came about as a result of two sisters in care being certified insane, and it turned out they weren't. Cassels, a Queen's Council, conducted an inquiry and, as a result, a lot of people have recently been released . . .'

'I heard nothing about it.'

'Well . . . he said they should never have been there in the first place. Of course, they made sure that Knucklehead, posthumously, was certified insane. The system knows how to cover itself. Bastards!'

Gloria Gaylord then told us a succession of stories about herself, most of which took place in or around Eve's Bar. She seemed to adore The Widow, who was apparently a legend on the streets and had taught her all she knew about the game. Gloria lived dangerously, passing herself off to punters as a girl, with none of them having yet discovered otherwise. 'It just proves that all they want is any old hole to poke into.'

The Widow allowed Gloria to use her patch at the Shore. The area had a notoriety as international as the ships that docked there. In the daylight hours the place teemed with activity as cargo was loaded and unloaded. Crews leaving the ships after months of floating captivity were warned that it would be in their interests to return to the ship before nightfall. If not, they must organise a meeting place so they could return in the safety of a group. The contrast between night and day was stark. Poor street lighting, fighting hard to create a presence, failed miserably. Wide open warehouses created an atmosphere of lurking danger. Weirdos, usually with harmless, voyeuristic tendencies, crept around. Others, more organised and vicious, waited to attack drunken sailors. The Shore was awash with rumour and mythology; one such tale was of its being a no-go area for policemen after two of them attending a call were knocked unconscious and one of them raped by all three assailants. Officially, the police now denied not patrolling the area but it was clear that theirs was a damage

limitation job. In such a place, with a predominantly tran-
sient population, crime detection was nigh on impossible.
Then, of course, they told me there was the more organised
part of crime in the Shore, very much the domain of the
Sylvesters, a father and son duo. It was in this cesspit that
the two women plied their wares.

'Aren't you afraid?' I asked naïvely.

'Don't have the time to be,' said Gloria.

'But every trick is a potential murderer,' said The
Widow.

'Since you told me that the only dagger I've had in me
is a meat one,' laughed Gloria.

Later, tucked into the warmth of my bed, I savoured the
glow of our encounter. They had spoken my name, 'Hero',
and that felt good. They made me laugh and feel almost
normal. I had met two women, had been invited into their
flat, and was now their friend. Bonecrusher knew something had happened but didn't ask. I wanted to tell the
world that I had just supped from the cup of life. All
the trauma of my past paled into insignificance as the warm
glow of The Widow spread through my belly into my loins.

'The Widow,' I whispered, as Bonecrusher snored. 'Widow,' I repeated slowly. Touching myself, I felt a sensuous
warmth in my groin: clutching my penis I tried to raise it
from its flaccid status. Alas, only the embers of the fire
glowed, the poker maintaining an impotence. 'One of these
days, one of these days,' I silently promised myself.

Friday night revellers, with their painted faces and lac-
quered hair, stumbled from pub to pub, their shrill laughter
and loud voices penetrating and obscene. I watched them
buckle, weave in a drunken haze, lean over to spew vomit
into the gutter, splattering their shoes and clothes in the
process. Their faces contorted, their lips puckered and

stained. These frequent violent eruptions. Drunken brawls, cursing and shouting, signs of their unhappiness. I recoiled at the ugliness of it all. Come Monday morning, most would tighten the stays of their emotional corsets and return to a prim, mundane office routine. Bonecrusher and I had to beat a path through this madness for our stint of late night hosing and washing of the Abattoir.

The bull, living out his last weekend on earth, was destined to fill the plates of top class restaurants five days after being hung on the butcher's hook. He pawed the cobbled floor as we passed; his commanding spirit remained unbroken. That in itself was remarkable considering he'd now been moved to the Killing Pen, a space designed for the convenience of the Killer and so narrow that it restricted all movement. Despite this, the bull managed to retain a dignity that reduced the killing machine around it to insignificance. I held out a sugar lump in the palm of my hand which he gently nuzzled into his mouth. Instinctively I felt that we understood each other. As did Bonecrusher, despite his craziness. Yet every time I thought of the bull, a sadness entered my heart. He was on the countdown to oblivion.

'I've cancelled my bet,' whispered Bonecrusher.

'Why did you do that?'

'Because.' He nodded bashfully towards the bull. 'You know.' He clearly did not want to talk about it. Seeing my puzzled look, he leaned across to speak into my ear. 'He'll hear,' he whispered urgently.

'Oh, oh, I see!' I said.

Alongside the bull's pen was a blackboard showing all the Killers' names and scores to date. C.P. and Pig were neck and neck, with three more working days left. Bonecrusher and I now trod a wary line, ensuring everyone was treated equally. Even then, we were subject to having things

thrown at us, or being cursed to the high heavens by those
Killers falling behind. The tension was high, as no competition had ever been this close. Pig Thompson in particular
fizzed with anger at C.P. Horn, the young pretender.

Playing my high-powered hose across the pens which
that very day had held sheep now reduced to dead meat, I
wondered if their ghosts ever came back to haunt the place.
(Come to think of it, I've never heard of animal ghosts.) If
ever there was a creepy place at night, it was here, especially
when the wind howled through, rattling the pen gates.

Mr Downie, the night watchman, usually soused in
booze, was oblivious to it, hail, rain or snow. 'A skinful a
night keeps away the shite,' he'd comment. It was often the
case that he'd be drunk so early that Bonecrusher would
lock the door from the inside and climb over the fence to
get out, to prevent him from getting the sack. The walk
home in the early hours was usually done in tired silence,
the late-night partying having subsided, leaving only the
stragglers, who gave the impression of attempting to climb
the face of the building, as they clung to it in a drunken
stupor.

'I wouldn't mind if the Killers had a competition over
that lot,' said Bonecrusher, nodding at two drunks shouting
angrily at each other.

I nodded. We walked a distance in silence, lost in our
own thoughts. I always associate alcohol with Fat Head
and Gorky. Their forays into our beds at night were fuelled
by booze. Smells, like old music, bring their own haunting
memories of the past. Alcohol pins me down in a bed while
others ride roughshod over me.

'Do you remember watching Gorky or Fat Head bugger
their way round the ward, knowing one night it would be
your turn?' I asked.

The pain of it saw us walk two street blocks without a reply.

'Did . . . did they get you . . .?' he asked tentatively.

'Yes, a couple of times, till I made a laxative bomb.'

He stared at me in puzzlement. 'A what?' I described it to him, causing him to break into loud laughter. 'Wish I'd thought of that.'

Later that night both of us lay awake in the darkness. 'They did me . . .' he whispered. ' . . . I hated it . . . hated myself worse, I've never felt clean since. At first I didn't really understand what was going on, they filled me with Largactil you see, but next morning my arse was burst wide open. I went for treatment'n they said I'd been shitting bricks, that's what caused it.'

This was our first experience of talking to anyone about it. In The Institution it was a non-subject, I guess because of the humiliation we all felt and the imminent likelihood of it happening again.

'I'd love to get the bastards back one day,' said Bonecrusher.

'That would be my dream come true,' I said.

Both of us had become so emotionally charged in that dark room, that we just couldn't get a wink of sleep.

'This is the sort of bedtime therapy I could do without,' whispered Bonecrusher.

Suddenly I sat bolt upright. 'I've got it, I've fucking got it!'

Startled, the midget also sat up. 'What . . . what's the matter?'

'The fucking bull, let's steal it,' I shouted.

'Nick a bull, you must be joking,' he shook his head at me.

'Just think of their faces, it would be a great way of

getting our own back. Just think of the way they've treated us — all of them.'

Bonecrusher lay down again. 'Yes, and just think what they'd do if we got found out.' He stared wearily at me. 'And for that matter, where the fuck will we put it, under the bed?'

I was stumped and sank back into the mattress. 'Hmm, you're right, I never thought of that one but, you must admit, the idea was great.'

Bonecrusher let out a laugh. 'Yeah, you can say that again. I can just see the gaffer's face. It would be to die for, seeing him having to hand back all that money to the punters. All bets are null and void.'

I could see Bonecrusher was letting his imagination run riot and I laughed loud as he continued.

'Think of that big bastard Sally throwing a fiver at us every week. D'you know, I watched him feed the bull a cabbage today and I thought, big rat, he's only feeding it for the kill. Him and Slates reckon they'll also make lotsa dosh from the competition. It's funny but, when I was in The Institution, I used to think that one day my time would come, that one day I'd get them back for the way they've treated me. Now I do the same thing with the Abattoir. In some ways it's like being inside again. You know, the way we're controlled by Slates and the others at work. I just want to get revenge . . . I'd just like to get my own back. It's the sort of fantasy that makes me put up with all the shit thrown at me. One of these days though, one of these days . . .'

'I'm the same, only, I don't want to spend my life living the dream and doing fuck all about it,' I replied.

Bonecrusher lifted his head sharply from the pillow. 'I've just thought of something. In the backcourt there are the old derelict washhouses that no one uses any more.'

'Yeah, so?'

'Well, we could stash the bull in there if we wanted,' he said, smiling.

'You reckon?'

'I reckon.'

In that moment, it was a case of forget the detail, damn the consequences and get on with it. In the blink of an eye we quickly got ourselves dressed. I felt a mixture of fear and excitement on the way to the Abattoir knowing that, if we were caught, we'd cop it from all quarters. At the same time, there was a compelling desire to do it. Having taken this snap decision, there was no turning back. It was almost as though something bigger than us was propelling us on. It could be described as a craziness but it wasn't entirely that. Silly as it may sound, it was like . . . like a blow for freedom.

Downie, the night watchman was, as usual, out for the count. Bonecrusher climbed over and opened the door to let me in. The bull snorted in recognition as we nervously peered in at him.

Suddenly a voice called. 'What the fuckin, shitting, pissin use is all this . . .?' It was Downie staggering to the door of his howff. We looked up startled but, thankfully, he was talking to himself as he pissed on to the cobbles.

Bonecrusher let out a loud sigh of relief. 'Thought he was on to us there,' he whispered.

Within minutes, Downie was again sound asleep and snoring. I placed a rope through the bull's nose-ring and he followed me placidly. The midget ran ahead to make sure the coast was clear. When a police car cruised by, we tugged the bull into a close-mouth till it passed. The only person we came across was a drunk, his back to the wall staring at us in disbelief. We had a tremendous sense of victory when we finally got the bull into the old washhouse.

He seemed at peace, almost as though he approved of what we'd done.

'Not so dumb, that one,' smiled Bonecrusher. Lighting a candle, we stood looking at the sheen of his hide. There he stood in all his glory – free!

'We've done it, we've fucking done it!' I whooped excitedly.

'I can't believe we actually have,' said Bonecrusher. He stood holding the rope with a look of exultant pride on his face. 'We've fucked them. We've well and truly fucked them,' and he let out a heartfelt laugh, the likes of which I'd never heard from him before.

I patted the bull on his wet nose. 'D'you know something? This moment alone makes it all worthwhile. I could get used to this.'

Next day we entered the Abattoir nervously at the usual time. The place was abuzz about the theft of the bull; a throng had gathered around the empty pen, speculation, accusation and paranoia was rife on the shop floor. 'Fucking ten grand's worth gone, just like that . . .' The crowd swelled as others came to start work. 'Some cowboys'll most likely be cutting it up in the back of a van,' volunteered a packer. 'I wouldn't be too sure of that. Looks like an inside job to me,' voiced another. 'Easy peasy, no locks or doors broken,' came the reply.

Bonecrusher squeezed my thigh nervously. I put an arm on his shoulder reassuringly and whispered, 'It's alright, don't worry.'

There were many disgruntled people. 'I want my money back. Where are Slates and Sally?' asked one. 'Yeah, salt'n pepper, those two. I wouldn't put it past them to have nicked the beast,' muttered another. 'Not so loud lad, the walls have ears around here,' cautioned an old man. 'I was only joking,' replied the man, a scared look on his face.

Above the crowd appeared the massive head of Pig Thompson. 'Where's my prize, where the fuck is he?' he demanded, ploughing through the crowd, tossing them aside like matchstick figures. He placed his hands on the pen door and tore it from its hinges. Like a huge trembling volcano about to erupt, he stood there before us showing an awesome fury. His fawning minions had ashen faces not knowing where Pig was going to dump his anger. In other circumstances he was always in control; the strong bully taunting the weaklings. Now it was different. Whoever had done this, he said, had done it against him personally.

Bonecrusher and I, now safely on top of the freezers, watched the big man foam at the mouth with frustration and anger. Turning towards the Killers' benches, he caught sight of C.P. Horn standing in front of a mirror combing his hair. 'I bet that bastard had a hand in it. He knew he was in for a beating hands down,' shouted Pig, pointing at C.P. who turned to look casually at his raging colleague. Horn's cool demeanour pushed Pig over the top with fury. In covering the distance to get to him, Pig tossed benches out of his way. As he wasn't the speediest of men, C.P. looked unimpressed. The entire Abattoir crowd stood still in an electrified silence. White lather had now gathered around the big man's mouth as he reached out a hand to squeeze the face of C.P. Horn. Pig Thompson's eyes widened in disbelief as the young man pulled a boning knife from the magnetic rack. The swift slashing motion of the finely honed weapon cut deep between the two middle fingers into the palm of Pig's hand. Blood spewed everywhere, as his huge bulk shuddered with shock, followed by an agonising bellow. The sycophants, at first being unable to believe what they had just seen, recovered sufficiently to wrap towels around the injured man's hand, while C.P. resumed combing his hair as though nothing had happened. Half the fun for us was watching them try to squeeze the distraught giant into the ambulance.

'He's lost a lot of blood,' said one Killer to me, forgetting that I was someone he normally wouldn't talk to. My guess was that Pig could fill a lake with the stuff and still survive. As the ambulance whisked the Chief Killer through the gates, a fitting epitaph was overheard. 'He'll never be responsible for as much as a hamburger again.'

The bosses upstairs, panic-stricken at losing their top Killer, called the police. The unmistakable bulk of Detective Inspector Iain Bull pushed through the Abattoir gates. Accompanied by his sidekick, Sgt. Bland, aka Captain Contempt, they scrutinised every face. No doubt it would be leaked to the *People's Chronicle*, whose headline would read: 'BULL INVESTIGATES BULL THEFT.' Rubbing the stub of his mutilated finger, it was obvious he was determined to wind this one up quick.

Bull, an old hand at the game, must have known that all the statements he'd gathered from the workforce about the Pig Thompson incident were tosh. On coming out of the office, he turned to Bland: 'He fell! These idiots think that's what I am. Pigs may fucking fly but not this one – too fat, that's why. Somebody downed him and probably nicked the bull too. Now I ask you, Bland, why would anyone want to steal a bull?'

'To farm it out most likely,' his colleague replied.

'Farm it out, my arse. I want you on the case immediately. Check out that bastard McGrory who's got the fleet of mobile burger vans. I've never trusted that fucker since all those cats and dogs were reported missing from the streets of Dundredge. He'd mince anything he got his hands on.'

'If that's the case, boss, I'll be in the queue myself for

an Aberdeen Angus burger. But seriously, you don't imagine he'd mince it, do you?'

'The point about having no taste, and that applies to McGrory, is that he can never tell the difference between what is good and what isn't. It's just fodder as far as that twat is concerned. But he's a near-neighbour of Downie, the night watchman. Probably as thick as thieves the two of them,' said Bull.

What they didn't realise was that I heard every word. His eyes flicked in my direction, showing no sign of recognition. Why should he, I thought. I was only one in a row of faceless men whom he passed in The Institution while there investigating deaths by suicide. Bull could always be relied upon, as far as the authorities were concerned. 'Good riddance to another piece of scum,' he was heard to say, on more than one occasion. These cops fought amongst each other like a wolf pack but, when it came to the likes of us, they closed ranks. He was one of those old-fashioned types with thirty five years' service to reflect on. He constantly reminded his colleagues, and anyone else within ear shot, that those were the days, when cops had respect and authority. Not like today when, in his opinion, the bureaucratic restraint on policemen was the equivalent of a tight pair of handcuffs. His part-missing finger was a typical example. Knucklehead, The Black Widow's brother, frequently attacked policemen for no apparent reason and, on this occasion, had been arrested. Bull, on going into his cell with some colleagues to teach him a lesson, had his nose broken. Knucklehead was sentenced to The Institution, where Bull was a frequent visitor. On one of these visits he colluded with staff to extract revenge on him, ensuring that he wouldn't repeat the offence – ever. The hammering was so severe that Knucklehead went do-lally, being placed in the notorious Refractory where he was subsequently bludgeoned to death. In one easy move Bull had reinforced the police motto 'The long arm of the law'. What he didn't predict was that Lockjaw, Knucklehead's brother, would later waylay him in a backstreet, biting off his finger in the attack. Not only that, but swallowing his wedding ring into the bargain. Lockjaw soon followed Knucklehead to The Institution, just prior to his death. Seeing Bull brought back a flood of bad memories; it was a relief to see him leave the Abattoir after taking statements.

Impatient to get home, Bonecrusher and I ran like the clappers to see our prize. He stood there, a magnificent beast, his black hide glistening in the candlelight. The floor was splattered with dung. We bought packets of hay at the pet shop, supposedly for guinea pigs, which we fed to him along with a heap of carrots.

'You big beauty, taken from the jaws of death,' I whispered in his ear.

He seemed content and less intimidating, his animal instinct, we imagined, telling him that all was safe, for the moment at least.

'It was a great idea at the time but what the fuck'll we do with him?' Bonecrusher asked.

'Damned if I know but it sure as hell was worth it, especially seeing their faces today.'

'Yeah, it was great seeing Pig squealing like a stuck pig. You, my beauty, gave us a taste of sweet revenge,' he said, patting the bull on the rump.

'He's gonna need some exercise, isn't he?' I asked.

'I suppose so, maybe we could walk him around the backcourt while it's dark.' Cautiously we led the bull round in a circle, keeping an eye on the windows that were lit up, knowing that discovery would be catastrophic. Having done so without detection, we settled him in for the night.

Lying in bed later, I reflected on my progress to date. Here I was on the outside with a job, a potential girlfriend, a flat and a ten-grand pet bull. It was way beyond my wildest dreams. Stealing the bull had boosted my morale. I could tell Bonecrusher felt the same.

'Hero . . . why did you want to be called that and not your real name?' the midget asked.

'I dunno . . . I suppose in a way I got whacked off being treated like shit'n especially when I know I'm not. Christ, the sweat box was a nightmare'n I suppose, at the end there, I felt I was a hero managing to survive it. I don't mean I am a great fighter or anything like that. It's more like, I sort of manage to get through things by being sneaky. But . . . I know . . . that I'm right and they're wrong. Why did you ask?'

He fidgeted under the blankets before replying. 'Just that I think it's a good name but I'd be too embarrassed to call myself anything like that, people'd say I was a bighead.'

I burst out laughing. 'But you are, lookit the napper you've got.' I could feel him shaking in silent laughter. 'What about you, how'd you get that name?'

'I did it for a bet, breaking bones I mean, when I first went to work in the Abattoir, but mostly to get myself in with Pig'n the others. It worked a treat at first, then they got bored with it, but I got stuck with the name.' He sighed. 'We're nobodies to them but what can we do about it?'

I laughed. 'We just did, we took away their ball and now they can't play their game.' Both of us settled off to sleep, more content than we had been for a very long time.

The following night the girls ambushed me as I was leaving the gates of the Abattoir. They escorted me away from the midget to the sound of whistles and catcalls from the Killers and packers. I was torn between pride and embarrassment.

'We'd like you to be our minder,' suggested The Widow.

'What could I mind?' I replied naïvely.

'You wouldn't have to be slave-driven in there for a start,' said Gloria. They ushered me into Eve's Bar. We slipped through the crush of bodies and found a table littered with glasses, around which sailors sat locked in an alcoholic scrum. Gloria pointed a finger down at them, and motioned to a buxom blonde, presumably Eve, standing behind the bar. Eve emerged with a wooden stave and tapped the sailors on the shoulder: 'Fuck off, come on, outta here,' she said. No one messed with Eve. They grumbled, sidling off to another part of the pub.

Our view across the bar was panoramic, leaving me wondering how it was possible to cram so many people into such a small space. Through a haze of smoke, the full range of human activity was enacted; one group hugged each other, while slavering a tuneless song; two small dogs copulated on a tabletop, to the cheers of betting onlookers; there was a fight, a card game, a passionate couple groping and kissing, others seated beside them.

'All you do is hold the money while we do the business,' explained Gloria. Nearby a loud voice growled, 'I'll blow your fucking brains out.' The man was holding a revolver at someone else's head. Eve looked up, leaned over with the huge stave, and bashed the gunman on the head. He sunk into the crowd, never to be seen again. The gun was magically passed over the crowd to Eve. Around her, eight bar staff served copious amounts of drink.

'You can still do your Abattoir work, if that's what's worrying you,' said The Widow. I was about to reply when my attention was drawn to a point between them where one sailor unzipped another and began masturbating him.

'I don't think I could do what you ask, anyway I've got this sod of a parole officer who'd send me right back at the drop of a hat. Though I would like to see how it all works,' I said, my attention riveted by the activities of the two sailors.

Gloria ordered drinks, including a beer for me. Looking down at the foam-topped liquid, I dipped a finger in to taste it. I grimaced at how awful it was.

'You could become my anchor,' whispered The Widow.

'What do you mean?' I asked.

'Well, you know, me and you. We could be going with each other.'

If ever, in my life, I felt overwhelmed, this was it. I couldn't believe my ears but, as we pushed through the bar doors into the street, she cruised close, putting her arm through mine.

'Oh, oh, getting serious is it?' called Gloria.

'I've got this amazing bull,' I blurted out.

'Hmm, I'd like to see that,' she whispered raunchily into my ear. 'No, straight up, he's huge,' I stuttered, trying to be serious.

'Well, I never! You are quite a Hero after all, aren't you?' she said in feigned mockery. 'I'll put you to the test later.' Oh fuck, I thought, this is all a bit of a mix up.

'Come on darling, time for business,' interrupted Gloria.

The spot where they hung around was approached by shadowy figures who would whisper into the ear of each woman then move into a nearby door, still within earshot. 'Twist it, tighter, tighter . . . oh fuck, even tighter . . .' a voice whispered before relinquishing a sigh so sonorous it gave me palpitations. Oh, for the want of infra-red eyes! One sad character with a dog on a leash approached The Widow.

'Masturbate my dog while I masturbate to you doing so.'

One after the other they popped the proceeds into my pocket, giving me a cash register mentality. Long into the early hours, Gloria finally muttered, 'God, I'm shagged!'

'So long as you're getting paid for it,' said The Widow.

This was the first time in two active hours that all three of us had stood together. I couldn't bring myself to say it but I was at a loss to understand how they could go off with these people and take their strange cocks, or whatever; all that stickiness and strange smells. The runt with the dog had a B.O. problem that was pretty nauseating. I guess maybe the girls were used to it all. It was cold and we stood there shivering.

'Is it okay to come to your place tonight?' whispered a voice from behind us. I almost jumped out of my trousers with fright.

'You shouldn't be near me, for Christ's sake. And no, you can't, as we're being watched,' said The Widow. Turning my head to get a look at who was talking, I was confronted by a man with a lower jaw the size of a JCB. The Widow put her hand into my pocket and fished out a bundle of notes, then gave them to him. 'Take this and lie low because Bull is in a china shop about you,' she warned.

'I heard.'

'This is my boyfriend, Hero,' she said. 'This is my brother, Lockjaw.'

His hand grasped my shoulder by way of introduction. 'I've heard all about you. Great to see you out.'

I was thrilled that he, a walking legend, had heard of me and totally blown away that The Widow had introduced me as her boyfriend.

'Let's go,' she said.

None of my business, I thought, as she sent him packing and we walked along the waterfront.

This bewitching woman was so streetwise. There was a

real tough side to her, hard as brass nails as they say, that much I'd seen in the short period we'd been acquainted. She had me well sussed out, but in a nice sort of way. It was almost as though she'd tuned in to where I was at, her intuitive part understanding without pasting me in it.

'I've met a whore with a golden heart,' I told her.

'You're talking to The Black Widow, honey, and I eat men for breakfast.'

' . . . and throws me the left-overs,' said Gloria.

'Have you really been married?' I asked nervously.

'Three times . . . and each one snuffed it. That's where I got my nickname, see. Rumour has it that I kill them after we've screwed, so keep that in mind. Aha, I bet that's why you're not doing it,' she joked, clasping my arm close.

'Have you really . . . I mean, did they really die or are you having me on?'

'Yeah, it happened. Two of them junkies, each overdosing shortly after we got married. The third, well, he was a pathetic sod. Battered to death trying to pick someone's pocket at a heavyweight boxing contest. Yours truly had to fork out all the funeral expenses, and gets The Black Widow nickname into the bargain. A man-eater, they say I am.'

When we reached the landing of our flat she turned to me. Gloria ran upstairs, smiling. 'I do like you, Hero,' said The Widow, snuggling up close and looking into my eyes. 'But you're not ready for me yet, eh?'

I fidgeted nervously. 'How do you know?'

'Well, I've tried to do enough favours for my brothers when they were inside. You know, give a few guys a bit who've just got out. It was like trying to raise the dead, most of them had me beat, or the drugs they had in there did.' She leaned over and kissed me before going swiftly upstairs. 'G'night,' she called, 'and don't worry, we'll put your bull to the test soon.'

Oh fuck, I thought, I'd forgotten to tell her about it, straight out of my mind it went.

A few days later Bonecrusher and I arrived back from work. On entering the flat we found a stranger sitting at the table.

'Hello lads, nice ta meet you. Just call me Sligo.' He said.

'Who the fuck're you?' demanded Bonecrusher.

'Your new flatmate of course'n sure it's a fine place we have,' he said with a fine Irish lilt.

I could feel Bonecrusher bristling with rage; he could never come right out and say it, but there was a tell-tale sign of disapproval, or resistance, that always came in the form of a verbal handgrenade. 'Spuds for breakfast, dinner and tea, I suppose,' he carped. I knew he'd thaw and acclimatise in his own time. Sligo was lean with an unshaven face and eyes that shone with a devilish glint. Good-looking in an abandoned sort of way, a crumpled cap sat askew on his head. He wore a thick black belt and knotted braces to hold up worn tweed trousers. His boots were treadworn.

'I'm ever so glad Mr Rafferty had the good judgement to put me with two fine fellows such as yourselves. I take two sugars, if you please.' He nodded at me making a pot of tea. I laughed. Bonecrusher went to the toilet, slamming the door behind him. 'Sleeping arrangements will be tight but I'll take the bottom end of the bed. Don't mind me, I'm used to the roads, the stars and the blue skies. Used to sleeping rough I am.'

That first night we lay in bed, whilst Sligo, still wearing his shirt and cap, polished up the darkness with endless tales of Ireland, eventually falling asleep as he talked, to the sound of Bonecrusher snoring. Listening to Sligo prattle away brought home to me how I stood alone, outside of everything; I didn't belong. He was the first patriot I'd ever met, someone who loved his native land. The very idea that he could weep over the tragedies of his country's past, and the problems of the present, stirred mixed emotions in me. The feeling of actually belonging somewhere is something I just don't have. All those years of isolation in The Institution had resulted in my old self being broken down, fragmented into a million pieces only to be resurrected in this new form. Although that long period of being alone provided me with a new belief in myself, that allowed me to get through what I had to, it also affected my relationship with everything else. It had wiped out any longing I might have had for my home, my community, or citizenship for that matter. I guess I had learned to live with myself and somehow that now seemed more important.

Sunday morning had us waking to the sound of Sligo singing to himself. This, accompanied with the mouth-watering aroma of fried eggs, bacon, etc., brought me and Bonecrusher swiftly to the table.

'This is heaven,' I sighed.

'Ah, you lads looked so tired and weary after a hard day's graft, I got up as bright as a button. My first day with you has got to be a good one, I says to myself.' He launched into a tale of sleeping in a barn on the Cork to Dublin road, where the farmer's wife brought in a steaming cup of coffee, and a plateful of what we were having. 'The wonder of it, that saintly lass with the heart of the Virgin Mary, she looked after us lads of the road as a mother would. Milk straight from the udder, butter fresh from the urn, jam from fruit she picked herself,' he reminisced. His words resonated inside me, exposing a hunger that no food could nourish.

Bonecrusher, still miffed at our new neighbour's presence, again went to the toilet, slapping the door behind him.

'I take it he has a bowel problem,' Sligo said, pointing the skillet at the toilet door.

'No, I think you could call it a head problem,' I explained.

'Oh . . . the awful migraine, I suppose.'

'No, a lobotomy.'

'Ah, a lobotomy . . . I can never understand star-gazing at all,' he said vaguely.

'No, a lobotomy is a brain operation . . . well, sort of. They cut two wee holes in your head, stick a tool in, twist it around and hope for the best.'

'And did it work?' he asked.

'What d'you think?' I said, raising my eyes to the ceiling.

In fact, Bonecrusher came round a lot sooner than I thought. Sligo possessed microwave qualities that thawed the midget that first morning. Indeed, it was he who suggested letting Sligo see the bull. With great caution, we showed him our prize possession. Opening the door he looked into the face of the beast.

'Bejeesus! What a handsome fella!' Without any hesitation, he took the bull by the ring and walked it around the small backcourt. 'He needs a bit of exercise, you see, and that pile of shit in his howff must be cleaned out. Come on lads, get to it and I'll rub this beauty down.' I watched from the corner of my eye as Sligo expertly lifted each of the bull's hooves to inspect them. With the palm of his hands he rubbed down its coat, then examined its teeth. The beast responded like an overgrown cat to this knowledgeable attention. All those years on the road, of sleeping on farms, must have given him a wealth of experience. Bonecrusher and I smiled at each other with relief. Having taken the bull on the spur of the moment, it was only now that we could acknowledge that we were out of our depth. Overtaken by the excitement of it, we had taken the plunge in rustling it. The place cleaned out, we settled the bull back inside then sat on the large white sinks looking at him.

'Sure enough, he's a beast to die for,' whispered Sligo. 'Yeah, and Pig almost did,' said Bonecrusher.

'What happens if someone finds him now?' asked Sligo.

'Well, we'll be in shit street,' I said.

'We can always say The Widow and Gloria upstairs stole him for you know what,' suggested the midget cynically.

I felt anger rise in me. 'Cut that out, Bonecrusher.'

'Only joking, only joking. The truth is nobody comes near this slum. They think it's about ready to fall on top of them.'

'Have faith lads,' Sligo brushed his cap further back on his head. 'God being a good Catholic works in mysterious ways. Don't underestimate Him.' A haunting tune from his harmonica seemed a fitting end to our first day together. The Irishman had shaken the cobwebs of despair from our souls. For the first time in my life I fell asleep laughing to myself, as he rabbited away ten to the dozen.

We wakened to the crash of splintering wood as our front door fell apart. It was as though a battalion of storm-troopers were coming through.

'Where's that Irish bastard?' screamed the voice of Slates. The light was switched on to reveal our landlords towering intemperately above us. 'You,' said Sally, pointing a finger as stiff as a poker into Sligo's face, 'have passed us a dud twenty quid note.'

Sitting up, his cap still glued to his head, Sligo noisily scratched his unshaven chin. 'Bejeesus, I couldn't tell a genuine forgery if I fell over it, lads.'

Holding the note to his face, Slates trembled with anger. 'Look, it's got a fucking lion's head on it.'

Sligo squinted at the note, 'Whose head should be on it?'

'The Queen's, you arsehole. Her Majesty the fucking Queen, dimwit.'

Taking the note from him, Sligo examined it. 'Sure and bejeesus it is a lion. But are you sure this isn't just a bad photo of her?'

Sally reached over, pulling the Irishman's face close to his. 'Don't be funny. There's not even a fucking watermark on it.'

Sligo tried to calm him. 'Well now, perhaps you should put it under the tap there then, but I'm fair affronted that you think I would even dream of taking advantage of two young lads who've been so kind, who put me in such a nice flat with two lovely boys. It seems to me that you lads, especially with your fine intelligence, should be looking at you-know-who.'

The two men looked at each other. 'You mean . . .' whispered Slates.

'That's exactly what I mean. Brought from door to door without so much as a foot on the pavement in between,' Sligo said, winking knowingly.

'I can't believe they'd do such . . .' started Slates but he was interrupted by Sally: 'I fucking well can, that mob are taking liberties with us.'

Sligo handed the note back. 'When I set eyes on you two I thought to myself, those lads'll get taken advantage of if they don't take care, and here you are.' The two men retreated out of the door.

'What the hell was that all about?' demanded Bonecrusher.

'Hush laddie, you more than any of us needs his beauty sleep.'

'Why were they on the rampage last night?' I asked as we walked to work. 'Eh, oh that, just a silly misunderstanding, me lad,' replied Sligo.

There was something odd going on that I couldn't quite figure out. It was as though he was hiding something behind an exaggerated Irish facade. 'Sligo, I don't mean to be nosey, but why are you walking to work with us?' I asked.

'Well you, me boy, will be pleased to know that I've got myself a little cleaning job here.'

We approached the building in silence.

'What wages are you getting?'

Pulling me aside, he whispered in my ear. 'We have a very sweet arrangement Mr Sally will collect my money each week for safety, take off my rent and give me five quid to keep for myself. Don't crack a light to anyone.'

On hearing this, the unease deepened within me. 'Sligo,' I began again. 'You know you told them you had travelled all the way in the van, without your feet touching the ground . . . did you come from The Institution?' He stiffened slightly, just enough for me to register it. 'It's okay, you can talk to us; we know, we've been there, both of us.'

He pulled me back into the street. 'Have you ever read Yeats at all?'

I shook my head. 'No, but I've read Steinbeck.'

He looked at me with sadness. 'Ah, but what a tragedy to meet someone denied such sustenance; you're bereft of the great man's solace, me boy. He was a very wise man, so let me recommend his work to you. In fact, me lad, you'll find one in the flat, amongst my wee bundle.'

'What sort of things does he say?'

'Aw, Hero, if only you knew the half of it. My favourite bit goes something like this: "Tread fucking softly or you'll tread on my dreams you idiot. They're all I've got." Now isn't that magic?'

We returned home that night to see the McCoy triplets, Doe, Rae and Mee – they came out that fast, said their mum – emerge excitedly from the backcourt. 'Mister, there's a monster in the washhouse.' All three of us attempted to shut them up but it was too late. Their shouts brought out the Mulhearn brothers, Blue and Red, both of whom were armchair alcoholics.

Mrs McCoy came running out. 'What's the matter?' she asked the boys.

'There's a monster in there, Ma,' said Doe.

'I came out for a piss the other night and thought I saw a bull myself,' said Blue.

Mrs McCoy burst out laughing. 'You've been drinking too much of the Bull's Blood, I think.' Sligo gestured for them to hush as footsteps approached. It was The Widow and Gloria.

'What's this then, a tenants' meeting?' asked Gloria.

Sligo put his fingers to his lips, 'Mum's the word mind,' and we escorted them to the washhouse door. Their faces looked on in amazement when I lit the candle.

'Is that the one that was on the news the other night?' asked Mrs McCoy.

I explained to them why we had done it and they expressed enthusiasm.

'What a beauty! And I thought you meant the bull in your pocket Hero, had me all hot and flushed at the thought of it,' said The Widow, batting her eyelashes flirtatiously.

'Can we feed it, Mister?' asked Rae.

It soon became clear everyone looked on the bull as a symbol of our having triumphed over our landlords, whom they despised.

'They'd have made a fortune out of it,' said Red.

'What'll happen if they find out that it's in here?' asked Mrs McCoy.

'They'll charge it rent,' replied Blue. We all laughed.

'It'll not get found out 'cause we'll guard it,' said Mee.

'Have you ever seen their likes in your life, eh?' said Sligo, smiling at the McCoy triplets.

'You handled that bull so well, have you ever worked on a farm?' I asked him.

'Born and bred in the slums, rats'n rust all me life. I've spent many a fine night dreaming of ploughing the fields, sowing the seeds and, if you think I'm good with a bull, wait till you see me with a combine harvester,' he winked. Afterwards I realised that this was the first time we had really met our neighbours. Under normal circumstances, we would scurry past each other. This was one thing we had the bull to thank for.

At the Abattoir the day after, Slates slouched against a pillar packed with parcels of meat I'd brought to him. 'This place hasn't been the same since Pig Thompson left. Where's the rest of the meat?' he asked.

'I got this amount from Deadeye, suppose you should ask him,' I replied.

His huge hand lifted a weighty parcel. 'That bull, have you heard who gave it the chop?' He scrutinised my face.

'We never hear a thing, nobody tells us the time of day,' I answered.

'Well, the cops are still sniffing around 'cause they think it's an inside job.'

A trickle of fear ran down the back of my neck. Fear was this big man's collateral; he worked on the assumption that weaker individuals like us would tell all, or else. Each of us living under his roof knew exactly what his intimidating potential was. But what he failed to understand was, how his fear and bullying generated contempt and loathing. Of course, we'd laugh and talk nicely to him, we had no option. He and his sidekicks believed in one miracle, that you could get blood from a stone, and that every attempt should be made to extract it. Each of us, on the other hand, had little or no way of protecting ourselves from any of this. But we had known worse; and it was uncanny the way the bull had become a catalyst, a symbol of our pride. Inevitably, as more of our neighbours got to know, the stronger we became. Whenever Slates or Sally abused us, we would think of the bull. Now we had something that gave us a lift.

'Right, load that into the mini – neatly,' Slates ordered.

As I did so, Sally turned up carrying a holdall. 'Is he around?' he asked his pal.

'Bang on time, if you'll pardon the pun.' Slates nodded at C.P. Horn approaching, cleaver in hand, Deadeye trailing behind.

'What is it?' he asked Slates.

'I take it you were bad at arithmetic at school.'

A puzzled look came over C.P.'s face. 'What're you getting at?' C.P. slapped the flat of the cleaver across the palm of his hand.

'I mean that trolley isn't as full as it should be. You don't seem to realise that we've had a good understanding with this place for some time now but, since Pig left, that understanding hasn't been up to the mark, so to speak,' said Slates, looking disdainfully at the cleaver.

'It may be that you've not appreciated my position as Chief Killer here. I am the man in charge now,' C.P. replied confidently.

Slates looked to Sally who shook his head ruefully. 'Look, son, had you told me the problem was money then that would've been fine, we could've sorted that out no bother. But you're not. You're trying to take liberties and that's not on. Let me put it this way . . . you are a . . . a sausage-maker let's say, and one of these days you'll probably be a half decent butcher. You come here carrying that cleaver without showing respect to me and, more to the point, you trail that one-eyed nonentity along, which further embarrasses me. Now to put this into perspective, Pig Thompson to you may have been the real competition but, to me, he was a big tub of fucking lard who did exactly what he was told. What he *did* have going for him is something you lack, half a brain.'

The longer Slates had talked, the paler C.P. became. Finally Slates grabbed the cleaver from C.P.'s hand. Sally pulled out two harnesses from the bag, stood up grabbing C.P. Horn to him and, with fluid movements, put a harness over Horn's shoulders before he could utter a reply. Slates casually walked to the freezer door, opened it, and made way for Sally to enter carrying C.P. Taking him to the nearest hook, he hung the Killer alongside the row of cow carcasses.

'I didn't mean it . . . I'm sorry . . . please, please, let me down.'

Grabbing Deadeye, Sally repeated the exercise then stood before the two men now suspended and pleading forgiveness from the rail. 'Learn from this, or you'll end up like that dead meat,' he warned, pointing to the cadavers alongside him.

Slamming the freezer door, they walked towards the mini where I was still loading meat. 'I told you he was getting too big for his boots. How long will we leave them?' asked Sally.

'That depends. How long did we leave the last one?' Slates asked.

'He went blue after an hour and a half.'

'How long till frostbite?'

Sally whistled to the foreman. 'Bob, how long till frostbite?'

The foreman rubbed his chin thoughtfully. 'About three to four hours.'

'Give them two hours. We need him to cut meat for next week,' said Slates. 'And before the bastards come down, mind and ask them what they know about that fucking missing bull. I still think that bastard's behind it.' Pushing me aside, he squeezed into the mini, driving off.

On entering my supervisor's office he lifted his gaze from the papers on his desk. 'Eleven years, nine months in all . . .' He turned a page, his eyes stealing every word from the report. 'Hmm, a troublemaker, to boot, and clearly eleven years in the sweat box didn't sort you out.'

Talked a lot to himself, he did. The impeccable dress, razor-sharp creases in the pants and spit-polished shoes had a definite whiff of neurosis.

'I despise would-be rebels, Ferguson, and you had better understand that. I've seen them come and go. Now then, what have you been up to, had a hand in nicking that bull, did you?' He gave me a cold, penetrating stare.

'Me, a bit heavy for me!' I replied, showing him my hands.

'Oh, a smart arse too.'

'Not a bit of it,' I said, shrugging my shoulders.

'Well, your landlord seems to think it was an inside job, not in your league though, but that you may just have a hint of who did; see anybody lurking around with a van or anything like that?'

He pulled out a hanky, unfolding it elaborately. Blowing his nose was a major exercise. Choosing a square between the folded creases, he attacked each nostril then refolded it to its original form, placing it back in the same pocket before inspecting his fingers. He looked at me coldly and was about to say something when a commotion outside his door interrupted. Crossing the room to open it he found two of his clients pushing and shouting at each other. Closing the door behind him I could hear him screaming at them to calm down.

I took advantage of his absence to look at the report:

JOHN ALEXANDER FERGUSON: AGED 12. PLACED UNDER CARE AND PROTECTION ORDER. THE ABOVE NAMED HAS SHOWN A PROPENSITY TO VIO-LENCE WHILE IN JUVENILE DETENTION. MOMENTARY PROGRESS WAS SHOWN AT ST. JUDES YOUTH DETENTION CENTRE WHEN FR. McGON-NIGLE TOOK A KEEN INTEREST IN FERGUSON. EMPLOYED IN THE LIBRARY TO ASSIST HIS LIT-ERACY HE SHOWED EXEMPLARY PROGRESS. A FULL REPORT OF THE INMATE'S SUBSEQUENT UNPROVOKED ATTACK ON THE PRIEST IS ATTACHED. HIS TRANSFER TO THE INSTITUTION LED TO A DETERIORATION IN HIS BEHAVIOUR. FERGUSON DID HOWEVER RESPOND POSITIVELY TO PROLONGED DRUG THERAPY. A LONER, HE SETTLED WELL IN THE ISOLATION BLOCK. HE WAS

OBSERVED BY STAFF THERE TO BE AN AVID
READER BUT NON-COMMUNICATIVE. STAFF CAU-
TIONED THAT THEY HAD TO BE WATCHFUL OF
HIM AT ALL TIMES. THE RECENT INTENSE MEDIA
CAMPAIGN SURROUNDING NON-CRIMINALS BEING
HELD IN THE INSTITUTION HAS INSTIGATED THE
SECRETARY OF STATE TO REVIEW ALL SUCH
CASES. MR HUGH CASSELS, Q.C., CHAIRMAN OF
THE INQUIRY, RECOMMENDED THAT FERGUSON
BE RELEASED WITH DUE HASTE SAYING HIS PAR-
TICULAR DETENTION IN THE INSTITUTION AS A
JUVENILE WAS A BLIGHT ON THE CRIMINAL
JUSTICE BILL. HIS ASSESSMENT DREW ATTENTION
TO THE RECENT CONVICTION OF FR. McGON-
NIGLE FOR A SERIES OF SERIOUS SEX OFFENCES
AGAINST YOUNG INMATES AT ST. JUDES DATING
BACK TWENTY YEARS. IT IS BELIEVED BY THE
DEPARTMENT THAT ALTHOUGH THEY ACTED
WELL WITHIN THEIR REMIT IN PLACING FER-
GUSON INTO THE CARE OF THE INSTITUTION AND
ALTHOUGH THEY HAVE TO BOW TO THE DECISION
OF THE SECRETARY OF STATE, THEY INSIST THAT
FERGUSON BE PLACED UNDER SUPERVISION IN
THE INTERESTS OF PUBLIC SAFETY. ALL THE RELE-
VANT REPORTS ARE ENCLOSED.

It was as though some mental block had immediately prevented me connecting to what I'd just read. In those first
seconds, it was as though, in one page, I'd read someone
else's entire life history. It was difficult to believe it was
me. Fr. McGonnigle, a name that burned a hole in my
heart. Who would've believed it, a priest sending me to
hell and damnation here on earth? Until I met him, I'd

had half a chance of making it. Once he had condemned me in my innocence, I was lost to all sense of decency . . .

'Right, let's get back to where we left off. You realise that part of the conditions of your release is that you must not fraternise with known criminals,' he said on returning.

'What kind of animal are you?' I asked.

Ignoring my question, he continued flicking imaginary dirt from his white shirt. 'Come on, answer the question, Ferguson.'

'Hero, my name's Hero,' I shouted.

'The problem with you, my lad, is that you're supposed to report everything to me and you're not. Now that isn't a very good start. I am very suspicious.'

I could feel the first tingles of it entering me as I looked into his dead, grey eyes. When it happened, it was like a dam bursting, spreading the anger surging through my body. His mace of authority began to evaporate. 'No one told me,' I whispered.

'Come, come, Ferguson, you know the rules, and they must be obeyed at all times.'

'No, no . . . I don't mean that . . . you never told me about THAT! Nobody did,' I said, pointing to the file.

'I want to say one thing to you, Ferguson, and one thing only . . .' It was the first and last time I was to experience power levitation. Lunging clean off my feet, I grabbed him by the throat, hauling him over the desk like a wet rag. 'Hero, my name's fucking Hero, geddit!' His specs dangled from one ear, his eyes bulged with fear. 'Say it, you bastard, go on say it.'

'Hhherroo . . .' he muttered.

'Say it loud and fucking clear, or I'll pull your tongue from your head.'

'HERO!' he shouted.

Grabbing the report, I pushed my face into his: 'This,

you fucker . . . none of you told me. My life typed out in one shitty page. Not one single fucker mentioned it . . .'

His grey pallor turned a sickly yellow with fear as his eyes pleaded with me not to hit him. ' . . . I'm taking this so you can charge me with theft. So that I can charge you sick fuckers with the same . . . theft . . . theft . . . of my fucking rotten life'. Taking the ink bottle from his desk, I poured it over his head before turning to leave his office for good.

Things were never the same after that. Instead of feeling as free as a bird, I felt the opposite. Returning to the flat, I put the report under the mattress. Almost as though I was in a comatose state, I pulled the blanket over my head thinking hard of what I'd read. In black and white, officialdom had exonerated me, but so deep was my mistrust of them that I couldn't take it in. The things they had written about me throughout those years had created so much agony for me, even though the substance of the documents was petty and mindless. The handwritten reports by the guards were often incorrect in spelling and child-like in their scrawl, and all of them had a similarity of content that lacked originality. Each reporter lifted from the previous one, changing the wording slightly. The night observations of me, over the years, were identical: 'The resident slept soundly.' To all intents and purposes, I never had a bad night. Huh, and what about Fat Head and Gorky, whose indecipherable scrawl repeated this phrase over and over. Shit, what is he doing tonight, what poor terrified bastard is copping it right this minute? Getting out of bed I leave the others sleeping soundly . . . I throw a coat over my naked body and enter the street.

The coldness of the night air stings my ears as I stand on the pavement watching two rats drag the body of a dead pigeon towards the sewer grill. Their beady eyes look into mine. No, these rodents, furtive and sly, possess a nature similar to Gorky and Fat Head, preferring prey that is defenceless. The heavy overcoat does little to keep the cold from my body. A draught of air is drawn from below, turning my balls into blue chestnuts. I should stamp some heat into my feet, but abstain till the rats dispose of the carcass; why should I spoil their impending banquet? There is enough misery around without me adding to this kill-joy mentality; people bent on heaping their wretchedness on others. There is no shortage of them; mothers, fathers, wives and lovers; policemen, judges, priests and ministers; politicians, nuns and, of course, guards. Each, no doubt, would at this moment stamp their feet to shoo the rats away. Heroes of the human race, defenders of dead pigeons. I wonder, if I piss down the grill after them, will they consider it ale to wash down the dead bird? There are rats, and there are rats. Biggies, and smallies; fatties and thinnies; some are rodents, some are human. Myself, well, I know more about the latter than the former. Had I a choice, of living life under there, in their underworld, I'd find it much better than here. I can see it plain as day. Me, trudging around, through mile after mile of sludge, knee-deep in putrid waste, all of it consisting of that which is rejected from above. Imagine me being the Hero, of the rats and the maggots. I could build up an army of all that is detestable, a shoal of reprobates, we'd swim the length and breadth of the sewers. Rats and rats, the four-legged furry ones, and the two-legged human ones, living cheek by jowl. Here, in this place, I'd be Hero of the Underworld. I like that, I like that very much.

My wandering takes me through the wide open gates of the graveyard where I now sit camped on a desecrated gravestone. I reckon the dead of the night is exclusively reserved for the mad and the bad and, of course, for those who have since passed away. Into what category do I fit? At times like this, I am just not sure. The wails from a nearby fiddle do nothing to elevate the atmosphere. Dead is dead, is dead. The Fiddler parades the narrow pathways, serenading those decomposing underground. Who is he, what is he doing? Rumours abound, but the sympathetic explain it away by telling a tale of melancholic proportions; a devoted husband lamenting nightly the death of a much-loved wife. Others less so, suggest a self-imposed penance for his past indiscretions that drove her to death. Others suspect him of necrophilia; this group swear to have seen him humping a corpse. As though to add credence to the lie, it was whispered that the glint of a Vaseline tin could be seen in the moonlight. Both sides vociferously defending the authenticity of their story are often brought to the point of violence. What did it matter, what harm did it do? Was he any different to those two creeping shadows over to my right, burglars returning with their booty? Together they dig a hole, depositing the bag of loot into the mound of a newly buried child. Perhaps, and this is more likely, the Fiddler has been mistaken for them. What on earth brought him into the world to live the life he does, to stand accused of what he does? I'll tell you, regardless of the suspicions of that lot out there about this poor bastard, the truth is he's got it sussed. He knows this fucking rotten system is into self-destruct and is fiddling, while Rome burns.

Huh, Rome – the Papal City. It was from here that Father McGonnigle was influenced to become a priest. Being brought up a Catholic, having in those innocent days of childhood worn out my fair share of rosary beads, I was intoxicated by the Father, the Son and the Holy Ghost – all three in one. I would look at priests as possessing a purity beyond reproach. What a fucking joke, how could I ever have done so? McGonnigle and his betrayal has scarred me beyond belief.

Relief comes in the form of a piss, where steam from hot urine rises before my eyes. Grateful for small mercies, I know at this moment, in this period of madness, I suffer from acute myopia; I'm someone who responds to the greeting 'isn't life great?' with 'I don't fucking know because I've never been allowed to live it.' I'm the sort of person whose knuckles are bruised through knocking on life's door, asking to be let in. Surrounded by people who have long since accepted their exclusion. I'm locked into this recurring nightmare trying desperately to throw off this blanket of failure, whose capacity to suffocate me is remorseless. The roar from the odd car heralds the beginning of a new day, even though the darkness gives no hint of daylight. My freezing cold bum warns me that it is time to go, to leave the madness and darkness of night behind, to return to the routine of convention that dominates everyone's existence. We enter and leave the world in the same way; have the common denominator of eating, sleeping and shitting. One would imagine that would be enough. But no, these people compete to dress, commute, work and socialise in the same way. Is this what I aspire to?

A paperboy runs to the newspaper board. Releasing the clip he slides in the latest headline: 250 DOWNED IN AIR CRASH. There you are, a bit of a drama.

As I entered the flat, Sligo and Bonecrusher stopped dressing. 'Lookit the state of you!' said Bonecrusher, eyeballing me from head to foot.

'Oh boy, you look like Paddy McGintey's goat with yir bleery eyes and tufted hair,' said Sligo, taking my arm and pushing me into a chair.

'Have you been out with *her*?' asked the midget, raising his eyes to the ceiling.

'Do you know I shouldn't have been in there,' I told them.

'My, my, was she too big for you? I bet you could get a train up it. Anyway, I told you about wee guys like me. One shout Hero, and I'd have appeared like Sir Lancelot.' Bonecrusher clutched his groin.

'I mean The fucking Institution, you stupid cunt. I should never have been in there in the first place.' I got up to retrieve the report I'd taken from my supervisor.

'What's new about that, none of us should've been there,' said Bonecrusher. I fanned out the pages of the report to show them. 'See, I took it from the bastard. It says it in here.'

Sligo pulled out his copy of Yeats. 'This will do more to cheer you up than that,' he said.

'But I could sue the bastards.'

'Hero, stop taking yourself so seriously,' said Bonecrusher, and they both burst out laughing.

'Come on, we'll be late for work.'

We walked most of the journey in silence.

'Cheer up Hero,' said Sligo, 'you're free, remember, nothing will bring back the years.'

'We're as free as the bull,' said Bonecrusher.

Throughout the day that remark stayed with me, as did my bad temper. All those dreams I had in The Institution were so simple and straightforward, but then our lives are full of broken dreams. Yet here on the outside there remained that claustrophobic feeling, as though I was still trapped.

The heat in the Offal Room was unbearable as I stood in the lung container, cramming organs, one after the other, into a plastic bucket. The thick red slush was tepid, giving off a smell similar to that of sour milk. Condensation created a hazy mist throughout the room, giving Bonecrusher a ghostly appearance, as he moved around the heart tank thrusting them into the small plastic buckets.

Sligo walked out of the door shouting over his shoulder, 'Your dad would be proud of you, lad.'

If only he knew, if only . . . An early memory I had of my old man was when I was drawn to the front room by the howls of Fred, my two-year-old kid brother. Dad, demented by the unending screams, lifted Fred by the right foot, swinging him head-on into the door, causing it to slam shut. Fred didn't stop crying. In fact he got worse but my old man could never get the hang of the equation, more pain brings louder screams. Dressed in his army greatcoat, which had been glued to him, he sunk into the hollow of his old fireside chair. Even at that age, my old man failed to impress me. He'd sit staring ahead in his chair, holding on to an old metal billycan. As I approached him, his fingers would tighten around the wire handle and, on drawing parallel, he'd swing it at my head causing me to duck as it swished past my ears. 'Bastard,' he'd mutter. Whenever I was within a few feet of him, my antennae latched on to any hint of movement, thus avoiding him. The truth was, he was too far gone. For years he'd hidden from the military police in a small niche underneath the floorboards, a hidey-hole that had saved his skin many a time. The only person to drag him bodily out of it was Aunt Letty, and she swung him around like a wet rag. He headed there at the first sign of her, and remained there on best behaviour while she was around. Maw eventually got the house changed to her name to prevent the police kicking the door down. She pleaded with him many a time to give himself up but he was immovable. His clapped-in jaws and unshaven face sticking out of the army greatcoat epitomised his bunker mentality.

It all started to come to a head when I was twelve. One night Maw bathed me and Fred before putting us to bed. As always she knelt at the bedside with us to say some prayers. Fred let out a mumble jumble of nonsense in lieu of the Hail Mary. Sometimes he'd get melodious causing Mum and me to smother our laughter. She'd then always apologise to God for it. That particular night I remembered looking at her, drawn and worn. She seemed to be filled with a weariness that burdened her like never before. Mind you, the old man being as batty as he was didn't make matters easier, and then there was us two. She lay beside us that night, something she'd never done before.

'Son, you be a good boy and always say prayers for your Ma, and look after your wee brother,' she whispered, stroking my hair in that familiar loving way. I fell asleep watching her scrub our clothes in the sink. My old man's continuous finger-drumming on the billycan sent me into a slumber.

'Mammy, mammy,' cried Fred in the morning. Rousing myself from sleep I peered up to see her swinging from the pulley alongside the newly washed clothes. At first, I thought she was playing some strange game.

'Da, Da,' I called, waking him from a deep sleep on the armchair.

'Oh my God!' he shouted, throwing the billycan to the floor and running towards her. Wrapping his arms around her legs he began to cry and we followed suit. Our neighbours were good; everyone minded their own business, but at times like this they rallied round. Aunt Letty was round like a shot but couldn't handle it. In fact she went on the booze in a big way. So, it was down to Mrs Maloney next door, who had eleven children. She handled *all* the funeral arrangements for us. The last of the great soup-makers in the street, being her neighbour was the equivalent to staying next door to a superstar. Twice a week she made a huge pot of the stuff, the aroma of which had everyone living in the close sniffing the air. This made her kids so popular all of us would stick to them like glue in the hope of being given a bowl of soup. Whenever my old man went over the top she'd take Fred and me in. Like us, they had a room and kitchen; their sleeping arrangements were eight in one bed and three in their mum's, which was where we'd squeeze into on our overnight excursions. 'Make way for the reserves,' she'd shout to her lot while heaving us bodily into bed. Her bulk and strong character left everyone in no doubt that she wasn't to be messed with, but for us staying, those nights were memorable.

'Hey, hey, what the fuck're you doing . . . leaving all this to me?' cried Bonecrusher, wading towards me. 'You've been in a dream and doing sweet fuck all. What's the matter with you, eh?'

'Oh nothing,' I mumbled, 'just cruising through old memories.'

'He stood up and scratched his huge forehead. 'That's the thing about me, I never have that. I can remember sweet fuck all before The Institution, d'you know that? You're such a lucky bastard being able to.'

I shook my head. 'That's what you think . . . well, in a way it is but sometimes it can be sore.'

'What d'you mean?' he asked.

'Just that . . . not everything is happy memories. Sometimes when I think back about my Ma, or my old man, you know, it can be pretty sad.'

'Na, that's piss. What I can remember from The Institution, I make sure it's happy. You know, there's a wee boss in my head that cracks the whip telling the mushy part to stop messing around. Even when I try to think about who my parents were. You're no longer there, it says, so let it be . . . and, although I try like fuck to think of what happened before, my wee boss tells me not to be daft as I'm here now, and what happened then is immaterial. He's in charge and, if you think about it, he does no a bad job.'

The three of us sat around the table discussing ways to cheer up the flat when Inspector Bull and his cohort Bland entered without so much as a 'hello' and sniffed around like a couple of bloodhounds.

'Have you seen that bastard Lockjaw?' Bull asked. All three of us shrugged.

'I know where you wide boys come from so don't think I don't. Now that cow upstairs is hiding her brother and you've been seen with her,' he said, pointing his finger at me.

'Of course I see her, it'd be hard not to as she's a neighbour, so what?' Bull is the type of cop who hates anyone being even remotely cocky to him.

'Listen, you idiot,' he sneered, tapping his finger against the side of his forehead, 'I know you've been in the barmy cane, but that's no excuse for being snide to me.' He punched me on the chin. The thump sent stars shooting through my head as I fell to the floor. As I got to my feet I saw Sligo shivering with fear in the chair. Bonecrusher stared at the wall.

Bull walked across the room and leaned against the sink, his back to the window. 'C'mere,' he ordered.

I walked towards him rubbing my head.

'Two things are getting right up my fucking nose. One is that bastard Lockjaw. If you see him, I want you to get in touch with me right away. Okay?'

I nodded my head in acknowledgement, keeping my eyes averted by looking into the backcourt. At that moment, I caught sight of Red Mulhearn, obviously blind-drunk, holding the bull by the nose. The triplets, Doe, Rae and Mee, were busy assembling a dustbin so that the equally drunk Blue Mulhearn could climb on to the back of the beast.

'Two, that fucking bull was stolen and it was an inside job. You and your two pals there are close to all this activity and are bound to hear something, just a whisper that's all I need.' Jesus Christ, I thought, please don't turn around. If he had he'd have seen Blue get up only to fall over the bull, much to the delight of the triplets.

Bull reached out, pulling me by the collar. 'You are the leader here so I'm expecting you to make sure those two do their stuff, d'you hear?' Looking past him I could see Blue making a successful mount, then leaning over to help the triplets on. 'I'll do my best,' I said, as Red tugged the bull out of my vision. 'That's a nice boy, just what I like to hear, good co-operation.' He rubbed his hands together as he and Bland walked out of the door.

Hurriedly, I opened the window and whistled to the triplets, urging them to get the bull out of sight. Fortunately, Bull and Bland didn't think to go into the backcourt.

I rushed up to The Widow's flat. She lay in bed looking ravishing.

'Come in and keep me warm,' she teased, snuggling into her downy.

'Don't be daft,' I said. 'Guess who's just been at our place?'

After listening to what had happened she sat up, her firm breasts bare to the world. 'He's a mental case, and fucking well dangerous. I keep telling Lockjaw to get away for his own good.'

'Why doesn't he?' I asked.

'He can't stomach the idea of running away, especially from Bull whom he hates. Truth is, he'll kill that bastard one of these days. I know it's in his heart.' She sounded worried.

'What the fuck can we do about the bull, we just got by with the skin of our teeth there?'

'I know a young trainee lawyer, Ruth Oliver, who recently inherited a farm. I'll suss her out,' she said.

'A lawyer,' I said suspiciously. 'Can she be trusted? Surely she'll run a mile from resettling a nicked bull?'

'Leave it with me,' said The Widow.

There was a sigh of relief when I told the others.

'I'm sorry it has to go, but so long as it goes to a good home,' said Sligo.

'Our success in nicking him will be complete if we can ultimately free him,' I added.

That night in bed I lay awake while the others slept. In a strange sort of way I envied Bonecrusher his lobotomy. Maybe, I thought, I'd like something a bit more accurate, that could extinguish those bits that brought me most pain. Fred, my younger brother, was one source of this. I could remember those early signs, registering that he wasn't quite right. One morning he woke up to discover that he had been struck dumb – just like that. I didn't realise it right away, but it suddenly dawned on me when it got to lunchtime and he hadn't asked for anything to eat. Now that was really something, as most days he could eat us out of house and home.

'Somebody stole the cat's tongue?' I asked, nudging him. Not a word.

'The best news in donkey's years, as he's a moaning-faced bastard anyway,' was my old man's response.

Fred missed Maw. For ages after she'd gone he'd point

to the pulley where she had ended it. This annoyed my old man fiercely. 'Do that again and I'll crack your head,' he'd shout at the boy. Fred's problem was, he could never master the art of avoiding the swinging billycan. I spent forever giving him lessons, but he was a dunce.

I did have some good times with Fred. He came into his own when one of our neighbours died, and his deaf wife gave us their old gramophone. Fred was obsessed and bewildered by it, and would sit for hours listening to the music. He was never the full shilling, Fred, but it wasn't his fault as we'd never had anything like this in the house before. I figured out that, in not knowing what a long-playing record was, he imagined that someone was inside singing. 'It's a bit crowded in there today,' I'd say jokingly when a band was playing. Suddenly, he would creep up on it like a panther, throwing open the lid to catch the person singing inside. This became a regular feature that attracted my pals. I could've sold tickets for it. 'Put that bastard Cliff Richard on,' they'd jeer. 'Yeah, I hate the fucker, set Fred on him,' they'd shout. One day, just as Fred was approaching the turntable to catch Cliff Richard, there was a knock on the door. A priest, introducing himself as Fr. Anthony, asked if he could enter and bless the house. I hesitated not knowing what to say.

'Is . . . is God not everywhere already?' I asked stalling for time, knowing my old man wouldn't want him in. My mind wrestled with that old conundrum: Dad would give me a hard time letting him in, God would send me to hell if I didn't. Fuckit, I'd prefer to deal with God later, than Dad now. Suddenly, as though God had read my mind, a blue flash, followed by a loud bang, filled the air.

'Jesus Christ!' said the priest, blessing himself.

'He's here?' I asked, shuddering. We entered the room. Fred lay on the floor, his face blue, his fingers clasping wires from the gramophone. The priest knelt at his side to check his pulse, then began administering the last rites just as Dad popped up from beneath the floorboards like the resurrection itself.

'What the fuck was that?' he asked.

After the funeral my family life began to resemble the song, 'Ten green bottles hanging on the wall'. Here I was, twelve years old and hardly seen the inside of a school; it was as though, officially, I was invisible. The whole thing came to a crunch when Dad wakened me in the middle of the night. This was after spending three days and nights under the floorboards without so much as a piss. Telling me to get dressed, he dragged me by the hand through the dark, deserted streets, his eyes bulging with paranoia.

'Are you okay Da? You don't look your usual self?' I whispered.

'I've fucking had it with those floorboards. Enough's enough,' he shouted.

'But Da, you've been there for years, you've stayed there through Ma's suicide, Fred's kamikaze . . . this just seems . . . well, crazy, so why do it now?'

'Right up my jacksy it went. One fucking splinter too many, that's why.' Pulling me into the police station he stopped at the front desk. 'I deserted from the army twenty-two years ago, and I've come to wipe the slate clean,' he shouted at the uniformed cop writing in a ledger.

The bored desk sergeant took one look at him and said, 'If you don't get out of here and take that kid home to bed I'll put my boot up your arse and stick you in a cell.'

There you have it: Dad, not having touched a street in years, now doing the decent thing, and being told to beat it. If they had taken him seriously and locked him up, my guess is he'd have returned to sanity, and been here today.

The response however was so far beyond his comprehension, that he held open his army greatcoat as though he was Batman before shouting at the top of his voice 'Geronimo!' and throwing himself over the counter, on top of the cop. The desk sergeant, used to such behaviour, pressed the panic button, which had immediate effect. A team of bluebottles buzzed out from behind a door and whisked my old man off.

I was taken to the canteen for a mug of hot tea, and a chocolate biscuit. Afterwards, they allowed me to sleep on a mattress on the floor in a vacant cell. I spent what was left of the night listening to my old man curse and swear while pounding his cell door. This cop shop, it seemed to me, was a zone where the rule of law was suspended. Drunks were heaped together in a tiny cell where they snarled and lashed out at each other. Young offenders were punched and kicked by policemen for no other reason than malice. These same cops sat with me at breakfast displaying kindness itself. Mrs Maloney called to collect me, and I was elated at the prospect of being the twelfth Maloney; but the cops had informed the Social Services who sent an inspector to find out more about me. Within three days, two staff from the local authority arrived to take me to a residential home where I was placed under a 'care and protection order'. As they dragged me into the car, chased by a posse of Maloneys, neighbours joined in to pelt the two officers with flour, eggs and brush poles. On arriving at the home, the two staff immediately set about punching me.

'You little bastard, it's all your fault,' they screamed.

Out of the corner of my eye, I could see a cluster of children's faces peering through a glass door. They laughed and heckled. This of course didn't make my lot any easier. However, I had long since learned that there is always an up side to every down. The kids in the place immediately put me on a pedestal; for them to experience two staff in this condition was a refreshing source of fun. They made me tell the story over and over again.

This was Dornywood, Home for Abandoned Children, its history dating back to the seventeenth century. The thing about institutions like this is that one simply walks through a doorway into a time warp. The traditions, rituals and customs consume everyone who enters. The staff are so-called free people but they themselves are different on the inside to what they are on the outside. The person I was at home wasn't the person here in Dornywood. I was cowed and afraid even in those rare moments of bravado when with the other boys. No, the thing was that here you had to abide strictly by what went before, there was no shaking free from it.

While Bonecrusher and Sligo slept routinely, my natural cycle had been broken since taking the disturbing report that confirmed my innocence from my supervisor. I often took to the streets. One night, I was walking along the footpath of the canal, the moon reflecting a perfect image on the water. Ahead, I saw a silhouette of two figures, sheltered beneath the bridge. Coming nearer I saw two men, their hands stretched towards the flickering flames of a bonfire; the aroma of a barbecue twitched my nostrils. Both men warily kept their eyes on me as I approached. Satisfying themselves that I wasn't a threat, one offered me a swig from the bottle he was holding. I gulped deeply, slaking my thirst, and was surprised that it was in fact water. Their faces were caked in dirt, from having spent many a year using the pavement as a pillow.

'What's your name, friend?' asked one.

'Hero.'

'Good one. My name's Warthog, this's my pal Skelly, a man who has never looked anyone straight in the eye in his life.'

Sure enough, he had the damnedest cross-eyes I'd ever seen.

'Used to be called Max Sennet but he changed all that, but then he's the best fighter between us,' winked Skelly.

'Looks as though you guys're having a banquet,' I said, nodding at the meat roasting on the spit.

'You're the sort that refuses nothing but punches, Hero. A man after my own heart,' said Warthog.

'Yeah, I can see he came just for the food,' added Skelly.

'No, not really,' I told them. 'I can't sleep so I just wander the streets at night.'

'Right Hero, grab this lot,' said Warthog, holding out the charred meat.

'That'll put hairs on yir chest,' said Skelly. The food was absolutely delicious, and I must confess to eating my fair share, thanks to my generous hosts, who also gobbled enormous portions.

'Where're you guys headed?' I asked.

'Wherever the morning takes us,' replied Warthog.

'You don't live any particular place?'

'Na, we're free and easy. Sleep where we can, eat what we can. Been like this for five years now,' Skelly explained, tugging away at a piece of meat.

'Well, the way you guys eat, you do well on it.'

'Oh, we're not always so lucky but we cracked it tonight,' retorted Skelly.

'Come off it, Skels, we live like kings! You see, he tries to make it all sound miserable, so that less people will move into our patch. My thing is, the more everybody moves out of the rat race, the better life will be for everyone,' said Warthog.

'I don't think that lot up there are going to be knocking you down in the rush,' I replied.

Warthog nodded. 'See, I told you,' he said to Skelly.

'Well I don't know, but I didn't start out on this by choice, mind you. Hit the booze, lost the job and family. I'll not bore you with it, as it's old hat. But it was tough in those early days, took some getting used to. I can tell you that now, but fuckit! I wouldn't change this life for a million pounds. I'm as free as a fucking bird, and it's just great,' said Skelly.

'Do you get social security money or anything like that?' I asked. Both of them laughed.

'Not on your Nelly, it would be an albatross around our necks; it ties you down, making you run round in circles till the next week. Can't do this, can't do that . . . Fuck! I did that for two years after being knocked redundant and it just about drove me crazy. Me, a master joiner, going in to sign on, being interrogated by somebody that'd hardly started shaving. Demoralising, that's what it is, fucking demoralising,' said Warthog.

'There you go, you've just proved my point. That's exactly what I've been trying to tell you, thicko,' replied Skelly.

'What, what did you say . . . I didn't hear you say a fucking thing.'

'Just that, it's only a matter of time, till all those fuckers living like that switch on. Think of it man, millions of unemployed, some of them right smart bastards. Now, can you imagine them putting up with that for years? I tell you it's only a matter of time till this place is packed to the gunnels,' Skelly explained.

'Hey, that meat was fucking brilliant. Will we put the rest on?' asked Warthog.

'What about tomorrow, I thought we were keeping some for tomorrow night?' Skelly reminded him.

'You're so fucking conventional, Skelly. Take a look at that moon, think of the crack we're having, feel the atmosphere and let's live for the fucking moment!'

'Ah fuckit, you're right. The night's young, and who gives a fuck if Hero there eats us out of house and home? Ring for the fucking chef!' said Skelly.

All three of us broke into loud laughter. Warthog pulled a red hot poker from the fire, spitting on it. 'Snared a lot of rabbits did you?' I asked.

'Are you joking, couldn't bear the thought of it,' said Skelly.

Warthog moved to a nearby box covered by a dirty blanket. Pulling it off, he leaned forward with the poker. Standing up, I crossed to see what it was; just then the agonised squeal of rats filled the air, as Warthog killed five of them with the poker. The cage contained about eight. Moving off, I violently threw up till my stomach was empty, staggering along the canal path.

'Hero, Hero, are you okay, chill out man! We're really sorry,' shouted Warthog as he raced after me.

'We really didn't think about it, sorry man,' said Skelly. They got to me just as I was about to retch up my stomach lining.

'Oh fuck, that was horrible. You should've told me,' I said.

Warthog pulled me by the arm, back towards the fire. 'We just didn't think, Hero, honest,' said Skelly.

'I should've sussed that you didn't like to see animals killed, it's just that we're used to it,' explained Warthog. My mouth opened as I gaped at them, still dazed. Gagging and spitting, I shuddered.

'Kill as many of the bastards as you want, it's fucking

eating them I'm on about,' I said leaning over to retch once again. It was their turn to gape dazedly at me.

'What, you mean the food!' said Skelly in amazement.

'You could've fooled me, the way you guzzled it down,' added Warthog.

'You are a bit of an ungrateful bastard, if you ask me,' said Skelly. I was now in the bizarre situation of trying to pacify them, while tugging strands of rat meat and spew, lodged between my teeth.

'Look, I know you meant well, but I'd never have eaten that in a million years, had I known what it was. I thought it was rabbit, not a rat!'

'Actually, it was three you ate; but what's the problem? It's not as though we got these out of the sewer, or something like that. These came out of the grain mill over there; these fucking things are fed on the best this country has to offer. Okay, so they may eat the odd pigeon but, fuck me, pigeons are a luxury food nowadays. The way you're going on, it makes me feel like a cannibal or something. I just can't believe the hypocrisy of it. Mr Outraged, quite happy to eat a wee bunny rabbit, that never did anyone a day's harm. It's shit like that that makes me glad to be out of the rat race,' said Warthog, who leaned over to lift the cage, showing three large rodents, their snouts covered in blood from cannibalising their dead companions. This time, I vomited over the cage. God knows where it came from, but it did, in thick lumps.

'Fucking Jesus, you've just ruined our fucking breakfast,' cried Skelly.

Warthog looked on in disbelief. The vomit, having covered the rats, frightened them; but almost immediately they recovered, to sniff and devour this new delicacy, their small, darting tongues lapping up every morsel of the vomit.

'Ah shit, that's it ruined, I'm not eating those now, not after them eating his vomit. Let the fuckers away, and we'll get new ones tomorrow,' said Skelly.

'That'll be right. I'll kill the bastards, just to make sure its not them we catch tomorrow, otherwise he'll get the impression we'll eat anything,' Warthog retorted.

While they discussed the next day's rations I sat with my head between my knees. 'Here, try some of this water,' suggested Warthog in a conciliatory tone. Checking it over, to ensure it was what he said it was, I took a large gulp, rinsing my mouth out before spitting it in the fire. It's funny how one's mind thinks at times like this, but I'd have given anything for a handful of my old saviour – laxatives – to purge clean my insides.

'You see, Skelly, let that be a lesson to you. The life we lead takes some getting used to,' Warthog remarked. 'Now, if you think back to when you first hit the streets, there's no way you could have tucked into a rat for supper. Had I offered you a choice between a fish supper and a rat supper, I know which one you'd have taken. That's something you tend to forget when you argue that the masses are about to join us,' Warthog remarked.

The end of another sleepless night spent walking the streets – I cursed my insomnia. On arriving home, the two of them met me on their way downstairs.

'You been depressing all those people in the graveyard again, Hero?' asked Bonecrusher.

'Oh you look a bit of a state, me boy,' added Sligo.

'You'll never believe it,' I replied, shaking my head.

'Don't kid yourself,' answered Bonecrusher.

'I had a rat barbecue on the canal.'

Both of them stopped dead in their tracks. 'A what?' they exclaimed in unison.

'A rat fucking barbecue.'

'On the canal?' asked Sligo.

'Yeah, that's what I said.'

Bonecrusher shook his head. 'And what the fuck is a rat barbecue, a crap carry-out or something?' he asked.

'No . . . next to the canal, I mean. These two guys I met, they're living on the streets, that's what they eat. I didn't know what the fuck it was and I ate some. It was fucking rats, they were as big as cats,' I explained, feeling my stomach begin to churn again at the thought of it.

That night they asked me to show them the rat eaters. 'They might not be there, these guys just wander off at a whim,' I replied.

As we approached the bridge, sure enough they were still camped there. 'Hello Hero, nice to see you again,' welcomed Warthog.

'Thought we'd seen the last of you,' hailed Skelly.

After the introductions, Warthog pointed to the spit. 'Just in time for supper, lads.' All three of us shifted nervously.

'It's okay, we've just had a Chinese take-away,' I explained.

'Ah'm fucked if I know how you can stomach that foreign food,' replied Skelly.

'Hope you lads don't mind us carrying on,' smiled Warthog, continuing 'we're a bit like royalty tonight, Hero. Look at this, some cracking plates, Skelly found them in a skip this morning. Our luck was in, so back to the grain mill to get a few juicy ones and, hey presto, we thought another night under the bridge was in order.' Skelly held his plate proudly, while his pal shoved three rat portions on to it.

' . . . and you don't have any place to stay at all?' asked Sligo hesitantly.

'Of course we do, here,' replied Warthog confidently.

'But how do you stand it, like now in the winter?' asked Bonecrusher.

'Take more clothes from other people's clothes lines and pile them on. Skips are full of burning material, and the span of the bridge keeps the worst of the frost away,' said Warthog.

Both of them knowingly pointed fingers at each other, in what must have been a well-rehearsed routine: 'But when our balls turn blue we weld ourselves together,' they said simultaneously. 'A tour de force we are, just like that old song,' extolled Warthog with gusto, as they both crooned, 'Oh we aint got a barrel of money, we may be . . .'

Together, still holding portions of rat, they wrapped their arms around each other, kicking one leg, then the other in a can-can dance. They did a neat little number, their gravelly voices chasing the few remaining pigeons nesting under the bridge. They were silenced by a ramble of drunken voices from above. All of us froze in unison; Warthog cautiously stepping forward to look over a wall next to the bridge parapet. We followed suit, seeing two luxury coaches disgorging people in formal black tie into the courtyard of an hotel for what turned out to be a wedding party.

Clambering over the wall we walked to the rear of the building; a row of long panoramic windows ran from one end to the other, revealing a sumptuous dining room. Tables were laden with cutlery in preparation for the dinner. The top table was decked with the most spectacular bunch of flowers.

'Lookit that!' exclaimed Warthog, pointing to a magnificent wedding cake, five tiers high.

'Have you ever seen anything like it in your life!' exclaimed Sligo.

As we stood with our faces pressed against the window, a figure appeared, causing us to jump back before realising it was Warthog. Very carefully he prised the top tier off then handed it through the window to Skelly, who teased as he took it, 'Go get your own now.'

Warthog did just that, returning for the next layer, and the next . . . till nothing was left. He carefully closed the window behind him, then all five of us retreated into the nearby bushes.

'There's nothing to beat a good bit of wedding cake after a rat main course,' quipped Warthog, burping loudly.

The guests entered the dining room. The newly-weds looked a picture of happiness sitting at the top table beside the in-laws.

'They look happy enough,' said Skelly.

'Wait till they find out their cake's done a runner,' warned Warthog, letting out a walloping fart, bringing all of us close to tears with laughter.

'Hog, that is fucking lethal!' cried Skelly.

'Sorry, wedding cake always does that to me. Right, no more farts please till we see the rest of this movie.'

Sitting contentedly amid the debris from the wedding cake we looked on as the guests swept through each course. The first signs of animated conversation began amongst the staff.

'Somebody knows all's not well in Denmark. Lookit that huddle of penguins in the corner . . . ah ha, here's the manager. See how he moves through the tables pretending everything's hunky dory . . . any minute now he's gonna shit himself . . . [BURP] pardon me. See the bride's old man, him with the military moustache. Look how he's jerking his head to one side. Now there's someone that's seen a bit of action in his time. Oh oh, he's giving the manager the eye. Ahh, now there's the cavalry in the form of the chef. Look at those hands flailing, there's a real maestro for you. Knows what he's talking about, pointing right to the spot. Ahh, now they've seen the crumbs. He'd make a good detective, that chef. Hmm, it's getting serious, look at the way the old major's grabbing the manager by the scruff of the neck ... oh ... ah ... jeez ... she's burst into tears. Fuckit, I hate movies with sad endings. Well lads, it's time we did a vanishing act,' whispered Warthog as he rose from the grass.

Cautiously we sneaked out on to the street. We had barely separated from the duo twenty yards away, when police cars came from all directions.

'Right you lot, against the wall. Who are you and what the fuck are you doing here?' asked one cop, all in a mouthful.

'We've just come home from work,' I lied.

Warthog and Skelly were shepherded towards us.

'Do you know these three?' a cop asked Warthog. He replied first with a loud burp before saying, 'Them, never seen them in my life before.'

He then began to pick lumps of icing from his woolly jumper, putting them in his mouth.

'Frisk the lot of them,' ordered the sergeant.

'What the fuck is this?' asked a cop, pulling the cake topping from Warthog's pocket.

'And this?' asked another, extracting a lump of wedding cake from Skelly's jacket.

'I know you're gonna find this hard to swallow, but I've just been married and that's the cake. You'll now have to congratulate me, you lucky thing,' said Skelly.

'And who in their right mind would marry you?' asked the cop.

'Well, if you really want to know, I did,' replied Warthog, taking the cake from the cop's hand.

At this point the old major emerged from the hotel

bursting with anger. His presence brought the police standing to attention.

'We've got them, sir,' said the sergeant, holding the small wedding figures.

'These two sir, they're the culprits,' added another.

'If I may make a point please. This is our first night on honeymoon and your behaviour is atrocious. If you don't release us immediately, I'll report you to my uncle who is the chief constable,' Warthog announced.

The old major grabbed Warthog by the throat, 'I am the bloody chief constable, and you've ruined the happiest day of my daughter's life.'

The other cops grappled to pull him off as a Black Maria arrived. Warthog and Skelly were thrown inside and it sped off.

'You three, fuck off,' said the sergeant.

Later that night we sat on the washhouse sinks looking at the bull in silence.

'What'll happen to them?' Bonecrusher asked.

'It doesn't bear thinking about,' replied Sligo putting both hands on his head.

'What fucking luck, the chief constable's daughter!'

'Mind you, the cake was nice,' observed Bonecrusher.

'All the same, Warthog and Skelly will be in for it.'

'Och, they'll get a decent bed for the night, a warm plate of porridge first then a good kick in the balls,' replied Sligo.

'Yeah, that mob'll string them up by the short and curlies, okay. The cops'll get their pound of flesh before they get near the court. That's their way of saying, do what you want to others but not to us,' I said.

'Boo!' shouted The Widow creeping into the washhouse.

'Christ, what a fright you gave me!' shrieked Sligo.

We told her about the arrests and she replied, 'Forget it, they'll never see daylight again.'

The idea of the two ramblers being locked up in such a confined space hit all of us hard. We discussed ways in which we would be able to help. The Widow suggested speaking to her lawyer friend, asking her to visit and defend them. I felt particularly affected by their predicament having known them that bit better than the others. Realising this, The Widow grabbed my arm. 'Hero, could you help me move a wardrobe in the flat?' she asked. Once inside her door, she closed it and turned the key.

'Where is it?' I asked.

'Here,' she said, pointing to herself. Snuggling close she kissed my neck.

'C'mon, let's get into bed.' Before I knew it we were naked on the bed with her lips hungrily searching mine. Like a masseuse she stroked me tenderly, sometimes lingering for the briefest of moments at a sensitive spot. I touched her with my trembling hand, letting my fingers rub gently against her hard nipples. She moaned. 'More, some more please.' Although my body felt the excitement as her hand expertly played with my cock, it remained dead.

'Hero . . . let your hands touch me . . . everywhere,' she whispered. I did as she asked, feeling self-conscious that everything she did to me failed to raise a gallop.

'Let me make you come at least,' I pleaded with her.

'Okay.' She placed my fingers on her clit. Once having built up a perfect rhythm she took off, huffing and puffing, bucking and rocking, till finally she fell off the edge into a body-twitching orgasm.

'I wish I could do that, I only wish I could do that,' I whispered.

'Oh Hero, one of these days we'll make it together – that was great, you brought me off so beautifully,' she said with a shiver, before kissing my lips. Her scented sweat was all around me.

'I'm glad, at least it doesn't make me feel altogether useless,' I replied, nodding towards my still limp cock.

'It'll take time, time's the healer,' she replied encouragingly.

'Will you help me with it?' I asked.

'Only if you promise to keep giving me orgasms like that.'

'Ha, this guy Graves said, to bring the dead to life is no great magic. But what a fucking liar he was,' I joked, looking down at my still limp cock.

'Aw Hero, laugh and the world laughs with you . . .' She nuzzled me with her wet lips.

'Fuck, it's hard putting up with this, when I think how in there I'd dream of this moment, imagining myself like a wild animal in bed with a woman for the first time. Look at me lying here beside your lovely body, and I'm fucking useless.' Immediately I said this I felt much better.

We lay together in silence, skin touching skin, and soon the sound of her even breath told me she was asleep. Watching her I felt lucky having her as a girlfriend, her beauty and strength, her finely chiselled features now so relaxed and calm. This still night was ours, two nearly-lovers at peace with one another. It was this moment that fed my hopes for a future with her, free from all that both of us had previously known. I drifted off with my lips on her flesh, into a haze of dreams about our laughter and joy, being free . . .

'Hey, waken up sleepy head,' said The Widow hugging me close.

'Oh fuck, there I go again, wasting valuable time,' I said, more to myself than to her.

'It's what happens from this minute on, big boy,' she whispered, her hand cupping my balls.

'You're a Catholic, aren't you?' I asked.

'Yeah, a lapsed one, but how'd you know?'

Reaching down to grab her hand, I whispered, 'Because you believe in the resurrection.'

When our laughter subsided, The Widow held me tight. 'Hero, let's get out of here, away from all of this.'

I stroked her hair. 'Now, there's a thought worth having. I'm as free as a bird, without a penny to my name, that is.'

'But if we put money away we could do it.'

'What, on five quid a week? It'll take us a lifetime to get the train fare.'

'If I go for more tricks we could soon get it together.'

'Then you'll really be saddle-sore.'

'I can't get enough,' she joked in return.

'Seriously,' I suggested, 'I could bide my time and see if Slates will give me a pay rise.'

'You'll sooner get blood from a stone.'

'Yes, but God loves a tryer,' I replied.

The night was bitterly cold as the bull pawed at the ground and we stood around him in the backcourt.

'Does he need to go?' bawled Rae and his brothers.

'He needs to go to a good home, so shut yir geggy,' shouted Mrs McCoy, losing her temper.

'But we gave him a good home, Ma!' yelled Rae.

'For Christ's sake, when are they coming to take it away?' asked Mrs McCoy in exasperation.

'C'mon then, up you lot get.' Sligo threw first Doe then his two brothers on top of the bull before leading them off around the backcourt for the third time.

'How do you know this lawyer won't sell it for hamburgers anyway?' asked Red Mulhearn suspiciously.

'The Widow said she's okay,' I replied.

'I wouldn't trust a lawyer for love nor money, if you asked my opinion,' said his brother.

'Same here. Remember that bastard that got me sixty days for pissing in the street. Now was that no' a case of me being thrown to the wolves by that lawyer?' asked Red.

Bonecrusher entered the backcourt, followed by two men wearing luminous white gloves. 'They're here,' he said, nodding over his shoulder.

'Who are they?' I asked.

'Don't worry about them, they'll never say a word to anyone. That much you can bet on.'

'How do you know?'

'Because they're from the Dummy Gang.' Almost on cue, the two men began to make rapid signals with their hands. 'They'll shift anything from a camel to a crane,' whispered Bonecrusher, holding a hand to his lips. One of the men approached the midget making signals with his hands.

'Oh fuck, they can't do it as the van's broken down.'

'Yippee!' cried the triplets.

'So much for the camel to a crane.' I mumbled in exasperation.

Slates' office was on the bottom floor of a tenement block, a single-room flat he had converted. Two huge rottweilers wearing muzzles surged forward at the sight of me.

'Sit!' shouted Slates from behind a desk. The dogs obeyed and Slates returned to counting wads of money which he casually tossed into a metal box at his feet. Sally sat nearby drinking a beer, his leg draped over another chair.

'What do you want?' he asked.

Taking a leaf from Sligo's book, I tried a bit of dip-
lomacy.

'Slates, I don't want you to think I'm playing on your
generosity. I'd hate you to think I was seeing you as a soft
spot as you've been really good to me. Is there, do you
think, any chance of me getting a pay rise?'

It seemed to work. Instead of booting my head in, he
puffed his chest, adopting a philanthropic pose.

'What I like about you, Hero, is that you're the only one
amongst that bunch of nutters that I can speak to. That
midget for instance, he's the cheekiest bastard on earth.
Fuck knows how you and that barmy Irishman stand him.'

Sally nodded in agreement. 'I'll squash the wee bastard
one of these days,' he said. 'Oh boss, big Morty called the
other day saying if we have anybody on our books, he's
needing somebody – there's your man.' He pointed to me.

'Brilliant idea,' said Slates. 'Right, my son, we've got just
the thing for you. It's a live-in job that'll put fifteen
smackers a week into your hand – not to be sniffed at, eh?'
He winked and threw another bundle of cash into the box
before leaning down to lock it.

'Sounds good, but I'm not sure about the live-in part,
especially as you've got me in a nice flat already,' I said,
lying through the back of my teeth.

'Don't worry, you'll love it. Sally, get Morty round here
pronto,' he ordered, dismissing anything further I had to
say.

Morty was tall with a pencil-thin body, and deathly grey
pallor. 'Hello Slates, Sally,' he said, tipping his lum hat on
entering.

'Morty, how're you? More to the point, how is business?'
asked Slates.

'Dead busy, dead busy,' he replied gravely.

'There he is, what'd you think?'

The tall, angular man turned to look at me, rubbing his chin thoughtfully. 'Is he reliable?'

'As a Rolex,' said Sally.

'Is he strong?'

'As a great big fucking ox,' replied Slates.

'Is he trustworthy?' enquired Morty, with a serious look on his face.

'As a Swiss bank. This young man will cost you fifteen smackers a week, the usual conditions applying of course,' said Slates, with a knowing wink.

'Fifteen! I could get an army of immigrants for that!'

Slates waved a finger saying, 'Not with the talents of this guy, you won't.'

Morty rubbed his chin thoughtfully, while looking me up and down. 'You do have a lost look about you, just the sort who would relish a very dead-end job with wonderful prospects,' he said.

'Does that mean you'll take him?' asked Slates.

'Yes, I suppose so,' he sighed resignedly.

The Mortician

On the way out he introduced himself. 'My name is Morty, I'm a mortician,' he said, pointing to the black hearse parked at the kerbside. 'The job will, you are aware, be live-in; food supplied, your first month's salary being repaid to your old landlord, by way of compensation, understand?'

I nodded, going along with it anyway, as the wage-rise would mean The Widow and I getting away from all of this sooner rather than later.

'Do you by any chance have good references?'

'Just what they told you.'

'Oh well, follow me.' The inside of the hearse had a sickly sweet smell.

'Will I get time off . . . to see my girlfriend, that is?'

'Dead right you will, so long as you do your work properly, your free time's yours to do what you will. There may, however, be busy periods when that will be impossible,' he added as an afterthought.

'Is it hard work?'

'Dead easy, dead easy. But, we do have our moments you know. I get up every morning and pray for a disaster. Good for business they are.' He smiled wryly.

Entering his funeral parlour, we passed four doors, each with signs saying Resting Room. We continued along a narrow wood-lined corridor, the end of which led downstairs to a basement. It was deceptive in that it was huge, cutting a swathe beneath the street above.

'This is where you will work. That section is for coffin infills, over here is the cold slabs reserved for washing the bodies before final preparation and dressing. Over here, behind the curtains, you'll see your residence, and next door is mine.' He slid back the curtains to reveal our respective areas, each housing a single bed with a neat bedside cabinet attached. 'I don't allow smoking here as it's detrimental to the deceased, as well as being bad for my sinuses.'

'It's okay, I don't have any bad habits,' I grovelled.

'You're breathing,' he muttered. 'You may, if you wish, go to your former abode to gather your remains, returning by six thirty sharp,' he instructed.

When I got there no one was at home, or at The Widow's, so I wrote a note telling them about the new job and having to live at the Funeral Parlour. I visited the bull, feeling guilty at leaving the others with the burden of looking after him.

On my return, trying to find Morty, I peered in all four doors along the corridor. Each had an open coffin placed in the middle of the room, surrounded by flowers: all of them contained a dead person, looking as though he or she had just lain down for a short nap. As I came out of the last Resting Room, a voice shouted, 'How dare you!' It was Morty, his eyes glinting. 'Under no circumstance must you enter the Resting Rooms during opening hours. At all other times, you will remain below. Do you understand?'

'Yes, well I am sorry but . . .'

'No buts. The basement – now!'

It took me all of two minutes to sort my things out. The bed had a nondescript downie and double pillow similar to that of Morty's. Apart from the discomfort of his close proximity, the living conditions were an improvement on the flat, though I wouldn't admit this to the lads.

'Would you like some tea?' asked Morty, creeping up behind me.

'Oh, yes please, two sugars and a spot of milk.'

'We only take black here,' he said. Handing me mine, he retired to his bed space. The sound of his chair grating along the floor was followed by an incredibly loud 'SLUUURP' as he supped from his cup. No doubt I'd have to get used to it. Still, I was the sort who was thankful for small mercies. Peering through the split in my curtain, into the dimly lit basement, I could see some books on a shelf. Tiptoeing across, I read a title: *Embalmed with Loving Hands*. Another read *Formaldehyde: How to Immortalise your Organs*. The others were dense, and technical.

That afternoon Morty took me aside, 'You must never – ever – get emotionally involved with your clients. Understand?' said Morty. 'Your behaviour must be impeccable at all times, your dress orderly and clean.' Walking to a cold slab he pulled the white sheet from a body. 'This,' he said, 'is Mrs Taylor, the local dentist's wife. Like most others in her condition, she forgot to let out her last breath, which means we now have to free it. This part of our preparation is called Fart'n Flush.'

She lay there grey and still, the skin on her face like a dried handbag. It was hard to believe this thin gash, that was once her mouth, had uttered words.

'Stand back,' warned Morty. Pulling off his tight-fitting jacket, he casually rolled up his shirt sleeves. Taking a large pair of scissors, he cut free her clothes with the expertise of a para-medic. In seconds she lay naked before us and as cold as marble now that death had frozen all her assets. Large folds of fat hung around her waist like treadless tyres.

'You, my lad,' he said, 'will proceed to wash down her body. Remember this, Mrs Taylor lived a good and useful life, so handle her with the utmost care. Having just recently gone, her spirit may still be with her, reluctant to leave because of her good deeds.' Placing his ear to her midriff, he beckoned me to do likewise. There was a peculiar rumbling of Mount Vesuvius proportions. 'Right, grab both her feet by the ankles lifting them high above your shoulders. Quick now,' he ordered.

I rushed, as keen as mustard, to obey his command, only to be sprayed by a ferocious spurt of liquid shit.

'Consider that your first lesson. Now then, start by washing yourself down first,' he said, taking his jacket before disappearing with the hint of a smile on his lips.

This being my first wash-down, I was quick to cotton on to the problem areas. In order to get into the jowls of her fat face, I had to grab, vice-like, her head, while my free hand wiped away the dirt from along the crevice. She burped loudly, causing me to step back, falling over the bucket of shit I'd just cleaned up. Trapped wind, I wondered to myself, or the reluctant spirit warning me to take it easy perhaps. On attempting to turn her over, gravity, like the Devil's embrace, defied my efforts to do so. At the halfway stage she lay, bum in the air, head off the slab, at which point she let out a massive fart. There's nothing more nauseating than the scent of dead fart, but even I had never before been this close. The sweat now pouring from me dripped steadily on to her back. When finally getting her face down and washed, Morty peered in.

'Good job, turn her over now,' he ordered, then he went quickly upstairs.

By this point I now hated Mrs Fucking Taylor. 'You big fat turd, you've probably eaten your way through a dozen bakery shops, without a thought given to those who have to deal with your dead weight,' I muttered to myself while heaving her over again. Morty glided alongside. 'Hmm, very good, very good start indeed,' Taking a strong steel needle he threaded it. 'This is to give shape to the face,' he said. 'In the old days we simply placed a hefty bible under the chin, to set a sombre, but peaceful mood to the face. Nowadays, it's a stitch inside the top lip, then through the bottom one, before a final figure of eight. It ensures that the mouth is kept shut, stitched up tight in other words. Remember that lad, in more ways than one. This place holds many secrets, bears witness to many strange things, and you come highly recommended. Here, discretion and silence mean a great deal. You'll go far by observing these rules.' Having finished the sewing, he stepped back to observe his work. Cutting the thread, he tucked the edges inside her lips. Mrs Taylor's eyes gazed vacantly at the ceiling. 'Now, unlike what you see in films, the proper way to close the eyes is as follows: Take a small ball of cotton wool, damping it like this, then squeeze out the excess water before applying to the eyeballs, like so. Once moistened slide them down,' he said, inviting me to have a go. Sure enough, they closed like well oiled lids.

'There now, guaranteed not to wink,' he said proudly. 'Mr Taylor, bless his heart, wants her embalmed. First things first, let's plug and seal all other orifices.'

This is where Morty's skills shone like a beacon. His hands moved swiftly, pressing together the appropriate amount of sealer to plug the various holes. Stretching and tugging dead flesh, he rammed the vaseline plugs into her rectum and vagina as quick as a flash. Dispensing the clotted blood congealed underneath the flesh on her face and body, he brought a hue of normality back to her appearance.

"The key to all of this, my lad, is balance. We inject

these chemicals, to make sure that the blood taken out of the heart is replaced by artificial colouring.' He rammed a huge needle into her chest. 'Too much gives her the colour of a beetroot, and we wouldn't want that, would we? They'd accuse us of putting her under a toaster wouldn't they?'

Together, we heaved her over to the preparation and dressing area. Having got her into the frumpy dress, Morty applied make-up that gave her demeanour peace and tranquillity. The artist that he is, Morty stepped back and walked around the body, scrutinising it for weaknesses. Dissatisfied with something, he undid her blouse, tugged down her bra, grabbed her nipples tightly between forefinger and thumb, and jerked them violently towards the ceiling. Re-doing the bra, and blouse, he stood back. The breasts had improved immeasurably.

By the time he had finished she lay there like Sleeping Beauty awaiting the Prince. I made a note in my memory bank, that if I wanted to look good before they cremated me, this was the guy to come to.

No sooner was she dispatched to the Resting Room when Shuffles, a colleague of Morty's, appeared with another client, Dr Simpson, a gynaecologist. As we removed the coffin lid, we saw that he lay naked with a massive hard-on.

'He died on the job,' said Shuffles dryly.

Morty, without so much as a blink, reached out, grabbed the dick and squeezed it tight, thus shrinking it immediately. White sperm oozed from the foreskin on to his fingers. 'His last shot,' he said.

After that first week, any distaste I felt about dead people soon evaporated. Although the bulk of what I did involved the odds'n sods of flushing'n farting, I looked forward to working alongside Morty; it was an education in itself. There seemed no shortage of bodies, as Shuffles carried

them in and out as though there was a full-scale massacre
going on up there. What was fascinating was the daily
turnover of dead bodies. We were a sort of indoor parking
lot for the dead – no sooner in, than they were out. It
wasn't till I had this job that I gave it any thought, it was
like a conveyor belt of dead people, a few so badly damaged
that we simply screwed the lid down, and that was that.
Morty had built up a good reputation because of the quality
of his work, so he was worth keeping an eye on; a bit like
listening to Granny. He knew all the tricks of the trade;
from plucking plukes to lopping off and filling wart holes.
With a twist of the fingers, he could turn the saddest client
into the happiest. People were heard to say, 'he must've
died a happy death', all because of Morty's skills. Mourners
of a suicide, who had thrown himself under a train, were
so carried away by the smile on his face, that they clean
forgot the dead person's previous unhappiness.

Shuffles, Morty's colleague, had been with him for many
years. He acted as front-man at funerals, starting first by
meeting the family, transferring the body from house to
parlour, then taking charge of the burial or cremation. A
strange old sod, he was nevertheless good at his job and
well thought of in the business. He was renowned for his
solemn shuffle (hence the nickname) when leading the
hearse on the journey to the church. Other funeral parlours
sent their trainees to study him and, rumour had it, he had
a following amongst mourners. It was certainly true that a
lot of the same faces turned up at different funerals. One
could never tell whether they were what is known in the
trade as professional mourners who like nothing more than
to attend a good funeral service, or indeed fans of Shuffles.
Whatever, he was proud of his position, knowing he made
a substantial contribution to the good name of the
company. A tall, almost skeletal man, he resembled Morty,

a shade thinner perhaps. People say the eyes are the window of the soul, until I met Shuffles I thought this was pure pap. But here was a man whose red-rimmed shifty eyes told me he was soul-less. I considered him someone capable of anything. Yet the minute he hit those streets, shuffling along in that deadly fashion in front of the hearse, his unique style transformed him in some illusory way, giving dignity to the funeral. It was the weirdest thing I ever did see.

One evening Morty invited me into his compartment for an evening meal, a sure sign that I was making good progress. He had a portion of chicken. Wearing a collarless shirt, he sat on his bed, inviting me to do likewise. It was funny seeing Morty look dishevelled, as he was always smartly dressed in that funeral way.

'You're doing a good job, my lad. Dead on I say.' He tore the chicken apart, then crammed it into his mouth. Cracking through bones he swallowed the lot in a one'er. No prisoners were taken.

'I'm glad you think so, as I really like working here. I'm learning so much. Being here makes me think of things I never thought of before.'

'Dead right it does, what sort of things?'

I thought for a bit, not knowing how to respond. 'Well, for starters . . . hmm . . . well, it's the strangest thing, doing what I do to these people who were . . . were sort of walking about hours before. I don't mean any disrespect, or anything, but it's just like working in the Abattoir in a way. I keep wondering, in fact I'm even dreaming, about where the other part goes; the part that thinks, walks, talks and does everything else. D'you know what I mean?' I felt quite stupid at the way I was describing it.

'My dear boy, you are indeed a thinker, so let me give you some simple advice. They come in here in all shapes and sizes, all creeds and colours, from every background you can imagine. Death is the great leveller. The thing to remember in life is this, that all of us come into the world in the same way, and we leave the same way. What sits here on this bed, eating this food, is our physical bodies. The vehicles, or let's say the packages, that will carry each of us through our lifetime. The other part, the thinking, talking, walking, feeling part, is the mystery. All we do here is clean up and dispose of the packages that carry that mystery around, in physical form.' He gulped down a mouthful of chicken. 'D'you get it?' he asked, to the crunch of chicken leg between his teeth.

'Yes, yes I do. That was very well put.'

'Dead on, dead on. Now then let's get back to my plan for you. Over the next two weeks, I intend giving you some basic tuition in embalming. But it's important that you get an overall picture of the business. I want you to start work earlier, so that your basement work can be set aside for the 11 a.m. funerals, following from start to finish. Observe and capture everything, including the magic of Shuffles McGuiness, that is truly worth learning. As well as giving you a good grounding in the practicalities, it will let you see the effort we put in to making this the finest funeral parlour in the city.'

'This is great . . .' I said, chuffed at his confidence in me.

Now, to expand your knowledge of the death industry, I've made arrangements for you to attend the City Mortuary, as we've many good friends there, especially Philip Bliss. A fine young man. The experience you get there will complement your work here. They will be menial tasks in the beginning, as one would expect, but if you want to get anywhere in this world, you've got to start at the bottom. Now, how is that girlfriend of yours?'

'Oh, well, I've been so busy here I've only seen her once but we're saving up and she's working extra hard.'

'Sounds nice, what does she do?' he enquired.

'Hmm . . . she gets . . . does riding . . . I mean she's a riding instructor,' I said nervously.

'Horses . . . ugh, can't stand the things myself, so she's a good rider I suppose?'

'I don't do a lot myself, but so they say.'

'Good, maybe you should get more practice. Remember that tonight, as usual, I do my fortnightly Rigor Mortis Course at the mortuary. Shuffles will assist you with the new client. Make sure you put all the lights out when you're finished,' he instructed.

Shuffles entered and gave me a curt nod. 'Let's get to it then.' Taking off his jacket, he folded it neatly on the chair then carefully rolled up his sleeves before putting on a white gown. Walking to the cold slab, he peeled off the sheet. His long fingers probed the body, a young woman in her early twenties. She was blonde, a natural blonde, and very beautiful. Her card indicated the cause of death as being suicide by an overdose of barbiturates. Shuffles, in his dispassionate way, took a flat stainless steel pan and placed it beneath her bottom. Moving to her chest, he pressed hard on her breasts, those shifty eyes of his whirling in all directions. The body let out two loud burps. Proceeding to the cavity below her rib cage, he gently, almost caressingly, stroked down to the top of her pubic hairs, causing dribbles of urine to fall into the waiting pan. He continued till it ceased. All of this was done in silence.

'Get the cleaning materials please,'

'You . . . you lead those funerals so well Mr McGuiness,' I said nervously, trying to break the silence.

'Hmm,' he replied.

'Morty would like you to teach me.'

'Get me some more scented water please . . . I decide who I teach,' he replied. I brought him the water. His eyes stared steadily at me almost as though he was looking deep inside me. I felt a great fear and discomfort. 'Do you know who Charon is?'

'Never, who is she?'

'Charon is a man! The ferryman who conveys the souls of the dead across the river Styx into Hades.'

Lifting his finger, he pointed ominously at me. 'Each day the wailing souls of sinners swoon and sway as I punt my pole, pushing that ferry through the mist and water to the raging flames on the other side. A journey of no return, for those passengers locked into perpetual torment, cursed for their sins against the Almighty. That short span of the Styx being the moment when those pleasurable sins of the past demand their price. That is where she will pay for her fornication and debauchery,' he raged, pointing at the dead blonde.

I stepped back nervously, suspecting he had flipped his lid, but he continued.

'Nothing crackles sharper, nor wails deeper, than a fresh dead soul pushed by these calloused palms into the intense heat. Their souls will singe in Satan's fire, not for a moment, but forever. Each day I do this for the Almighty, knowing that the evil deeds of the Devil will keep me employed in perpetuity.' Agony burnt into his brow, as he stared, hollow-eyed at the blonde. I coughed loudly, nervously. He turned and looked vacantly in my direction. Gone was the demonic menace that had so recently gripped him. It seemed as though he was emerging from a strange personality change. Turning to look for his jacket, he said, 'Oh there it is,' and proceeded to dress himself in silence. 'Cover her please,' he ordered, walking to the sink to wash his hands. 'Where's Morty?' he enquired over his shoulder.

'He's gone to the hospital, then he's going straight to the City Mortuary to instruct the Rigor Mortis Course,' I replied.

'Damn!' he remarked. 'The City Mortuary, will you go there and ask the superintendent for some shrouds? I need them for tomorrow.'

'I'll do it right away.' I hared off through the door, only too glad to be away from him.

When I got back from the mortuary with the shrouds, I entered the parlour through the basement door as Shuffles would have locked the front door on his way out. He was always so keen to impress Morty. On this occasion he had turned out all the lights. Placing the bundle on the table I suddenly heard a strained voice coming from the slab area. Tiptoeing to the door I peered through the small pane of glass. My eyes were drawn to a flickering candle. Pressing my forehead to the glass, I could see a hazy shadow. I closed my eyes to get them used to the dark. When I reopened them I caught sight of Shuffles shagging the dead blonde.

'Grab it you bitch or you'll end up in the Styx . . . c'mon . . . c'mon . . .' he was muttering.

I was so shocked that I fell forward and tumbled through the door as he ejaculated.

His face registered surprise at seeing me. Dragging himself off the body, he fumbled with his fly. 'You dirty little bastard. So, your wickedness is at last being revealed . . . little voyeur . . . pervert.'

In a state of panic, I lifted myself off the floor still speechless, not believing what I had just witnessed. He stood there, swaying drunkenly, a menacing look on his face as he drew himself to full height.

'Whenever I am in the act of chasing the Devil from a lost soul I expect you to respect the Lord's wish for privacy.

Now cover that poor creature.' And he walked out through the door.

Hurriedly, I tossed the shroud over the dead blonde, got into bed pronto and pretended to be asleep in anticipation of Morty's return. 'How could he have done that?' I muttered to myself, lying in the dark. The all-pervading silence was broken by farts coming from the direction of the dead woman. I froze with fear at the sound of Morty switching the lights on when returning.

'Ah Charlie, what a night. Had them spellbound I did. It was a wonderful audience, mostly young folk too, university types though,' said Morty, seemingly speaking to someone. 'Holy Christ!' thundered his voice in anger. 'Hero! Hero!' he shouted at the top of his voice, while swishing back the curtain.

Pretending to waken, I blinked. 'Wha . . . what is it?' I said.

'Has that bastard Charon been in here?' he asked, his voice trembling with fury.

'I don't know a Charon . . . only Shuffles . . .' I confessed nervously.

'You must've heard it . . . he was at it with her, wasn't he?' He pointed at the dead blonde.

'He sent me to the Mortuary for shrouds . . .' I said, sitting up.

Morty turned to pick up a large jar. 'He's been guzzling the formaldehyde again.'

'Not that, it's poisonous surely?'

'To anyone else yes, but to Charon no, though I wish to hell it was.'

'But how do you know he's done anything?' I asked, pretending ignorance.

'C'mere' he said, taking me to the blonde. 'See this, when I last saw her, her belly was flat as a pancake. Now it's as though she was nine months pregnant. This young woman's had something rammed into her, blowing in air, thus inflating her belly like a balloon. If you move your eyes to the right, you'll see finger marks in the vaseline tin. I think that's a fair assumption that Charon's been at it, wouldn't you say?' He sighed as though speaking to a half-wit.

'But who is this Charon?' I asked, continuing the pretence.

'Shuffles, with fucking formaldehyde in him, that's who.' He held up the half-empty bottle. Morty pressed both hands on the blonde's belly, causing a loud prolonged fart as the air rattled out of her. 'Don't worry dear, I'll make up for it,' he whispered. Then he went out to make a pot of tea and invited me to sit down with him. 'Now you see why I wanted some help here, Hero. Running this place is a big responsibility. But Shuffles, bless his heart, the truth is the job has gotten to him. I've known it for ages, it's the young ones that tempt him. God knows, if he so much as laid a finger on young Charlie, I'd have him good and proper.'

'Who's Charlie?' I asked.

'Oh, you've not met him yet, have you? He's my little brother, he's lived here for years now.'

I looked around wondering what he was getting at. 'Where does he live?'

Opening a nearby cupboard, he carefully extracted a large jar, inside of which floated a pickled baby. 'This is my wee brother Charlie. A late birth, he died in my mum's belly. They buried her and I pickled him. Just a young chap when I did the job too, one of my best ever.'

The wrinkled, almost walnut-like baby with his little hands folded, peered out at me. Morty placed Charlie on the nearby table, while we sat drinking our tea.

'I was so excited about him being born, I so much wanted a brother to play with. He'd probably have looked like you by now.'

He had an air of sadness about him. I guess it came with the job, a strange old creature, so insular, so alone. I felt this strange affinity with him. He perceived himself as being a servant to the dead whereas I, having been surrounded for years on end with insanity and suicide, occasionally felt the same on witnessing close-up this human tragedy. On a night like this when shadows created hidden corners, I glanced at Morty's grey, death-mask face and felt mixed emotions at having lived, while Salacious Sam and his like had died. All those sad creatures who went under, screaming, mad in despair. Remembering those joyous moments I had, of willing them to death, helping to push them over the edge, and for what reason? Was it simply a break from the monotony, or a small notch of recognition telling me that I was okay while those around me wilted and cracked? It made me wonder how much of Charon was in me . . .

'C'mon Hero, it's bedtime.'

As I closed the curtain behind me, he popped his head through. 'Remember, keep it sewn up,' he whispered, dangling an imaginary needle while pointing to his sealed lips.

Although I had only been employed by Morty for a short time it felt as though I had been there for months. The reason being that I seldom got out. The work was very intense and claustrophobic, I was always in the basement with the bodies. I did miss The Widow and my friends and feared for them and the bull. It was a great surprise when the lads came bursting in.

'Ah, me boy, 'tis us come to see you,' said the welcome

voice of Sligo, coming through the door followed by Bone-crusher.

'Brought you some nice steaks,' said the midget cheerfully.

'No pigs balls?' I asked laughing.

'Too good to give away; lookit the size of this.'

'Are you back with Debbie yet?' I asked him.

'Na, don't feel like patching it up just yet.'

'Your timing's good, as my boss is away.'

'Let's see the place,' said Bonecrusher.

On seeing the coffins, Sligo remarked, 'Oh, it must feel cosy being buried in one of those.'

I took them to the cold slab and did a Fart'n Flush for them.

'Phew, they're really honking, but you learn the ropes quick,' said Bonecrusher admiringly. 'But, it's all the same, whether it's here or there, we're all in the flesh and bone business.'

Sligo nodded, 'And death.'

Taking them to the wooden cupboard, I introduced them to Charlie. 'This is Morty's kid brother,' I said, watching their jaws fall open.

'Fuck, if that's the state he left his brother in, what'd he do to the rest of us?' gagged Bonecrusher.

'No, honest, the guy's a genius.'

The tour finished, we sat having a cup of tea. 'What's happening with you guys?' I asked.

'Well, the gruesome twosome have cut our wages; they've been unable to get somebody to fill your place. If it wasn't for The Widow and Gloria helping us out we'd be in soapy bubble. We're also worried that word of us having the bull will get out. But, despite the risk, that fucking animal is the one consolation prize we've got over those two bas-tards,' said Sligo.

'Yeah, thank fuck we didn't get rid of him that night. But, Hero, we all need to get out of this, it's doing our heads in,' Bonecrusher said angrily. 'It's just like we're still tied to The Institution and can't get away from it.'

'Those big bastards are loaded as well,' I said, telling them about the strongbox in their office. 'Maybe the way out of this is to nick their money.'

'You must be joking, they'd feed us to the rottweilers,' warned Sligo.

'If we're smart enough we'll never get caught.'

'They'd never imagine it was us in a million years, specially if we planned it properly, and you could do that, Hero me boy,' Sligo encouraged.

'How much do you think they have?' asked Bonecrusher.

'I don't know but it looked a fortune to me. Wads that would choke a horse and, as Slates says, all of it tax-free.'

'Do you think they leave it in the office?' asked Sligo.

'They've got everything so sewn up, they don't believe anyone would attempt to steal from them. My guess is it's still sitting right next to his desk as we speak.'

'When should we try taking it?' queried Bonecrusher.

'We'd better speak to The Widow first,' I advised.

The Widow and Gloria sat drinking a bottle of gin as we arrived. We discussed the possibility of robbing Slates, sending them into roars of laughter, a response that sent us immediately into depression.

'No, no, don't take it that way,' reassured The Widow. 'It would be brilliant, but the thought of nicking everything from them is just too much.'

We cheered up at her encouraging response.

'The thing about it is, darling, they can't go to the police. Most of it's there because it's all under-the-counter, think about it, it's there for the taking,' said Gloria.

'But, fuck me girl, I'd hate to get caught by those two with my hand in the till,' said Sligo. 'It'd be a fortnight in the freezer then all they'd do is tap yir hands off.'

'Hmm, worth remembering before we get too carried away,' I said.

'It seems such an easy touch to leave alone. I mean, if it was legal, we'd have the cops to worry about,' said The Widow.

'Could we do it?' Sligo asked, looking at me.

'Fucking right we can, otherwise we're stuck with these bastards for life,' I said, staring at The Widow.

'What a thought!' said Gloria.

'What?' asked Bonecrusher. 'Being chained to those two, just like their poor rottweilers.'

'What do we do about the dogs?' asked Sligo.

'Oh, I guess the easy part is getting rid of Slates'n Sally, but we'd need the cavalry to deal with the dogs,' said The Widow.

'That's it, General Bird's Eye,' said Bonecrusher.

'Who?' asked Sligo.

'You know, General Custard, he could throw pies at them while we got off with the moneybox,' said Bonecrusher, making the rest of us glance nervously at him.

'I was thinking more of Lockjaw, now that's my type of cavalry – with teeth!' said The Widow, ignoring Bonecrusher who trotted off to the toilet.

'I think his lobotomy's playing up,' I suggested.

'Hmm, funny you should say that. The other night I wakened to find him sitting up in bed, arguing with the wallpaper,' Sligo said.

'Well, let's keep that in mind, but maybe The Widow and I should work out a way to get this money so that we can all get outta here. My guess is, this life isn't good for our health.'

★

Walking through the windswept streets, the cold air nipped my cheeks as I thought about the money, wondering how much they had, one thousand, two . . . maybe even more. Whatever it was, it would be a fortune that we could only dream of possessing. I could feel myself getting all fired up at the possibility of stealing their money. Never in a month of Sundays would they believe it was us. I could just picture their faces, and the mere thought of it sent a warm glow through me. It would be a terrific way of getting back at them.

The thought of robbing the landlords took time to sink in but it did fill me with a flow of thoughts about it while I washed down the bodies. Morty took to sending me out more on errands and this added to a feeling of things changing for the better. At last things were happening.

'Round the back!' shouted the uniformed receptionist, as I approached the mortuary door. On entering, I descended a long flight of stairs, the tinny echo of my footsteps rattling around the enclosed space. Opening a heavy metal door, I walked into a large grey room; my steps clattering on the white tiled floor breached the pre-vailing silence. Twelve trolleys standing alongside each other all had bodies on them, one of which was uncovered, and in these surroundings his skin was similar to white marble. Around the table stood a series of buckets filled with bloody water, one showing part of an arm with the upper part of a palm and fingers sticking out, the remainder beneath the water. Another had a foot extended. The bulky envelope in my hand slipped to the floor with a thud that echoed around the room, causing a head to pop out of a nearby door.

'Over here, lad,' said the attendant before casting a glance at the envelope. 'Ah, you must be Hero, I'm Philip Bliss, the superintendent of this place.'

'Hi Philip,' I said, waving.

'Come on in,' he replied.

'Morty asked me to give you this.'

Tearing open the envelope, he counted the money inside. 'Right son, it's tea break, get yourself a cuppa.' He replaced his feet on the table. 'That's what I like, a wee Johnny,' he said happily.

'A what?' I asked.

'A wee Johnny Cash – cash in hand, stupid!' Lying beside him were the pathologist's bloodstained coveralls. Before taking a bite from a mutton pie, he said, 'That's a very smart man you're working for, I hope you appreciate it.' I nodded as he took an enormous bite, parts of it spilling down his front. 'A man that looks after people,' he mumbled.

'Yeah, that's why he sent me here, to get more training,' I said.

'Don't worry about that, I'll take care of you. Take care of him too though, there's not a body that comes here that I don't earmark for him,' he said, 'Most families don't know their arses from their elbows at a time like that, so a nudge in the right direction does no harm,' he winked.

In actual fact, Bliss turned out to be a miserable sort of bastard but, nonetheless, he allowed me to get on with my work without interference. The Autopsy Room was frequently reserved for sessional work to train students from the medical school. My job was to ensure that each trolley holding a towel-wrapped corpse was adjoined to a white sink to allow body fluids to run away. Bliss' job was to clean and lay out the tools for the job, including the buckets to hold body parts. Prof. Rufus Thorburn, nick-named B&D (Black & Decker), took the classes, attacking the corpses with a relish that would've put Dracula to shame. He had a wry sense of humour; he'd start each class by saying, 'May I introduce you to Mr Disposable, the one patient never likely to complain.' Interestingly, it would put the class at ease, forcing them to laugh when, in reality, all they wanted to do was to be sick. Placing the scalpel at the throat, he'd slit a perfectly straight line all the way to the navel. A gleam would come into his eye, however, when it came to his speciality; using the Black & Decker with a new saw blade every time, he'd place it against the forehead and lift the lid off. 'Just like opening a boiled egg for breakfast,' he'd say, looking at the students. 'Now then, all you do is rummage around checking all the organs like this.' He put his hand inside the dead man's stomach. 'Now in here there's a jumble of intestines, just like putting your hand in a snake-pit, only in this instance it's slimey tubes. Let your fingers investigate for intestinal blockage. Prepare notes on C.o.D. (cause of death) and, when you're finished, patch it up, before passing your papers to me for correction.'

Thorburn had warned me to be on the lookout, particularly when dealing with a new class, for students turning a tinge yellow. Observing for any excess sway, I quickly moved in to shore up the faint-hearted. Some though, were as cold as ice. It was here that I first came into contact with Cathy Spencer; a serious twenty-one-year-old, she was Prof. Thorburn's top student. No heavyweight cadavers for her. No, old Black & Decker gave her the thin reedy ones. That's favouritism for you. Cathy's father ran Hepper & Hepper, a rival funeral parlour to ours, whose clientele was mostly from the working classes. In assisting her father, she learned a lot.

'Daddy taught me always to keep in mind that fateful phrase, "Oh death where is thy sting?" when going into a house where someone has just died. As a man of great experience, he always wants to know if they are insured and, if not, he says, look for cracks in the lino, the porcelain dogs on the mantelpiece; quite often, he says, you'll find the most expensive item in the house is the logs on the fire. This keen sense of financial assessment is crucial for, as Dad puts it, if they can't pay us, we can't pay you,' she explained with a look of pride.

She was impressed by my position in Morty's. I think she fancied me, because at tea breaks she would dash for the kettle and always make mine. Smiling, she'd bring out a small packet of biscuits to share. The most intimate experience I had with her was when the Prof. instructed me to assist her with approaching exams. We both examined the corpse of a man who had lain in a putrid stream for an unspecified number of days. Her instructions were to identify precisely for how long the body had been there by studying the algae growth in his orifices. Cathy was studying his rectum with a magnifying glass while I collected algae-covered snot, with tweezers, from his nose.

'Hero?' she whispered.

'Yes Cathy.'

'Do you like Indian curries?'

Pretending to be immersed in his nose, I panicked, not knowing what to say. What could I say, never having had one in my life before! 'Yes, yes Cathy, I do.'

She smiled warmly, looking up from between the corpse's legs, the magnifying glass giving her eyeball a leering expression. 'I have a passion for them,' she declared. I returned her smile, saying nothing.

'One of these nights we'll share one,' she invited.

Over lunch, she produced two cartons of pot noodles, Indian curry flavour. 'This'll do meantime,' she smiled. Pouring the hot water into the plastic containers, she waxed lyrical about the algae and the hue it cast over human flesh. Sometimes she would provoke me with spontaneous questions. 'How long does it take the blood to harden in the arteries once the heart's stopped beating?' she'd ask, holding an imaginary stop-watch. Her whole world revolved around mortuaries, funeral parlours and the dead. I guess that, on sharing a Tandoori chicken, she'd turn it into a post-mortem, she was that kind of woman. At every opportunity, she'd invite me to visit Hepper & Hepper to meet her father and some of the dead clients.

'Some of them are so sad and depressed when they come in, but my dad works miracles on them, making them look nice for their families. Do come and see, Hero,' she pleaded.

The pace of change I was experiencing was daunting and difficult to cope with. There were times when I was so caught up with the excitement of the present and the plans for the future that I would suddenly find my thoughts reversing into the past, almost as though I was trying to unravel something. Flashbacks that took me back to Dornywood. That place was the start of my troubles. Victorian in stature, its outline sprawled over land adjoining the Olivetti typewriter factory. This modern building with its high-tech machinery sucked workers in at 8 o'clock each weekday morning, and spewed them out at 5 p.m. A glimpse of them going about their normal lives was enough to send spasms of yearning racing through my body: the desire to be one of them caught up in a normal day. These two buildings stood side by side as neighbours, yet they were chalk and cheese; one stood as a tribute to twentieth century engineering skills, the other was caught in the inimitable institutional time-warp, its regime reminiscent of years gone by. The headmaster, Mr Coolidge, proudly announced to new boys that some of Dorneywood's practices had been in place since the first day it opened.

'Respect, cleanliness and good manners are the back-
bone to a useful life,' he would point out. On my arrival,
he informed me of the weekly line-up in the yard: 7 a.m. on
Mondays, for lysol treatment, to ensure that any forelock
touched was lice-free. Once he'd finished his intro, I asked,
'Where's the care and protection then?' Out popped a staff
member from behind a curtain, his face as blunt as a
sledgehammer, and hauled me through the door by the
scruff of the neck.

I was soon to discover that my old man was sanity
personified compared to this lot. Coolidge strutted the
corridors, thumbs tucked firmly into his grey waistcoat
pockets. Behind him traipsed a clique of lackeys, listening
attentively to his monologue and nodding acquiescently to
his every word.

'The problem with the world today, is that it is hurtling
full steam into the future without respect for the past.
These boys must, at all costs, have a clear understanding
of our heritage and history, the importance of our country's
values and achievements; indeed the very disciplines that
made all of this possible. It is no good telling them
that fame and fortune lurk around the corner, when we
have neglected to build within them the very foundations
that lead to this. You chaps have a duty to be sharp of
tongue, and not to spare the rod in keeping shoulders to
the grindstone. Remember, what they dislike you for today,
they'll appreciate you for tomorrow. Such is the rugged
journey from adolescence to manhood . . .'

Each day Coolidge would continue this diatribe, passing
classrooms, knowing that it kept everyone on their toes. To
reinforce this, he would on occasion enter one, letting his
eyes wander over the heads of the children who, in a state
of trepidation, kept their eyes to the task at hand. Once,

in those first weeks of my being there, he strutted up to a boy sitting next to me, grabbing him by the hair.

'You malingering little sod. Your eyes, you raised them from your work, didn't you?' He shook the boy by the hair.

'Sorry sir, I've got a sty in my eye.'

Coolidge shook with anger. 'A sty, a sty did you say? What kind of excuse is that?' he demanded, looking from the boy to the teacher. 'You sir, what kind of a class do you run, what kind of indiscipline do you encourage for pupils to make feeble excuses when lacking in concentration?'

The teacher turned white. 'I beg your pardon sir.'

Coolidge stared coldly at the teacher. 'All my efforts, the valuable time I contribute to ensure proper standards of classroom discipline, at times seem to be in vain. You sir, will see that this pupil is brought to order, and you in turn will report to my office before you leave for the day.'

He then left the classroom shaking his head in despair at what had taken place. The boy had to bare his buttocks for ten lashings of the cane, while we simultaneously recited the Lord's Prayer for the reparation of his soul. My problem was that I didn't know the prayer, and could see that, in between lashings, the teacher fearing his appointment with Coolidge, was looking for another victim. I was terrified it'd be me. The funny thing about terror is the strange effect it can have on a person. Others in the class stood frozen to the spot, but I suddenly pissed myself. The splatter of water on the wooden floor brought the lashings to a halt. I remember looking at the faces of the others, their jaws having dropped open. I could hear the sound that reminded me of rain water, but terror obscured the fact that I was the source. The teacher, a look of disbelief on his face, staggered back from the bare buttocks, his eyes fixed on the puddle of piss.

It was at this moment that I realised what had happened. One thing led to another, and before you know it, I became my dad. Running down the aisle, I jumped on the teacher's desk, flew off it on top of him, shouting, 'Geronimo!' The teacher collapsed in the corner with me on top. Grabbing the cane I smacked at his hands and legs, causing him to bellow so that it echoed along the corridors. Well, that was it. Coolidge stood on the threshold looking in. Before you could say 'Belt up,' he fainted right there on the spot. Keeled over just like that.

On being ejected from there I was placed in St Judes. On entering I was taken aside by Fr. McGonnigle.

'Welcome to St Judes, lad. You're off to a new beginning here, the slate wiped clean. What happened at Dornywood is in the past. Here we have a nice bunch of lads, but I won't pretend we don't have some bad apples. Last year we took a crowd to the Convent of the Helpers of the Souls of Langside. Rogues that they are, they raided the stall, flogged the pictures, crucifixes, rosaries, medals and what have you; and then, would you believe it, took them to the priest to be blessed, before trying to present some of these trophies to favourite teachers like Mr Solomon, whom you'll soon get to know. My advice to you, lad, is to steer clear of the troublemakers as your life will become a misery. This is your opportunity to make a new start,' and he made a sign of the cross above my head.

His introduction lulled me into a false sense of security that was blown apart on entering the long corridors. Dull eyes and blunt features were spread like marmite on the faces of the kids in St Judes Youth Detention Centre. Society had imprinted its mark, consigned them to an impoverished and brutal existence. Knowing this, they bullied their way through each day and I watched them spread like lice, entering every corruptible seam in the

Centre. Having barely reached puberty, they behaved towards each other like depraved adults. The weak amongst them were taunted and teased beyond endurance; the frail, battered and broken; the infirm and mentally subnormal stripped, and often sodomised. In contrast to this, there were those few who were bright of eye, sharp in cunning. The nimble-footed, as opposed to the plodders. Knowing the corridors of the place were rife with anarchy, the kindly Fr. McGonnigle gave me a library job, encouraging me to read books. On introducing me to the place he pulled a book from the shelf.

'This is Marc Connolly's Negro play, *Green Pastures*. It is really a book about St Judes, lad. When God and the Archangel Gabriel are looking down at the earth, at you lot and others too, Gabriel says: "How about cleanin' up de whole mess of 'em and sta'ting all over ag'in wid some new kind of animal?" "What," says God, "an' admit I'm licked?" Now lad, that is my position here in St Judes. I'll stay with you and the others through thick and thin, I won't be licked either.'

That was the first time I'd heard of Marc Connolly, and it seemed he'd written that just for me. I was immediately impressed and affected by Fr. McGonnigle, a youngish man with slick black hair. He never seemed to lose his temper throughout the time that I knew him. Indeed, as a favoured son, he placed me in a position of responsibility by intimating that I knock on the door of his library office should anyone want him. It was he who introduced me to the value of books in expanding one's knowledge and understanding of the world. I read copiously, knowing that in the library I was shielded from the brutality that seemed to exist within this institution. It was here I was introduced to the writing of Steinbeck, Dickens and Russian authors like Gogol and, of course, Dostoevsky. I admired and respected Father McGonnigle for introducing me to all of this, and was so proud when he invited me to be an altar boy when he was serving Mass. Now and again he would pass by the library desk where I was seated, leaving a piece of cake, or a sweet. Although I considered myself a favourite of his, I did notice how he seemed to work privately with one or two other boys. I was always under strict instructions that he must never be interrupted during these sessions. One day, he uncharacteristically popped his head out of the office to warn me.

'This place is sacrosanct. No one should enter.'

I nodded, though did think it odd as that was the abiding rule anyway. He spent a great deal of his time there with another boy, Lance Teirney, an illiterate, whom he was teaching to read. Lance was a bright spark. Eyes like diamonds, they shone with a fiery intelligence. Although he could neither read nor write, one look was enough to bring home that this kid had it. What I didn't know was that Fr. McGonnigle had lost his frock to Lance. This came to light that morning while I sat reading a book. Loud voices came from the priest's office followed by the sound of upturned furniture. Lance came rushing out, throwing a pointed letter-opener on to the floor beside my chair. The priest emerged, blood running from stab wounds to his hand and chest, and he collapsed on the floor. While trying to help him I got covered in his blood, a sight that made the other staff pounce on me as the culprit. While pinning me to the wall, they asked Fr. McGonnigle if I had done it.

'Yes, it was him,' the bastard said.

'Liar, fucking liar,' I screamed, struggling fiercely, surrounded and dragged along the corridor by priests, one of whom wagged an ominous finger shouting, 'Your second attack on a staff member. You left the other from Dorny-

wood in a fine mess too. The Devil's got into you but we'll
be rid of him and you.'

I was hastily plucked from there, to be deposited in the
nearest psychiatric ward, where staff constantly mentioned
my father's mental illness. More than once, I heard, 'It
runs in the family.'

'But it had nothing to do with that, nothing at all,' I
screamed at them. 'The priest is a poof and a liar, a liar,
a fucking liar.' At first I believed that Fr. McGonnigle had
made a mistake because of his injury and that he would
tell them the truth. Each time the ward door opened I'd
look longingly, hoping it was him coming to apologise. It
was never to be. Indeed, the psychiatrist informed me that
the priest had made a lengthy statement confirming that I
was his assailant. I went berserk with anger and attacked
the psychiatrist. I didn't mean to do it, honest I didn't. It
was just that if there was anyone in my life, whom I considered to be a good and saintly person, it was
McGonnigle. It was this same perception of him by others
that doubly damned me. The one lasting memory I have
is of being universally despised for attacking a man of the
cloth. The ears around me were deaf to my pleas. I knew
all was lost and sort of withdrew into myself.

My transfer to The Institution was processed under the
existing Detention Order, which rendered a court appearance unnecessary. It was all concluded with my case file
being transferred from a desk in one department to a desk
in another. The familiar blunt faces from St Judes also
filled the corridors of The Institution. On entering that
first day, I was pinned by the arms and bent face down
over a table by Gorky and Fat Head.

'None of yir shenanigans here lad,' warned Fat Head.

'What a nice wee arse,' taunted Gorky. The click of

high-heeled shoes echoing down the corridor was my first
introduction to the Queen of Needles – Dr Snider. Hands
in the pockets of her white coat, she stared indifferently at
me. Being no match for those bearing down on me I cried,
'Don't hurt me!'

She looked askance, a brief sneering smile crossing her
lips. 'Hurt you, my staff never hurt anyone. They simply
prevent residents from hurting themselves. During your
stay here, Mr Ferguson, you will discover the ingenuity of
evil, when witnessing the extremities that residents will go
to in order to do themselves harm,' she said, the sneer
returning to her lips.

I remember that moment so well, she was cold, arctic
cold, as her bony fingers held the syringe high to the light,
while pressing the plunger. Turning towards me, she gave
the two bruisers a cursory nod. Never having previously
had so much as a drink of alcohol, or a drug of any kind,
the implosion of this substance, as it infiltrated, shattered
the privacy of my temple. Others with whom I have since
discussed it talk of an uplifting high, before careering down.
This was never my experience. The first prick of Snider's
needle, followed by its massive infestation, chased me for
my life, chasing me from myself. The first ever injection
reached deep inside of me, where not even my father could,
and made me a stranger to myself. This frightened part
which seemed to have raced off somewhere was something which I have since constantly searched for. I know
that it is somewhere near, yet far.

'Help! Help!' I yelled.

Gorky shook his head: 'This one is worth watching
M'am, a troublemaker if ever I saw one.'

But perhaps in a perverse way, in a positive sense, this
prevented me from succumbing to the horrors of institutional life. I was far too busy looking for the lost me, to

play with them. Strapped to the bed those first few days, I was gagged with a sanitary towel, thus preventing me from expressing whatever my need may have been. In this, the guards were very experienced. Those first weeks were filled with expectation, as I awaited the return of that wayward soul. I often wonder if I've lost that piece of me, forever.

Perhaps that lost piece of me migrated, went and took up residence in the conscience of the priest, tossing him from the divine to the demonic. Those well-worn knees of his will be dragged, knocking a Samba, as Shuffles punts him across the Styx. He burned a hole in my brain those first months, he did. I knew he would still be taking people's confessions, saving their souls, while carrying out his nefarious deeds. Once again, my fresh start was no start and, again, someone I thought was the good guy, turned out to be the bad guy. My life at this point was like a downed spitfire careering out of control, with me on board and unable to intervene. This, I was soon to discover, would be what life in The Institution would always be like.

Sligo came to the funeral parlour to warn me of Bonecrusher's deteriorating condition. 'He's getting worse,' he whispered.

'C'mon Sligo, aren't we all?' I joked.

'No, no, I'm not panicking, simply saying that others are beginning to notice it.'

'But they already write us off as being from the loony bin anyway, what's new?'

'Look me boy, we are tolerated, because we are seen as loonies who behave normally.'

'Give or take a few flakies, but what's so different now?' I enquired.

'When he touts his trolley around he makes this fucking great whine like an engine, even when he's parked it at a bench for filling. At first I thought he was winding them up but, this afternoon he had three sheep heads on the bench, tongues out, eyes open, whilst he was singing, "Baa, Baa, Black sheep, have you any wool?" When I had a go at him, he was deadly serious at my interrupting his choir practice. It's that fucking lobotomy, I tell you,' he warned.

'Well, when you think about it, he's the marathon man compared to some of the others that have had it,' I said. 'Look, there's nothing we can do except try to camouflage it, as much as possible, otherwise they'll cart him back into The Institution and that will be the end of him.'

'I know, I know, that's why I'm here,' said Sligo. 'At the end of the day, we're in the hands of the Gods.'

Lockjaw came in at this point, as had been arranged by The Widow. A man of few words, perhaps because of his massive jaw, he listened, his small peering eyes looking straight through whoever he focused on. 'Just leave him,' he said with an air of finality that let Sligo know there was nothing to be done.

'Right, let's get some tea on,' I suggested, by way of changing the subject. We stood at the stove watching the kettle boil. Lockjaw lifted the lid of the steaming kettle, placed his finger into the boiling water and stirred it without a flicker of pain. Sligo and I stared open-mouthed.

'How can you do that?' I asked.

'Boyyo, boyyo, boyyo,' whispered Sligo in amazement.

'I lost my pain way back,' he said with a strained smile.

We spent the best part of the evening talking. When they first hit the streets, the two brothers had struck unparalleled terror. One had a lethal head butt and fists like mash hammers, the other a physical body strength, combined with a ferocious bite. Rumour had it they had set about four rough guys, tearing them to ribbons in a backstreet. Everyone was wary about tackling the brothers, all except

Detective Bull that is. Mind you, rumour also had it that he was a crazy man with a black heart.

Lockjaw told how their mother was a hooker and had the three children by two different foreign sailors. The Widow was their step-sister, the brothers sired by the same man. 'Fuck knows what concoction was in his sperm bank,' he said. He described how she called The Widow her flower and the two brothers her weeds. Despite the revulsion his mother had felt towards the boys, all three of them were very close.

'I remember you in The Institution, how long did they keep you?' Lockjaw asked Sligo.

'I didn't think you'd remember me as none of us look the same in civvies, bejeesus. I guess it was something like eighteen years in all. I may even have lost a year or so along the way, the place gets to you in that way.'

'Whaooo,' I exclaimed, 'but what did you get put in for?' Almost immediately I regretted asking him. A blankness entered his eyes, as he pushed back the tipsy cap on his head.

'Not opening old wounds at all, at all; dead and gone, 'tis buried in the past, me boyyo. It's a long story but I'll cut it short. My mum and the three of us, my two wee nippy brothers that is, all slept in the one bed. I woke up one morning drenched, thinking the wee ones had pissed the bed again. Stuck to the bed sheets I was and, God almighty, it was blood. Sitting up, I pulled bits of my brothers and mum off me. They were dead, had been for hours. It was like wakening up on a butcher's bench, I tell you. My old man did it. They found him later, dead in the toilet, having swallowed a can of rat poison. I went nutty as a fruitcake, the worse I got, the more they transferred me. First it was a psychiatric ward, then a locked ward there, and so on, until I ended up in The Institution. Spent many a night there I did, roasting in torment, wondering why?' He closed his eyes as he gripped his mug of tea.

'He must've liked you,' I said.

'Oh, I turned on the rack with that one too. Maybe my being his blue-eyed boy made the others look bad, who knows. I just feel having come through the worst of it that I cannot understand, even now, why he did it. I suppose the thing about madness is, what you do when trapped in it can never be understood or explained. I got better only because the bloody thing burnt itself out of me,' he sighed.

'Still, you've come through it well though.'

'Ah, but for most of my early years there I didn't even know who I was or where I was, and it didn't really matter. I was there to get better,' he said, letting out a nervous laugh.

'But I heard all these stories about The Refractory, were they true?'

'Ah, the Refractory, burnt-toast-island we called it.'

'What d'you mean?'

'When the Watchdog Committee decided food going to The Refractory needed heating, Gorky told the cook to burn it so that it would be hot when it got there. And boy, I was working in the cookhouse and was it burnt, hmm frazzled more like,' said Sligo.

'Gorky said to get used to it, as we'd be going to hell anyway,' said Lockjaw.

'And he would know, being the devil incarnate that he was,' added Sligo.

'The stories I heard about it terrified me,' I said. 'Always when patients I knew were taken there, it was as though they entered some black hole in space never to be seen again. I guess, in a strange way, fear of going there kept me alive.'

'Aye, I know what you say me boy, but I was the harmless type who was never likely to go there, but the rumours . . . the rumours were enough to terrify the Holy Ghost himself,' said Sligo.

'Well, we're all away from that Evil Empire,' I said. 'But bang smack in the middle of another.'

'Or is it part of the same one?' asked Lockjaw.

'I wouldn't be surprised,' I said, 'but we all want to get away from this, and if we can blag some money from Slates then that would be great.'

'Do you want me there?' asked Lockjaw.

'Yeah, I would as they've got two rottweilers that could cause us problems.'

'They won't be a problem. Let me know the time and place,' he said, as he got up to leave.

'You've come through it well, old son,' I said to Sligo. His chirpy face lit up.

'Oh me, boyyo, there's times when I didn't think it, those gruelling mornings when I'd line up with the others at the medicine trolley to blank it all out, what happened to my family, I mean but, for some strange reason, my soul found refuge in Ireland, and that always puzzled me,' he said, with a twinkle in his eye.

'But you're not from there?' I queried.

'No, never been there in me life. Family did way back in the Potato Famine I think.'

'Ah, that explains it, it's all in the genes.'

'The what?' he asked.

'The genes, you know, those wee things that your mum'n dad pass on to you.'

His face took on a puzzled look suggesting the penny hadn't dropped. 'And I thought I picked up the accent and knowledge from reading Yeats,' he said, scratching his chin.

The Widow and Gloria approached as I stood against the

wall outside Eve's Bar. The Widow's dark, wild eyes stared, observing how I was bearing up. This pale, haunted face was staring intently at me; how, I thought, could someone so ravaged by a lifestyle of abuse, retain such fathomless beauty?

'How are you?' she asked.

'I'm . . . okay . . .' I said faltering. I was in reality torn about telling her that Cathy Spencer fancied me but was afraid The Widow would think I was two-timing her.

'Are you sure you're okay?' she asked, peering at me.

'Yes . . . okay,' I said, conscious of Gloria's presence.

'You're not getting a bad time from those stiffs I hope,' remarked Gloria.

'Where're we going?' I asked.

'To see a man about a dog,' she replied. The journey through various back streets and dimly lit lanes soon brought us to Camp Hill, our destination.

'This is the crotch of the gay scene, so watch your arse,' warned Gloria.

'But who do you know here?' I asked.

'Ruth Oliver, the dyke lawyer who wants to look after the bull for us, and another friend, Sudsy, who won this year's Belle of the Ball.'

'What's that?'

'Well, the people here have a festival each year that ends with a Belle of the Ball competition, and Sudsy won it this time round.'

'He must be beautiful then,' I remarked, letting my eyes fix on Gloria's lovely face.

'Beauty, my darling, is in the eye of the beholder,' she said, in a rather harsh tone.

Sure enough, one became distinctly aware of entering an area swirling with strong undercurrents of erotic activity,

as couples stood locked in steamy embrace, or on the brink
of advanced sexual engagement.

'This is the nerve centre of Camp Hill. It draws them
like flies round a hot arse,' whispered The Widow. No one
personified this more than Laser Cohen, Q.C., known here
as the Queen of Queens. With a keen sense of the the-
atrical, he lounged in a high-backed wooden chair, wearing
an alluring cabaret costume, vermilion in colour, an oyster
cigarette-holder hanging from his fingertips. In contrast to
this colourful, brassy dress, his face was whippet-thin, and
serious to boot. His eyes, sharp and penetrating. 'He's
pretty famous,' I whispered into The Widow's ear, as
Gloria threw her arms around Laser's neck.

'You'll see a lot of known faces here, I tell you,' she
replied, as Laser greeted her. 'Who's the big boy then?' he
asked smarmily.

'Gloria, Gloria,' shouted a shrill, lisping voice from
behind. A small round man with glasses minced towards
us.

'Oh you look so lovely, sweetie,' he said, kissing Gloria.

'Darling, what brings you here, with such a hunk too?'
said Sudsy looking at me. Sudsy was encased in tight
leather hot pants, with red-coloured braces.

'How did he win the competition?' I whispered to The
Widow.

'It was for personality. I reckon it was a sympathy vote
myself,' she replied.

'This is enough to put down a herd of elephants, so be
careful sweetie,' said Sudsy, handing Gloria a medicine
bottle. 'You'll never believe who I stuffed today?' he whispered with an air of secrecy.

The Widow looked at him saying, 'I'm all ears.'

'Bonzo, remember the cat that did the Whiskas advert?'
he said, pausing for the others to react.

'You didn't!?'

'Honest, and did he look a satisfied customer, when I'd finished with him?' he said proudly.

'You *are* an old Queen, stuffing the arses of those poor animals,' scoffed Laser.

'Somebody's got to do it darling, and the money's good too,' said Sudsy.

We were joined by a pretty young woman, dressed like a man. 'Ruth!' said The Widow.

'How did they get on at court?' I asked.

'Bad news,' said Ruth.

'Why, what did they get?' The Widow enquired.

'Well, I tried to advise them to tone things down, but you know what they are like; when the judge asked Warthog his occupation he said he was a nomad, informing the judge that he had special dietary considerations if he intended keeping him inside. When the judge asked what these were, he said rats had been his staple diet for some time. The judge, of course, almost threw up. Both Skelly and he were sent for Psychiatric Reports.

'Psychiatric Report, my arse, fat lot of good that'll do those two. One session with them will be enough to drive any psychiatrist mad,' I said.

On the way home I remarked that Sudsy must've been sick in the head.

'Why?' asked The Widow.

'Having sex with Bonzo, the cat,' I said. Both Gloria and The Widow folded in laughter.

'What's so funny?' I asked.

'Bonzo's dead, silly,' Gloria replied.

'That's even worse,' I said, shivering with disgust.

They looked at me before collapsing in laughter. Eventually Gloria recovered to say, 'Sudsy's a taxidermist, he stuffs animals for a living, you idiot.' We all burst into laughter.

'There you are, two of the juiciest steaks you'll ever see,' said Sligo, slapping the meat on to the cold slab. The two blood-red lumps lay next to an old lady's crushed head; she'd recently been knocked down by a bus.

'Good,' smiled The Widow, reaching out her hand, protected by a latex glove, to lift them. On the slab, at the opposite side of the bloody head, sat the small brown bottle given to her by Sudsy.

The Widow carefully sliced through each of the steaks with a scalpel, sprinkling the liquid from the bottle into the cavity she'd cut into the meat.

'Remember,' she said, 'don't lick your fingers after feeding them to the dogs.'

I looked closely at it. 'Why, what is it?'

'Strychnine. Right,' said The Widow, 'is everybody straight about what they've to do tomorrow?' Lockjaw, Bonecrusher, Sligo, Gloria and I nodded tensely.

That night I tossed and turned in my bed with worry, pretending to be asleep when Morty came in.

'Another splendid class, Charlie,' he said rummaging around, 'Knocked them for six tonight, I did. You would've been proud of me. Mmm, I could eat a horse I could, Jesus, bless my soul. Two lovely steaks. Hero, my boy you're my hero,' he said to the sound of rustling cellophane.

Startled, I jumped out of bed and peeped through the curtain. Slapping the steak, still wrapped, next to the cooker, he reached for the frying pan. I stood frozen to the spot in fear. 'Oh fuck!' Lighting the gas, he tossed some butter into the pan then proceeded to take off his jacket. I ducked, as he passed to go into his bed space to take off his boots. Quick as a flash, I dashed out, grabbed the steaks, kicked open the basement door causing a loud bang, then rushed back into my bed steadying my curtain.

'Hey, what's that?' shouted Morty.

'Wh . . . what?' I asked, pretending the noise had wakened me.

Morty stood outside his curtain wearing only one boot, a puzzled expression on his face. 'What's that noise?' he asked, walking to the door. 'Goddam! Somebody's stolen the steaks, the miserable shits!'

'I heard the door slamming right enough,' I replied.

'Buggers stole my dinner. Who'd believe it, a smash and grab for two steaks. Things must be bad out there,' he moaned.

'You should've locked the door behind you,' I said.

'I thought I did,' he said scratching his chin, a puzzled look still on his face.

I sighed with relief as I returned to bed, the steaks tucked inside my underpants. That was a dangerous slip-up, one mouthful of meat and he'd have been as dead as a doornail, joining his brother in the jar. Imagine doing a flush'n fart on Morty, I thought to myself, shuddering as I faded into sleep.

'I didn't recognise you, darling,' Gloria said to The Widow who was now wearing a blonde wig with a bouffant hairstyle.

'You either, sweetie,' said The Widow mocking Gloria, who was looking fat in a head-scarf, pushing a large old-fashioned pram.

'It's putting me in the mood for one, I tell you,' joked Gloria.

'What about me,' cried Bonecrusher from inside the pram, a large hairy shawl covering him. The only one not disguised was Lockjaw, as it would've been impossible.

'Sligo has planted the gun in the Mini,' whispered The Widow to me. 'I've just called the cops to tell them it's there. Slates and Sally are at the Abattoir anyway.'

I approached the office door with Lockjaw, cautiously opening the letterbox. Both dogs, minus their muzzles, rushed to the door, barking ferociously, clambering in an attempt to get at us. I dropped in the two pieces of steak, listening as the dogs sniffed silently. Lockjaw had his back to the wall opposite. We watched for a minute, before he signalled for me to step aside, then crashed his boot against the door, knocking it clean off its hinges. I was about to rush in, when the two rottweilers came hurtling out at me, the steaks lying untouched on the floor. I panicked, as one attempted to sink its teeth into my arm. Lockjaw, quick as a flash, grabbed the two dogs by the scruff of the neck, opening his own mouth to reveal the most godawful set of teeth on earth. He bit one of the dogs on the nose so viciously both of them cowered, whimpering in fear. In order to quieten them, he dragged both into the house, threw them into a cupboard, and locked the door. Together, we lifted the heavy metal box, heaving it into our getaway pram. Bonecrusher jumped in after it, and Gloria patted the shawl smoothly over him. 'Fuck, this is heavy!' said Gloria.

'Mama,' said Bonecrusher, in a baby voice. Gloria struggled up the street, followed at a discreet distance by The Widow and me, her arm through mine. Lockjaw made off through the backcourt. Just as we were priding ourselves on a clean job, Slates' Mini turned the corner passing us; both him and Sally were laughing.

The two men entered the building. Minutes later, they were running out of the close screaming, 'Fucking bastards . . . who . . . where . . .?' They were hopping around like lunatics. At that moment the cavalry came in the form of two police cars, screeching to a halt.

'Up against the wall, c'mon,' said the police, pushing Sally and Slates.

'You dickheads, we've been robbed, lookit the door crashed in,' screamed Sally.

'I'm a business man, you plonker,' shouted Slates.

'Got it, sir,' called the cop who'd been searching the Mini. Holding up a sellotaped bundle in the shape of a pistol, he looked proudly at his senior officer.

'You must've planted that on me, you arsehole,' screamed Slates, foaming at the mouth.

Just as Gloria was about to turn the corner, Inspector Bull came around. 'Oh fuck,' I said despondently.

He stopped, saying something to Gloria, then cast a suspicious glance at the pram.

'Fuck off, you big shit!' came the sound of Bonecrusher's voice.

'Oh Christ!' said The Widow. Bull, nosey bastard that he was, bent over to investigate. At that moment, the hairy shawl sat up, head-butting Bull into oblivion. Falling backwards, he tumbled into the doorway of a closed shop. Looking over my shoulder, none of the cops had seen it. We continued on our way, passing the unconscious Bull.

'Doesn't have a way with children, does he?' quipped The Widow.

The cop unwrapped the sellotape and sheepishly held up a toy pistol towards his superior.

'You fucking wankers, you've done your best to aid and abet a robbery,' bawled Slates at them, jumping up and down in fury.

Back at the Funeral Parlour, we took advantage of Morty's

absence by trying to open the strong box. On turning it over we heard the contents move, but no sound of coins.

'Shit, I wanted to hear a fortune rattling inside,' said Gloria. 'Real money doesn't rattle,' said The Widow.

'I know, but it does sound better than nothing,' replied Gloria.

Lockjaw appeared, carrying a huge hammer and chisel. The force of his blows reverberated around the basement.

'Enough to waken the dead,' said Gloria.

'That'd be poetic justice!' I muttered. 'Poor Mrs Damson there, she died of fright too,' I pointed at the old lady on the cold slab.

Finally the box fell open to reveal bundles of neatly tied notes and sealed packages.

'My fuck, there's a fortune. We're set up for life,' said The Widow. So overcome by excitement, we ignored the packages, concentrating on counting the money. In total, we had one hundred and twenty thousand pounds! All of us were stunned into silence. 'We had better play this right,' said The Widow soberly. 'This is money those two will kill for, so we'd better find a good hiding place, and get back to our usual routines. Gloria, are you sure Bull didn't recognise you?' Gloria looked up from the pile of cash. 'Positive. Even I didn't recognise me.'

'Right, any suggestions where to stash it?'

'Our bench in the Abattoir?' said Sligo.

'I know, Mr Waddington, the bank manager,' I suggested excitedly.

'You must be joking – a bank manager!' The Widow sighed.

'He'll not say a thing, I promise,' I smiled, nodding at the nearby coffin. 'He gets taken upstairs for viewing this afternoon, and buried tomorrow.' We gathered around the coffin, looking down at the round, bald head of the deceased; conservatively-dressed he looked the typical, discreet bank manager. Taking the notes, I placed them round his buttocks all the way down his trouser legs, ensuring that the money was undetectable.

'What'll happen if Shuffles tries to give him one?' Gloria teased.

'Not his type,' I said.

'What about these packages?' asked Gloria.

'Let's open them,' suggested The Widow. One contained photographs of an elderly man screwing a young woman; another was a well-thumbed notebook with names, addresses and phone numbers.

'Hey, this is worth a gold mine,' The Widow said flicking through the photographs. 'There's cops, businessmen, politicians, must be the ones that do deals with Slates. Let's stash it with the money. Who's the old guy in these?' No one knew. 'Let's put them in with the dosh. Mr Waddington, you're still in business,' she said, patting him on the chest.

As they were leaving, Sligo said, 'Hero, me boy.'

I looked at him. 'What is it?'

He rubbed his chin nervously. 'Well, you're sure now, that the bank manager chappy isn't going to be cremated?'

The menacing fall-out from Slates sent tremors through the streets. They were desperate to find out who had attacked Bull, suspecting rightly that it was the same robbers who'd done them over. He, however, was in hospital, still unconscious with a fractured skull. Meanwhile, the two big men were throwing violent tantrums with anyone who got in their way. Our worry was that, when Bull regained consciousness and told his story, they might put two and two together, knowing there weren't many head-butting babies around. They wouldn't have to look far for a wee person with a deadly head-butt. These were worrying times for us. The Widow kept an ear to the ground, getting all the latest news so that we could act quickly in an emergency. Mind you, what we heard wasn't too pleasant. For starters, Slates kicked both rottweilers to death, an indication as to what would happen to those who nicked the cash.

Following Morty's instructions, I observed Mr Waddington's service and funeral with more than a passing interest. The minister gave him an appropriate send-off.

'Right to the end Bill Waddington was a man to be trusted, someone who looked after people's financial interests with a selfless dedication . . . loved throughout the world of charity, he walked thousands of miles to raise money for them. It is a measure of the respect in which he was held when the director of one charity told me that Bill's legs were worth a fortune . . .' It was the one burial I lingered over till the last shovelful, and agreed with the sermon entirely. Everyone was touched when I told them what the minister had said.

'Do you think he was on to us?' Bonecrusher asked suspiciously.

We agreed to let the money lie low for a while, going about our usual business till we were ready to move.

The shriek of the Mini's brakes shuddered to a stop beside me. Slates and Sally jumped out, grabbing me by the lapels. Lifting me like a sack of feathers, they crashed my head through the window of a nearby house.

'You shit, you stole our fucking money!' Slates screamed. I shouted that I didn't know what they were talking about, when the householder, whose window my head had broken, told them to pull my head off for smashing it. The householder's pit-bull terrier growled dangerously nearby. 'Watch that dog doesn't get cut,' said Sally. Dragging me to the car, he then tossed me into the back seat where a strong smell of body odour and bloodstains permeated the interior. They grunted violent threats.

'Put his head in a vice, that's what we'll do,' suggested Sally.

'It's broken,' Slates reminded him.

'Since when?' grunted Sally.

'Oh fuck, you've a memory like a sieve. Abie Stern's kneecap last week, mind? I went to crush Reno's foot this morning but the vice was fucking knackered. I had to pick-axe him instead.'

Sally turned to punch me on the ribs. 'We could burn his balls with a Bunsen if you want. There's plenty of petrol left.'

'Look, there's Dan Doran, that bastard might know something. Get him,' urged Slates. Again, the car screeched to a halt, the two men hauling in their latest victim.

'Let's go to the butcher's and chop their hands off,' threatened Sally, as Dan Doran landed on me. Both men were totally beyond reason as they pulled up outside the tenement. Blood was already spewing from Doran's head wound. After dragging us into the office, both men laid into us with their boots.

'You pile of dung!' screamed Slates, searching my pockets, finding nothing. Doran had sixty pounds, a sum that confirmed their suspicions.

'That's all the proof we need, scum!' said Sally, thumping him on the head.

'I've just cashed my giro,' cried Doran. A firm knock on the door momentarily distracted the two men. Slates opened it to reveal Morty. 'Aw fuck, it's you, I told you to use the special knock,' he warned the undertaker.

'Sorry about that,' replied Morty. Seeing our condition,

the tall man began to look paler than usual, something I could never have previously believed.

'You wanted to see me, I hear?' Morty said ingratiatingly.

'What did I want to see you about, eh? You haven't got my money have you?' he asked accusingly.

'Slates . . . you wanted to see him about a few homers,' said Sally, nodding at me and Doran.

Morty turned an even paler shade of white, 'Boys, boys, be careful. The streets are ablaze with rumour, and it won't do any of us any good whatsoever. Things need to cool a bit, and Hero there's the best assistant I've got, or had . . .'

'Fat lot of good that is to us. For fuck's sake man, somebody out there is blowing our money good style, so get your thinking cap on. Who the fuck did it?' screamed Slates hysterically.

'Me, how would I know such things? I'm only an undertaker. Soon about to go out of business because I'm losing my best assistant. I trained him myself too,' pleaded Morty.

'Aw, what a shame. Look after this weasel while we work on this cunt, Doran,' said Sally wearily. They dragged him out of the room to the nearby workshop where the muffled sounds of torture struck terror into us both.

'Stay calm son, stay calm,' whispered Morty, his outstretched hand shaking violently. Sally and Slates returned, their vengeance slaked on poor old Doran, whose agonised screams sent a chill racing through me.

'Let that half-wit go, there's more chance of a blind man doing it than that loony. But hear me, Fuck Face, if you find out who stole our money, come here right away, okay?' Slates said, holding a clenched fist to my face. I nodded dumbly. 'And you,' he said to Morty, 'Get the midnight oil burning 'cause we're back in business.'

Limping into the street, I shook with relief, knowing that I'd escaped by the skin of my teeth. Once inside the hearse,

Morty let out a long sigh. 'Phew, do you know they've
beaten up and tortured half the district? God help the
thieves when they do get them. Mind you, they'll probably
be a long way from here by now, otherwise we'd have to
pick up the pieces.'

During this period I was grateful at being able to lose
myself in the monotony of routine between the basement
and the mortuary. At least dead people are harmless. There
was also an absence of superficial chitchat which is a
blessing when your nerves are frayed. At the same time,
there was a fear, deep in the pit of my stomach, that
someone would break. Maybe they'd grab Bonecrusher or
Sligo, purely by chance, just as they had done me, and
they'd cave in. The thought of it brought me out in a cold
sweat for, who knows, had Morty not appeared when he
did, would I have kept my mouth shut with a Bunsen
Burner roasting my balls?

'Hello Hero, you look so cute next to Mrs Morgan,'
cooed Cathy Spencer, dispelling these awful thoughts from
my head.

'Hi Cathy . . . yeah, well Philip asked me to do a good
job on her, for old time's sake.'

'She was such a nice person. Say, would you like to
share a pot noodle?'

'Honest Cathy, I'd love to, but I'm up to my armpits in
bodies. Another time huh?'

'Are you sure now, it's Tandoori?'

I was glad to see her move off, allowing me to return to
sorting out the old mortuary receptionist, Mrs Morgan
who, having slipped on a bar of soap, fell down the back
stairs, breaking her neck. A kindly soul, she was discovered
by Philip Bliss who, back in his trainee days, had had an

affair with her, their secret liaisons taking place in the Autopsy Room.

'We grew out of it though,' he reminisced, while eating a mutton pie at tea break. 'You look troubled these days, Hero, as though you've a lot on your mind.'

'Well, I do have a problem,' I said. 'You see, I've got this girlfriend but when I'm here, Cathy . . . you know, Cathy Spencer, well, she fancies me and well, I don't want to hurt her feelings.'

I couldn't very well tell him that I'd just ripped off Slates and Sally so at least this was a neat diversion.

'That Cathy, now there's a girl to watch out for,' he said, tearing off a piece of pie.

'In what way Philip?'

'Strange, strange person. In fact, apart from the Prof., you're the only other living person she's warmed to, and that should worry you, because the only obsession she's shown other than that is to the punters wheeled in here. I've never known a student to show such keenness in the dead. Talk about workaholic, I've seen her locked in till the early hours, sticking her fingers everywhere, sniffing samples like a bloody connoisseur, even tasting whatever she's extracted. The mind boggles, when I think of it. I tell you Hero, that girl's not the full shilling so keep to your steady girlfriend, I'm sure she has better habits.'

'What does the Prof. think of all this then?' I asked.

'The least said the better. There are certain things, my son, that one keeps one's lips sealed on, especially when one's job and pension are dependent on it. He's a powerful man and, in his eyes, I'm the gopher, so I'll gopher. There are things I've seen here that would make your hairs stand on end, but that's between me and the four walls. Self-preservation we call it. All I can tell you is, that I've put in my will that if there's a need to send me to the mortuary when I go, not to let it be this one.'

The Widow was waiting for me as I left the mortuary. 'Hero, come on in here,' she beckoned from a dark alleyway.

Snuggling up to me, her perfume singed my soul. 'It's so good to see you,' I whispered. 'The world's been going mad.'

'I know, I know all about it, but we've got a problem. The rain's been falling hard, and I'm wondering if coffins are waterproof as we don't want a pile of soggy money.'

'Oh fuck, I haven't a clue,' I replied.

'Can't you ask Morty?'

'No way,' I said. 'The slightest hint of anything could get back to Slates' ears. They are so fucking paranoid. No, let's take whatever precautions we need to.'

'You and I can dig it up,' she suggested. The very idea of going near the money, when those two galoots were still on the rampage, sent tremors of fear racing through my body. The Widow sensed my apprehension. 'Look, we've come this far, we're fucking rich, but we have to safeguard it. Only you and I can do it.' She was right.

In the early hours of the morning we met in the graveyard, the wails of The Fiddler playing in the background. The Widow stood on a nearby gravestone as lookout while I began to unearth the coffin of Mr Waddington. Two feet under I hit metal. 'What the fuck's this?' Probing deeper with my hand. Catching hold of a heavy duty plastic bag, I hauled it out.

'What is it?' asked The Widow coming over.

It dawned on me. I remembered the burglars I'd seen on my previous night-time wandering in the cemetery all those months ago. 'Those fucking cat burglars, they've stashed their booty here.'

'Who . . . what was that?' asked The Widow.

'Oh, I'll tell you later. Let's see what they've got.' Tearing open the metal box, I pulled out a small bag. On opening it, two wads of one-hundred pound notes lay on top. Underneath was a diamond necklace, rings and three gold watches. 'These must be worth a fortune!' I whispered excitedly. Handing them to The Widow, I continued digging till finally I reached our bank manager.

'Have the maggots got there yet?' The Widow asked.

'No.'

'Is it flooded?'

'No, but look at the water gathering.' Without much ado, I retrieved our loot, replacing the earth so that the cat burglars wouldn't notice the disturbance.

'I'm so pleased that the money is okay,' said the Widow, pushing all the loot into her bag.

'Not only is it okay, but we've made a profit thanks to investing it with our bank manager friend. If that's his performance when dead, he must've been shit-hot when alive.'

'Where can we take this lot then?'

'I know, we'll seal it in small waterproof bundles, and rebury it with Mrs McCann.'

'Who the hell is she?'

'An old lady on the cold slab, about to be buried the day after next. Used to work for The Samaritans.'

'Good,' whispered The Widow, 'our wee problem will be in safe hands then.'

The journey through the dark streets was not without danger. At every footstep, every passing car, we trembled, fearful it was Slates and Sally. Eventually we parted. I took the money and jewellery, and The Widow took the other packages to suss out if they were worth anything. I warned her to be careful.

Morty snored loudly, as I slipped into bed, having tucked the loot into Mrs McCann's knickers. Tomorrow I'd seal them in waterproof packets. It seemed as though I'd only had forty winks when a loud banging roused us. As I opened the door, the voice of Sally boomed loud.

'Here's the first homer for you,' he said, dragging an unconscious man into the basement.

'What, who is it?' asked Morty.

'No questions, no answers,' said Sally, heaving the body on to the cold slab. 'That, I tell you, was hard fucking work, get the tea on cunt,' he snarled at me. 'That's one fucker who'll not be spending our money.'

'How do you know he did it?' asked Morty.

'How do you know he didn't?' Sally retorted.

Nervously, I spilled the hot water over the table, trying to keep myself together.

'It's the law of the jungle,' said Morty.

'Law of the jungle, what about her then . . .' Sally laughed, pointing to Mrs McCann.

'Died of natural causes, as most decent people do,' replied Morty.

Sally leaned over and pinched her cheek between thumb and forefinger. 'The law of the jungle is life itself. What difference does it make if you go her way, or his?'

Trembling, I handed Sally his tea.

'Well, she led a good and useful life, helping her fellow citizens,' said Morty.

'And it did her no good whatsoever. She's as dead as he is; good, bad or indifferent. Ah well, there's better things to do. As for him, don't give him a minute's thought. You see, even if he isn't the culprit, his death'll give the real thieves something to think about. Don't worry, this nose'll

sniff the money out sooner or later,' he said before walking
out of the door.

I was faint with fright as Morty hurried to lock it behind
him. 'Hurry, give me a hand,' he urged.

'Why, what's the matter?'

'This man isn't dead.' He undid the man's bloody shirt.

I watched him wipe the dried blood from the man's face.
Sure enough, he was breathing. Using a pair of tweezers,
he lifted off a small piece of metal imbedded in the man's
forehead, the brand name SONY. Morty set about reviving
the man, ordering me to make strong tea with plenty of
sugar. He turned out to be an unlucky car thief caught
forcibly removing the transistor radio from Slates' Mini.

'Fuckin' hell, I didn't deserve this, I mean it wasn't as
though I was taking his life savings or something,' the thief
spluttered. Little did he know.

Morty and I, saturated in sweat due to all that we'd
experienced, sat wearily on the bed. 'I thought you were
brave taking Sally on in the way you did,' I told him.

'Goodness, he needs me to dispose of his dirty work, it
was the least I could do.'

'How did you get mixed up with them in the first place?'

'It's a long story son, but somewhere along the line it
made sense.'

'But you're a successful businessman, what did you ever
need the likes of them for?' I asked.

'Hero, Hero, Hero, you're like a dentist's drill, whining
away . . . These guys are like a bad virus, they get you at
that moment, when you're vulnerable. It's just that they
are opportunists . . . you know, people who take advantage
of unfortunate circumstances. It's second nature; think of
a vulture swirling in the sky, just waiting, knowing that
soon some creature will come by, weakened by some incident, and then they'll swoop.' He shook his head.

'What're you saying, these guys are vultures?' I asked.

'No, they're worse than that. You see, we're supposed to have intelligence, to be the conscience of all life but, as you witnessed tonight, we've failed miserably.'

'But surely that's what you were doing tonight, telling him that Mrs McCann was a decent person, and that he wasn't?'

'Oh, come off it, the truth is, that was pathetic. You don't deal in my business without knowing about right and wrong, life and death. These guys, in their own eyes, have made it, they're successful. Fuck, they've clawed their way up the ladder, doing anything to get there. Therefore they'll do anything to prevent it being taken from them, why shouldn't they? They see no difference between me and them. Truth is, I scraped and strived to make this a successful business, bringing it through the bad times and the good times. Once or twice I cut corners to get a new hearse or a back-hander here or there.'

'Like what you do with Philip, in the mortuary?' I asked, interrupting him.

'That sort of thing . . . it's what I call, the Faustian drip, a little bit here, a little bit there, its accumulative effect gradual, once it's done, there's no turning back.'

'You're losing me, what's that?'

'It's not a what, it's a who. Dr Faustus did a deal with the devil for a better life but it all came to a sad end. Most of us who succumb to those same temptations tend to delude ourselves, just like Faustus, the only difference being, we do it bit by bit. In my case, it was the burial game. Not that people ever stopped dying, mind you. But more people competed to bury them. Put simply, I bought Peter to pay Paul. Bugger it, why not! But do you know something, Hero, I've become a slave to it, that's why someone like that brute can barge in carrying a body whenever he likes. That's life, I suppose, but I'm just not enjoying it anymore. I know I've built up a good reputation, just as I know people think I'm a crank for keeping Charlie up there in a jar. Truth is, he reminds me of, well, the past, when there was sweetness and light.' He looked dreamily into the distance.

'I know what you mean, I used to dream of it all the time,' I said.

'Hero, we've only known each other a short time, but I've lived long enough to know a real person when I meet one. If you stick in at this business, I'll give it to you, lock, stock and barrel. I can then live my life out at the seaside, where the air is a lot cleaner . . .'

'Hmm, well, I don't want to sound ungrateful, but soon I hope to be moving on with my girlfriend. We want outta here, away from all this.'

'Son, let me tell you something. In the early days when building this business up, I had the contract for disposals at The Institution. I lifted more broken bodies from that place than anywhere else; another example of my Faustian drip, a time when sealed lips equalled a full purse. The poor souls kept there reminded me of pet mice in a maze. I could see it in their eyes, in their body language; always they were looking for a way out, but under the control of their masters. It was nigh on impossible. If you intend getting out, then do so, but don't delude yourself only to find you're a mouse in a maze,' he warned.

Mrs McCann's burial went according to plan, once again the money going down into the earth for safekeeping. This having been secured, gave us much needed breathing space. The Widow brought further good news. Laser Cohen had identified the old man in the photographs having sex with the young girl as the Lord Chief Justice. A stern, sombre man, he was apparently fond of capturing the moral high ground when debating with opponents. The girl, it so happened, was under age. The Widow asked Laser to do a deal of some kind, perhaps obtaining the release of Warthog and Skelly. A small price to pay, she was sure that Laser would pull it off. As for the book of names, they could see no immediate use, everyone knew the cops and politicians were corrupt; Laser would, however, put it in safekeeping for the future. In our desperation to get away from Slates and Sally, we asked The Widow to get advice from Ruth Oliver on what we should do with the money. Her view was that a small amount could be used to buy a property, the remainder to be invested to bring in income for us to live on. Indeed, Ruth was considering selling some disused, but habitable, property on her farm. She would explore the possibilities. Suddenly, a new horizon had appeared, one that until now had eluded us. The Widow returned from her meeting ecstatic, throwing herself upon me.

'Oh Hero, it's all gonna happen. At long last we'll be away . . . Just imagine us and the bull living on a farm.'

I couldn't shrug off Morty's image of us as mice in a maze. The Widow and I agreed that in taking up Ruth's offer, we should plan to leave as a group: Bonecrusher, Lockjaw, Sligo, Gloria and the McCoys. If it was a go'er, then we'd have to keep it all hush hush for fear of the gruesome twosome finding out. Hesitantly, I put to her the idea that, if we could pull it off, we should offer a place to Morty. After all I liked him.

'But can he be trusted?' she asked. 'He has, after all, done business with Slates.'

'They've had a gun to his head but I'm positive he can be.'

'Then do what you think best,' she advised.

I could feel a momentum gathering at the prospect of

our departure. But this was brought to a grinding halt when the inevitable happened. Bonecrusher flipped his lid. Sligo filled me in. It was early Friday morning when Sally arrived with the pay packets, giving the midget and Sligo one pound each, throwing in his usual snide comment, 'Don't spend it all in the one shop.' As usual, Bonecrusher retreated to his spindly chair outside the freezers. Then suddenly, in the middle of scrubbing a freezer, he stopped, and walked towards the slouching Sally.

'Betcha a bundle, I can snap in two the thickest bone on earth.'

Sally stared coldly, recognising something was amiss. 'A bundle, what would you call a bundle – a pound?'

'No, a real bundle, enough to choke a great big bull, the sort that goes missing, geddit?' Bonecrusher wiped the smirk from Sally's face.

Sally looked around, to see if anyone had noticed him being challenged, before attempting to rise. As he was about to, Bonecrusher brought his lethal forehead crashing down on to Sally's shin. The crack resounded around the Abattoir, attracting everyone's attention. The big man collapsed with a scream, the chair splintering under him. One thing for sure, no one but no one cries like that just for the fun of it.

The Killers standing nearest threw themselves on the midget, burying him under a heap of bodies. The manager, seeing the mayhem, immediately called the police. Although writhing in acute pain, Sally had pulled a huge meat cleaver from the bench and was now screaming at the Killers, 'Get the fucker over here till I chop him into bits.' Sligo said that never in his life was he so pleased to see a policeman. It turned out to be none other than Sgt. Bland. Bonecrusher was hustled into a Black Maria, and locked into a small cubicle. While the injured Sally was being carted off on a stretcher, Bonecrusher crashed his head through the door panel of the police van. 'I want some pig's balls!' he demanded, his head protruding from the door. The army of police re-entered the van which then sped off.

An ominous silence descended on us; if, at that moment, we could have willed him out, he would've been with us. The task of liberating him would be formidable. But now we had friends like Ruth Oliver, who would immediately move in to represent him.

'I'm afraid there is little chance of preventing him being sent back to The Institution,' explained Ruth quietly.

'Fuck, if that's the case, can we get Laser to do a deal for him with the photographs?' I asked.

'It depends ... these people are funny; at least that's what Laser thinks. You've got to tread carefully, it's not like trading stamps. Someone in the position of The Lord Chief Justice will carefully weigh up the pros and cons before committing himself one way or the other. You see even when you think you've got them bang to rights, these people still find a way of turning it around. They just don't give an inch, it's down to their breeding and education, I suppose,' Ruth explained. 'Show no emotion, give no quarter.'

'We could get him a decent psychiatrist who will give him a favourable report,' said The Widow.

'How do we do that?' I asked.

'We'd have to pay for it. But keep in mind that he is up on a serious charge,' said Ruth.

'Ruth, there is no danger of Sally hopping into that court to give evidence against Bonecrusher,' said The Widow. 'Just picture it, that giant of a man with a fearsome reputation to protect, hobbling into the court to accuse a midget, hardly big enough to reach his kneecaps. It would be hilarious, and Sally knows that. He also knows grassing is against the rules. That, more than anything, will keep him in line. The only thing on Sally's mind is ensuring Bonecrusher's release so that he can exact revenge,' said The Widow.

I found respite from Bonecrusher's predicament in talking with Morty. The fact that part of the farm was on the coastline appealed to him greatly.

'Right, I should start making it known I'm retiring, then sit back and wait for the offers,' he said.

'Who'll be interested?'

'That old skinflint Desmond Spencer, over at Hepper & Hepper, I guess.'

'Oh, I met his daughter, Cathy, she took a shine to me.'

'Did she now?'

'Could he afford to buy you out?'

'If he couldn't, I don't know who could,' he replied. 'He's a greedy man. His greed might get the better of him in wanting to buy me out. That in turn, my boy, means you spending a little more time at the mortuary.' He smiled, winking knowingly at me.

Cathy, of course, was delighted to see me again. To please her I agreed to open up a dead body. The flesh was cold and hard but surprisingly I didn't baulk as I had previously thought I would.

On her instruction, I peeled back the layers of skin as one would pages of a damp book.

'The thing is Hero, I've had this one for almost a year now and he's taught me many fine lessons. It's much better though when you move on to the limbs. If you make a mistake on one you can move onto the other,' she said, matter-of-factly. Taking a sharp-toothed bone saw, she began to remove the corpse's left leg. 'I know this isn't allowed but I think I'll take this for some homework tonight.'

At her invitation I agreed to visit her parlour, much to the joy of Morty. In actual fact, it wasn't as grand as ours, being located in a seedy back street. On arriving, I descended the basement stairs, first surreptitiously peering through the window before knocking. Desmond Spencer, a small rotund man, sat still at the table with his eyes closed, giving a good impression of being dead. Not one movement or breath did he make. There was a long pause after my initial knock on the door. Perhaps he has passed away, I thought, but then the door opened. After the briefest of introductions, Mr Spencer whispered, 'Come in,' his voice barely audible. Squinting his eyes, he scrutinised me critically, before letting out a deep sigh. Pointing a pudgy finger at a chair, he indicated that I should sit, before approaching the dresser to pour himself a tumblerful of whisky. Throwing the liquid down his throat with a loud gargle, his body convulsed in a spirited shiver. Returning to sit opposite me, he closed his eyes like a Buddha in meditation.

We sat like this for a full ten minutes. Finally, Cathy entered the room, dressed in a shroud-white dress. Her father opened his eyes, smiling approvingly.

'Has Dad been entertaining you?' she said, kissing her father lovingly on the cheek. Coyly, she beckoned me to their 'working chambers' as she called it. What they lacked in grandeur, they made up with business; bodies were everywhere, sometimes two to a slab. Cathy danced around them, pulling off sheet after sheet to reveal a series of ghastly faces and contorted bodies, pock-marked and ravaged by life's wicked excesses.

'Aren't they sweet?' she said smiling sadly. Looking up at me, her eyes suddenly turned steely. 'Hero, are you intending to remain in the job when the new owners take over?'

'Goodness Cathy, how do I know that when . . . when the new owners may not want me.'

'We would . . . I just know they'd be a fool not to; who could possibly leave out someone with your talent?'

'She is a fruitcake, if ever there was one,' I said to The Widow, giving her an account of my visit to Hepper & Hepper.

'A bit dipsy maybe,' suggested The Widow. 'Obviously she's a shy girl who lacks confidence.'

'What d'you mean?'

'That's why she gets on with the dead so well. You're probably the first live person she's had a relationship with, and last night she wanted to share her friends with you. It's not unusual you know; it is the sort of thing people do, invite you around for tea to meet their pals.'

'You're having me on, surely.'

She wasn't. 'Hero, you lack a certain empathy, when it comes to others. Imagine it, brought up with a miserable old bastard as a father, probably denied any toys, living in a house constantly filled with dead bodies. I bet when there was a dead baby there she'd go and play dolls with it. I can see her plain as day, changing nappies, probably fart'n and flushing the poor thing till its insides fell out.'

'You don't think so, do you?' I asked incredulously.

'I bloody well do. Nothing surprises me, under the guise of parenthood.'

'I know what you mean, it's something that's been twisting my head for a long time. Since I got out of The Institution, I've never met one person who is normal . . . D'you know what I mean, just an ordinary person. Sure I've met people, and initially it's been fine, and just when

I think they're nice, they show another side of themselves, reveal some bizarre or weird habit.'

'What d'you mean?' The Widow asked.

'Well, some of the things people get up to,' I said.

'Who, and what things?' she persisted.

'Aw Christ, where do I start? There's Morty and his wee brother in the jar, Gloria not being what she seemed.'

'Hero, you've been away for a while so you have an excuse, but ask yourself this, what harm are they doing?'

'Okay then, Shuffles shagging a dead body. What about that?'

'It's only dead meat.' She shrugged. 'What's the difference between the abuse there and that in the Abattoir?'

'Fucking hell, one's a human being, the other's a dead sheep.'

'*Was* a human being but, anyway, one man's meat's another man's poison.'

'But it's against the law.'

'Oh, talking about the law, Ruth did get a psychiatrist for Bonecrusher, so fingers crossed.' She pushed herself closer to me.

'We need to get him out of there,' I whispered.

'We all need to get out of here, I'm frightened now that Bull's on the loose. Hero, why can't we just take off?' she asked.

'Don't let him dictate the pace,' I warned, surprised at my own coolness.

'It's not only him I'm worried about, it's Lockjaw, he's always on a short fuse, particularly when Bull's in the picture.'

It was the first time she'd ever sounded vulnerable. I held her tight.

The Underworld

Sealing lips tight had become my speciality; a strand of knotted cat-gut at the end of a needle, a deft figure of eight through the upper and lower lips followed by a firm tug, closed forever. The only time in life when one can say with certainty that something is forever. These lips will never utter another word. This face, its stillness, its silence, permanent. A young man with slick black hair, teenage years barely begun, his body gangly but well-formed, taken before his time. For this kid, one pill too many, popped when the feeling was good, put out his lights – permanently. Morbid as it may be, this job focuses the mind on the meaning of life. Morty sees himself as a simple servant, disposing of packages now emptied of their contents. I want to know where this young guy's smile has gone, his voice, personality, the movements, his breathing life. Sometimes, like this youngster, it feels as though they've nodded off for a few minutes. I often think how wonderful it'd be if the person opened his eyes, smiled, got dressed and walked out. Imagine the sad, mourning faces of relatives and friends changing instantly as he walked through the door.

'If only I had a camera to catch that look,' laughed Morty, rousing me from the daydream.

'Just a boy . . . what a shame,' I said.

The sound of the door being kicked open brought us to

an abrupt halt. Sally came hurtling through the opening in his wheelchair quickly followed by Slates. Sally, his face purple with rage, pointed at me. 'That fucking, bastarding stump of a midget with his cannon-ball head is going to get ripped apart into tiny fucking pieces when I get a fucking hold of him, and you, imbecile, tell the little arsehole that I'm going to do it personally with my bare hands.' He gesticulated with his huge fists, emphasising just how effective he would be. He brought this brief cameo to a violent end by swinging a fist into the dead head of a client lying on a nearby slab.

'Calm down boys, calm down now,' said Morty, holding out his hand.

Slates swiftly about-turned, wheeling the chair back into the street, and they were gone as suddenly as they had appeared.

'Why did he do that?' I asked.

'Just be thankful it wasn't you,' answered Morty.

Inspector Bull had been released from hospital, the doctor having diagnosed mild amnesia as a result of concussion. This meant he couldn't return to work. His amnesia story was simply a ruse, concocted by Bull himself. He'd be the laughing stock of the police force, if it became known he'd been done over by a baby in a pram! Truth was, Bull didn't leave the hospital the same man who entered. It was as though the incident had pushed him over the edge. The knowledge that his personality had become more volatile spurred us on to pressure Ruth Oliver for a date when we could move into the farm. There was also the question of Bonecrusher and obtaining information on his appearance in court. With Slates, Sally, and now Inspector Bull, rampaging on the loose, we were living on the edge. The nutty cop was a particularly nasty piece of work. Known for his unconventional methods, his superiors tended to sideline him to the lesser crimes, such as illegal gambling, back street fist fights, or bull rustling. Now Bull was a loose cannon, patrolling the streets seeking revenge. Rumour had it that the ever-alert Lockjaw was stalking Bull, waiting for the right moment to pick him off. This in turn made The Widow extremely nervous. Although The Widow and I were close, she never talked much about her brother, nor did I probe. It was said that he bent nails with his teeth. He was someone not to be messed with. The street gossip about these two protagonists revealed a diversity of perception regarding their original clash. Bull, it seems, took the view that, by losing part of one finger, including his wedding ring, he had been hard done by. What really added insult to injury was the idea that anyone would challenge his authority in the first place. Lockjaw, on the other hand, had never forgiven himself for not savaging Bull in entirety. Had it not been for a cluster of bat-wielding cops coming to the rescue, he would have bitten the detective's face off. Still, there was always the next time.

Being with The Widow overnight was a great release from all the tension and nerves. I returned to the parlour one morning after being with her to find Morty in animated conversation with two well-dressed men whose taut, pugilistic faces had seen better days. They stood motionless before him, their bodies fluid, in that confident, boxer style. Morty was in a high-pitched state of excitement, the very opposite of his usual, calm demeanour. Catching sight of me, he motioned that I should disappear.

No sooner had I done so, when Shuffles followed breathing hard, carrying a smart black suit, white shirt and black tie. 'Put these on quick . . . hurry!'

As I re-entered the basement, Morty excused himself to

scrutinise me, tucking in my shirt collar, straightening my elasticated tie.

'I'll be back in a minute,' he waved to the men, vanishing behind his curtain. The taller of the two walked to a nearby slab and pulled the sheet from the head. His huge hands grabbed the chin, moving it to one side, then to the other. His fingers flipped open an eyelid, before closing it again. Tugging at the lips, he attempted to part them.

'Why won't this guy's mouth open?' he asked me.

'We seal their mouths shut, when they die that is,' I stammered.

'Good idea, trust nobody.'

We left the parlour and followed their smart car in the hearse with Morty driving.

'What's going on?' I asked.

'Joe Sylvester died early this morning.'

'Joe Sylvester, my God!'

Joe Sylvester is a very important man around here. He used to be a boxer way back, and his son Tony won a championship, then they went into business down at the docks. Well, old Joe runs the place. Everybody does what the Sylvesters ask, or else.

'The highways of this country are paved with people who refused to obey them, which is a pity when you consider the amount of business I lost,' said Morty. 'But, it's indicative of how seriously they treat their line of work, so keep that in mind. I intend to pull out all stops on this job, and you'll assist me all the way. Just do everything I tell you, nothing more, nothing less. They are known to be very generous to those who serve them well.'

We turned into a sweeping driveway leading to an enormous house. Following the two men, we entered a spacious hallway, where we were told to sit. Four other men, similarly dressed, with well-punched faces, lounged on chairs.

Two double doors opposite lay ajar. Inside, a man sat at a desk, talking loudly into the phone.

'How many containers . . . how much? Piss off, tell the fucker it's my old man that died not me. The price is high because I said so . . . tell the scumbag that . . . yes, well get back to me on it.' He slammed down the phone. 'Bring them in,' he ordered.

We were ushered into the room.

'Right gentlemen, I've heard that you're the best in the business, and I want only the best for my old man. Sit down and I'll put you in the picture, so that you will be able to make the best of a sad occasion. That way, there will be no fuck-ups. The old man left clear instructions about his funeral and I want you to follow them to the letter. During these final preparations I want, at all times, for you to treat him with the dignity he deserves. I've already done some research into all this, so will start with the don't do's. I don't want you plugging anything up his arse. My old man's never had it up his arse in his life, so it's not gonna start now. My old man loved a good joke, enjoyed telling a good story, so leave his mouth unsealed, as he'll want to crack a few wherever he ends up. He was a good chanter, especially the opera, great voice he had. His eyes are to be left open, so he can see where he's going. Did you get all of that?' he asked.

'Mr Sylvester, it will be the high point of my long career to follow your wishes to the utmost,' said Morty, in his most reassuring tone.

'Good, meet my father's personal assistant, Victor Russo, who will accompany you from start to finish. Victor, meet these two gentlemen,' he said, waving a tall dark man into the room.

Victor Russo stepped forward, dressed in the by-now-familiar style, with a face so badly scarred it was like a map of the city. He shook our hands in a friendly manner.

'Victor's parents came from Italy, here we call him the pally'taly, and pally he is too. Right Victor?' said Tony.

'Yep, that's me,' he winked at Tony.

'One other thing, Victor will select the music as he knows the old man's taste. Anything you need, any problems, he'll sort it out. I want no expense spared. Just get it right.'

Victor stepped forward. 'Tony, we need to get the old lady out,' he said quietly.

'Fuck, is she still in there crying over him?'

''Fraid so . . . it's pretty delicate, you know.'

'What am I gonna do? She fucking cried over him so much those two days before he went, I'm pretty certain she drowned him.'

'Hmm, if I could interrupt, Mr Sylvester,' said Morty, stepping forward. 'May I suggest you let me sort it out? Part of my job is dealing with distressed widows.'

The relief on the men's faces was a sight to see. 'I told you he was the best, didn't I,' boasted Tony.

Victor led us to Joe Sylvester's bedroom where the grieving widow lay prostrate on top of him. Sure enough, the old guy was covered in her tears. Morty led her out quietly, much to the admiring glances of Victor Russo.

He restored Joe to his former youthful self. Victor approached to have a look. A tear came to his eyes as he muttered, 'Just like the old days.'

My heart was thumping with pride, witnessing Morty's finest hour. Throughout the day we worked. The one break we took was for him to visit the florist's in order to supervise the floral arrangement. He instructed me to return to the funeral parlour for some white sheets. My cautionary manoeuvring to avoid Slates and Sally paid dividends as I approached. On the way out I peeped into the street. They were both loitering at the nearby corner like vultures scanning the horizon, searching for a victim, Slates' hands gripping firmly the handles of the wheelchair; Sally holding onto the sides in preparation for sudden action, his plastered leg protruding like a cannon on the turret of a tank. Both of them still seemed poised between a nervous breakdown, or committing mass murder. Perhaps both. It was obvious that they were both at their wits' end, trying to identify who was responsible, and wouldn't rest till they did. The more time that passed, the more frantic they became, knowing they were less likely to recover their money. A prospect too awful for them to contemplate. Although I was to blame for their present state of mind I, strangely enough, felt a twinge of sorrow for them. It lasted barely two seconds while I took evasive action by exiting through the backcourts.

On approaching my destination with my arms full of white linen, I started to whistle a tune when suddenly a loud bang erupted in my head. All I remember is a fog clearing, and me lying on my back, looking up to the stars. Suddenly, the face of Slates, then Sally, peered down at me.

'You piece of shit, tell the midget we're gonna stretch him in two,' snarled Sally, as Slates rolled the wheelchair backwards and forwards over the sheets strewn on the ground.

'Ha, ha, ha, ha,' came their manic laughter, as they took off along the street.

Sitting up, I touched my face. The pain was excruciating. Gathering the badly soiled sheets from the street, I weaved my way dizzily back to the Sylvester house. As I staggered into the bedroom, Morty, looking startled, stepped back from old Joe.

'What on earth happened?' he asked. I shrugged.

Victor walked over, taking hold of my chin to inspect the damage. 'Who did this?' he asked.

'I fell,' I replied, looking at Morty helplessly.

Victor turned to him. 'I'm leaving this room for a sip of water. I want the name when I return.'

He returned shortly afterwards, accompanied by one of our earlier escorts.

'Slates Rafferty and his friend,' said Morty.

Victor nodded curtly. 'Can you tidy his face up for the occasion?' he asked Morty.

'Yes,' Morty replied confidently.

'Fine then.' He turned to his companion. 'Get Docherty to sort him out, that suit's ruined,' he ordered. I was whisked off to the tailor, who hurriedly took my measurements before returning me to Morty, who was now in the library. What he had done with it in such a short time was extraordinary. The new white sheets, the floral arrangements, the seating and coffin table, was all of a piece. Add to this the mournful, classical music that was playing, and you had a man's death elevated to God-like status. It had to be seen to be believed. The coffin bearing Joe Sylvester was finally brought in to be placed in position. Morty, perfectionist that he is, then tended to the last minute details.

Tony invited us back to his office to run through the final details.

'The day after tomorrow is the burial, which means he has two nights here. First, you have to make available someone for the constant vigil. Second, we designate tonight as Reparation Night; it's given over to those who want to visit my father, to ensure he's not carrying any ill-will on his final journey. The last night, tomorrow, is Farewell Night, for those nearest and dearest to contribute gifts for the after-life enabling him to make his final journey in the style to which he was accustomed. Do you understand what I am saying?' he enquired.

'I do Mr Sylvester, I do indeed. May I, with your permission, volunteer my colleague here, Hero, for the vigil; I do know he will accept this duty with full honours,' suggested Morty.

'Hero, that's a fitting name. My old man would've liked that, a nice little touch. A Hero at his vigil. Now, this man Shuffles, I hear he's something special, so I want him to lead the way from the house to the grave.'

Reparation Night began quietly enough. Tony entered with his mother holding on to his arm, looking more composed. They were followed by a long stream of confessional wrong doers who entered, each one admitting to anything, from a lie to a dirty stroke. I couldn't believe my ears, and yet there was something touching about absolving past transgressions, thus enabling the deceased to travel with a lightened load. I was staggered when, last but not least, Slates entered, followed by Sally, hobbling precariously.

'Mr Sylvester, I apologise profusely for desecrating your passing by doing what I did. I've come here today to seek your forgiveness,' fawned Slates, a petrified look on his face. Sally made a similarly grovelling statement, though he was having problems maintaining his balance throughout.

After they left, Tony, seated nearby, leaned across and whispered to one of his minions. 'Those guys seem to enjoy playing in wheelchairs. Make sure they get one each.'

The man nodded, then slipped out of the room.

Farewell Night saw women join the male contingent to say goodbye. Each of them approached to touch the body, the men placing sealed, often bulky envelopes into the coffin, the women a neatly folded written note. Tony made a final farewell to his father early next morning, after which Morty and I set about sealing the coffin. While doing so, I noticed one of the many envelopes torn, revealing bank notes. I glanced at Morty, who gave no hint of having seen the cash. Old Joe was being sent off with his fortune, no doubt to bribe his way into heaven. Right to the end there was no wavering in their belief that 'everyone has a price'.

A thick haar covered the Shore as I walked along the quay, my footsteps echoing around the open warehouses, causing pigeons to flutter and coo. The Widow, recognising my steps, let out a long wolf whistle. 'Am I glad to see you!' she called, her faint outline shivering against the wall.

'Any word yet?' I asked.

'Ruth Oliver's meeting us at Eve's Bar tonight to give us an update on Bonecrusher,' she explained.

'I'll join you,' said Gloria coming over, 'let's call it a night.'

Spontaneously, The Widow and I took hands, as the three of us walked along the quay.

'Hero, what'll happen if Bonecrusher gets sent back to The Institution?' asked Gloria.

'It would kill him, but let's hear what Ruth has to say.'

As usual, Eve's place was packed to the gunnels, the punters welded together by dry land and booze.

'Hey, you look very formal,' shouted Gloria over the noise to Ruth, now pushing her way through the throng.

'I've been working late,' she shrugged, squeezing into the seat.

'What's the news?' I asked.

'Surprisingly good. His behaviour has been, let's say calm, and quite communicative. I chatted informally to one of the hospital staff. He said he's the best on the ward. Truth is, that wouldn't be difficult given the crowd that's in there. The other two are driving everyone up the wall,' she sighed.

'Warthog and Skelly?' I said.

'Yes, the ward is now filthy and smelly. They sleep on the floor, shit on the floor, and eat off the floor. They've got everyone into a new game, called Passing Through. They have a race after mealtimes to see whose lunch is first to come out of their arse, and I gather there are all sorts of arguments, when they're checking the contents, to verify authenticity.'

'I'm amazed Bonecrusher's doing so well, what's the secret?' I asked.

'Well, it's possibly down to the medication he's getting.'

'Oh, oh, they've not got him on the heavy gear surely?' I said.

'No, no, not at all. I've a friend, a doctor who prescribed me mild sedatives that should keep him in good nick. The psychiatrist interviewed him today. I expect the report to be on my desk at the end of the week.'

'Any idea how it'll go?' asked The Widow.

'We're paying for it; if it's a bad one we'll tear it up and start again.'

'If he is lucky and gets out, Slates and Sally will be waiting,' warned The Widow.

'I know but I guess the way things are going, we should be about ready to move anyway,' I said.

'Okay, next week it is then,' I said, feeling strong and determined.

That very next day, Morty was expecting Desmond and Cathy Spencer, from Hepper & Hepper. I could see Morty was nervous. The big man paced the parlour, inspecting every nook and cranny, knowing that his rival would give microscopic attention to the finest detail. He was that sort of fellow. Just prior to their arrival, he handed me a filthy bundle of crumpled clothes.

'Put them on please. Just for me, Hero,' he requested.

On entering and catching sight of me, Cathy tightly clasped her hands, a look of shock on her face.

'You! Malingering sod, get a bucket and clean that filthy floor,' yelled Morty to me angrily, turning to Desmond. 'Difficult to get reasonable staff nowadays. I'll make sure he's replaced before the new owner takes over.'

Cathy grabbed her father's arm. 'Daddy please!' she moaned.

'I do think the question of staff and discipline would be a matter for me, sir, if I decide to make an offer,' retorted Desmond brusquely. Morty knew that his action would appeal to Desmond's devotion to rigid discipline, while simultaneously setting the man up in the eyes of his beloved daughter as a knight in shining armour for rescuing her dear prince. Thinking it was one up for him, Desmond's wariness relaxed. The father and daughter soon adopted hound-dog propensities in sniffing around the premises. He counted and felt the fabric of every shroud while Cathy, rather predictably, sniffed the armpits of the recumbent clients. Meanwhile, I pretended to be hard at it, a slave to the wishes of my master.

'What's this?' asked Desmond, pointing to Charlie in the jar.

'My younger brother,' replied Morty affectionately.

Cathy, on approaching to have a look, melted at the sight of the pickled baby. 'Oh, oh Daddy, it's the most beautiful thing I've ever seen in my entire life,' she said, swaying in a sort of delirium.

Turning to Morty she asked 'May I?'

He smiled softly. 'You may, my dear.'

Stretching her hand she ever so gently lifted the jar, holding it softly to her breast. 'There, there,' she cooed, 'isn't he sweet,' she murmured, as she rocked him back and forth. It was like the Widow said, all Cathy wanted was a dead baby to play with.

'Perhaps we should have a seat,' suggested Morty, ordering me to bring some tea.

The two men proceeded to discuss the various ins and outs of the business; although there was friction around the sale price of the transaction, both of them, on a surface level, got on surprisingly well. They reminisced about the various fatal disasters each had had to deal with, with more than a hint of restrained joy. It was this common ground that brought them close to an agreement. This was cemented by the entrance of Shuffles. Cathy swooned before his eyes. It was apparent that she had a similar effect on Shuffles, as his eyes momentarily sparkled. It was a marriage made in their kind of heaven as I watched them leave the parlour together.

Once they had all gone, Morty rubbed his hands eagerly. 'Hero, let's have a celebratory dinner; a pot noodle in honour of Cathy, a Vindaloo to honour Desmond,' he said, an open hand crossing his heart in salute.

In the dead of night I went to the graveyard with Sligo to dig up the loot. I was expecting we would be met with nothing more than a hooting owl. Suddenly someone spoke from a few yards away.

'Right it's safe now. He's gone, let's do this one here.'

'Why that one? How do you know that's it?' said another voice.

'I just know, I can feel it in my bones.'

'But you've said that so many times. At this rate we'll be digging up the whole fucking graveyard.'

We listened as their footsteps moved off.

'That's the cat burglars looking for the loot we nicked from them. Be careful you don't fall down one of the holes they've dug,' I cautioned. We skirted the graves until eventually we arrived at Mrs McCann's. 'You take the first shift, and I'll do my copwatch,' I said to Sligo.

'I can't do it, Hero,' he said, agitated.

'What the hell does that mean?'

'It's bad luck.'

'Bad luck! Fuckit man, it can't get any worse.'

'Don't bet on it.'

'But the money's down there,' I said in exasperation.

'I don't care. Desecrating a grave will put a curse on me. I can't do it, I can't.'

'Alright then, you watch, I'll fucking dig,' I told him.

Recent rain had made the earth wet and heavy. Soon I was drenched with sweat and exhausted. Sligo sat calmly, listening intently for anyone coming, while I did the donkey work. I was so angry at him I kept heaving shovelfuls up in his direction. Having at last reached the coffin, I then had to clear every bit of earth in order to open it. There lay Mrs McCann, her knickers still intact. Sitting on her face I began hoisting up her skirt which, because of the wind, began blowing into my face. I was so whacked that I fell back just as lumps of soil from above fell on my head. Here I was knackered, filthy and trying to get into a dead woman's knickers. Yet, try as I might, I couldn't.

'Sligo, Sligo,' I whispered.

'What is it?' he asked.

'You'll need to come down and help me, the bundles are stuck under her arse.'

'Jesus, Mary and Joseph, I can't do it, Hero.'

'Please, please,' I implored, 'it's important if we want to get fucking away from all this.'

'Honest Hero, I can't do it, I just can't do it. I'll be cursed for the rest of my life for touching a dead woman.'

'You'll be cursed for the rest of your life if you don't,' I yelled back. Ignoring my anger, he stood up to leave, his foot slipping on the wet soil, sending him backwards, falling into the grave and bang on top of Mrs McCann's thighs. The coffin lid, now dislodged, fell on us both, making an almighty noise.

'What's that racket?' one cat burglar shouted to the other.

Placing my hand over Sligo's mouth, I stopped him screaming, sandwiched between me and the Good Samaritan.

'Please don't make a sound.' When I took my hand away, he immediately began praying: 'Hail Mary full of Grace, hallowed be thy name . . .' Still seated firmly on the face of the dead woman, I listened intently for the approaching burglars. Nothing!

'Right, help me lift her arse, it'll not take a minute,' I ordered, lifting up the coffin lid and adding, 'Now get her drawers down for fuck's sake.'

'I can't, they're stuck.'

'Right then, lift her legs high in the air and I'll do it,' I instructed. He did so, still repeating his prayers, over, and over, as I tackled her drawers. I had to rip each packet off her flesh. Sligo shot out of the grave before I could finish.

'Give me a hand, you Irish bastard!'

'I told you, I'm not Irish.'

'I don't give a shag what you are, just help me.'

By this time he was scared stiff. A combination of tiredness and wet soil meant I couldn't get out. Turning to Mrs McCann I heaved her into a sitting position with her forehead against the soil. This allowed me to stand on her shoulders to place the money on the surface then clamber out. 'A Samaritan right to the end,' I thought. I found Sligo cowering behind a nearby gravestone. Just then a car, with dimmed headlights, appeared. It was Morty, on schedule. The two cat burglars, startled, ran in our direction and fell headlong into Mrs McCann's open grave.

'Fuck, that's two full houses she's had tonight,' I muttered.

Morty drew to a halt outside Joe Sylvester's tomb. Dangling a key at me, he laughed, 'Let's see if Charon has been to collect him yet.'

'You cunning old bastard!'

He cackled with laughter. The tomb door opened with a creak straight out of a horror movie. Opening the lid, we took our time lifting the money from the envelopes, placing it into our sack and returning the empty ones to Joe. 'We've all had it up the arse at one time or another Joe, so join the club,' I said.

Replacing the lid, we made sure everything was as it should be. Morty slowly drove out through the front gate, the hearse being the perfect alibi.

'Do you think they'll check to see if the money's gone?' I asked.

'I doubt it, these guys believe that no one would dare do them over. But if they did, they'd give him a refill, proud that he's the last of the big spenders.'

Back at the parlour, we counted all the money, totalling just over one hundred and fifty grand. 'Fuck, that graveyard's better than a gold mine,' said Sligo.

'Add my nest egg to it, and you could say we're rather well off,' said Morty.

Although it was only days till our departure, we were still

living on a knife edge while some loose ends were being tied up, amongst them the bull who would finally be leaving for the farm. However, Lockjaw was another kettle of fish, being inexorably linked into a clash with Bull. This devotion to absolutism, on his part, drove me to despair.

'He is off his rocker,' said The Widow, fear in her eyes.

'I know, I know,' I said, hugging her.

'Hero, we can't let this crazy man Bull ruin everything.'

'I know, we need to be more active,' I agreed. 'I know how to get the bastard. If he's as crazy as that, let's use it against him.'

We persuaded Mrs McCoy to dress up identical to Gloria the day Bull was head-butted. Using the same old-fashioned pram, we stuffed Doe inside. Someone conveniently passed an informer some useful information, which he immediately passed to Bull. Positioning ourselves at a discreet, though ideal vantage point, we waited for the action. Mrs McCoy minced down the street, wheeling her pram. Stopping near the telephone box where Bull lay in wait, Mrs McCoy turned her back on him. He crashed out of the door, kicking the pram over, sending Doe tumbling on to the ground, and finally, pouncing on top of Mrs McCoy. Suspecting it was a mugging two passing policemen ran to help. Pinning Bull to the ground, they called for reinforcements whilst grappling with him. Bull was dragged, shouting and screaming, into a Black Maria.

'I could watch that over and over in slow motion,' said Gloria.

'Oh Hero, you are my Hero,' The Widow said excitedly and, for the first time in my life, I believed that's exactly what I was.

Mrs McCoy, having been given a check-up and sent home, arrived full of excitement.

'Guess what I've just seen? I can't believe we're so lucky,' she said.

'What are you talking about?' I asked.

'Slates and Sally, I saw them in hospital, somebody has broken both their legs now,' said Mrs McCoy gleefully.

'This is the night of the long knives!' I shouted, whooping with joy.

I stayed home that night with The Widow. On going to bed, my drift towards sleep seemed to stop just below the surface, in that restless place that is neither one thing or the other. I was troubled and unsettled, wandering into what seemed to be a turbulent space . . . it was a room, filled with ugly, black stumps, knotted with bad memories, seared and scarred by past events, almost a . . . a petrified forest, luring me . . . Help me! . . . beyond the forest shone a pale blue light, its neutral presence offering neither attraction nor repellance . . . My back, however, was to the wall, leaving me no option but to go forward, into, and through the petrified forest, in the direction of the light . . . Help me! . . . Trembling, I weaved a path between the stumps, now pulsating, like shivering abscesses straining to explode over me . . . accumulated over many tortured years they clung, like limpets, a burden beyond measure . . . Help me! . . . No succour awaited, when, finally, I reached the clearing . . . The pale blue light had a familiar deadness, an ominous hue, that served only to illuminate my old bed in the ward of The Institution . . . Obediently, I slid under the covers, pulling them up tight around my chin . . . from the corner of my eye, I caught the first signs of movement behind the opaque, office window . . . Faces, first one, then another, and another . . . men without features, men without identities, flesh pressed hard against the glass . . . Help me! . . . The handle of the door slowly turning struck fear into me . . . Deviously, and with stealth, I breeched my stash, releasing a cascade of laxatives gathering protectively next to my body . . . Help me! . . . Just then, at that very moment, a fair and gentle hand appeared, reaching in to brush away the laxatives, to shoo away the demons . . . ssshhh, she whispered, ever so softly . . . ssshhh . . . her hair fell gently on my face as her lips lightly brushed my forehead . . . kissed my eyes . . . finally resting on my lips, giving a warm, sensuous kiss . . . of life . . . Ohhh . . . It was then that I felt something stir, a long forgotten ripple of recognition . . . an absent feeling returned as her hands caressed my body . . . her fingers lingered playfully on my penis, provoking a slight prickle of the nerve ends, encouraging waves of arousal, causing me to moan a sound of deep, deep pleasure, as my penis hardened as never before. Still stroking me, she guided my body in one fluid, silky movement, so that I was between her open legs. Her dark triangle of pubic hair was black, lush and shiny, her stomach flat and firm, her breasts soft and nipples erect. Gently she eased my penis inside her. I could feel myself throbbing with life, bordering on rapture. At this moment, the physical touch became irrelevant, it was as though our bodies and all our senses melted into one, as we moved together with a harmony that finally exploded in ecstasy.

'It wasn't a dream, it wasn't a dream,' I said afterwards in amazement.

The Widow let out a warm, gurgling laugh. 'Yeah, I can assure you it wasn't a dream. That, Hero, was the real thing.' She kissed me fully and passionately on the lips. 'I always knew that when it happened, it would be like this,' she whispered, her lips touching my ear.

We lay there in silence. My thoughts turned to what my mum had given me, even though she went before her time.

My Aunt Maggie and her brown leather bag and she-devil look; my Aunt Letty with her big loom, her kleptomania and her fighting prowess. These women, all strong in their own way, had brought me to this point. And now The Widow, making a quartet of endurable strength that helped shore me up through the lean and tough years. Lying in that bed I knew we would win.

I tiptoed into the crowded courtroom for the hearing, and sat next to Ruth. In the well of the court sat Laser Cohen, defending, and nearby sat the prosecution counsel. At that moment Bonecrusher was hauled unceremoniously into the dock by two burly policemen. Once seated, he seemed to vanish, hidden by the rail around the dock. The proceedings lost no time in getting under way. These learned men, bewigged and begowned as in ancient times, what a farce! Laser Cohen swaggered to and fro, while the judge sat behind the desk looking like a sticky bun. How could anyone take this seriously? What, I wondered, was Laser wearing under his striped trousers. A pair of fishnet stockings with a red garter, or bright red crotchless panties? And the judge, was he making notes about a lewd photograph of him in a compromising position? This world was mighty strange. The disadvantage being that they had power and made judgements on ours. If only, I thought, I had a big wishing stick, what fun I'd have. Bonecrusher's medical history, minus the lobotomy of course, was hung out to dry for those of us on the benches to hear. The Prosecution was conducted by a scruffy man whose shoulders were covered in dandruff. He did however have a rich plummy voice.

'He has, your honour, a regrettable record of suicide attempts,' he murmured.

These men were masters of the cut and thrust of courtroom battle where the truth is discarded and the game is all. Watching this, I could understand why Ruth wanted out of it. For a moment I imagined I was hearing music from a pantomime and that all these were actors in character.

'We've got the bastards,' whispered Ruth.

'What . . . what did I miss?' I asked, being shaken from my dream.

'Not a lot, but I can tell from the play of events, he's out.'

'How can you tell, was something said?'

'No, I can tell from Laser's face and the play of court that a deal's been done.' She smiled.

I realised then that Sally, the missing witness, had caused the assault charge to be dropped. He was the only straight one amongst the whole shebang. His failure to appear might be so that he could destroy the midget, but there was no hidden agenda.

'Dr Olive Snider, whose care my client was under for many years, has herself added her weight to the fact that he is *compos mentis*, your honour,' Laser was saying.

'Fuck me, you're right,' I smiled. 'Never in a lifetime would I have fucking believed it. Dr Snider saying a good word about anybody. This is the fucking business,' I told her.

Without so much as a pause for thought, the judge hastily dismissed Bonecrusher, who left the court bewildered by it all.

'Hero, will you get me a puncture outfit,' were the first words he uttered. 'I'm gonna try and patch it up with my Debs.' Grabbing his arm I rushed him out.

'Who is Debs?' asked Ruth.

'It's a long story, I'll tell you another time.'

Morty and the others sat in the hearse, at the bottom of

the court steps. On seeing Bonecrusher, they gave him a cheer. Hugging Ruth, we left her, driving off in the hearse.

As we disappeared to our destination in the countryside, the beautiful scenery surrounding us was a welcome sight. Morty shook us from our dreams by putting on the brake to avoid hitting two dossers pushing an old pram along the road.

'Stop, it's Warthog and Skelly. Hey, how did you get here?' I shouted, overjoyed to see them.

'Hero, great to see you. I guess they didn't like our company. We had the time of our lives though, great fun it was, great fun,' laughed Warthog with a twinkle in his eye.

'Except for yesterday when they washed us down with a hose for our court appearance,' said Skelly, wrinkling his nose.

'Took me many years to get that dirt on, like a second skin it was, kept the cold out too,' Warthog agreed.

'But what happened, did you get any punishment?' I asked.

'Plenty of that, the food was the worst punishment of all,' said Skelly.

'No, I mean at court?'

'Well, we were blessed by the Virgin Mary herself, if you want to know,' quipped Warthog.

'You were!' exclaimed Sligo.

'Calm down Sligo, it's just a figure of speech,' teased Gloria, kissing him on the cheek.

'Her name was . . . what was her name again?' Warthog asked Skelly.

'Mmm, a psychy woman . . . Dr Snider, that's her name,' he replied.

All of us in the hearse looked at each other knowingly.

'Ah, so you lot know her as well. A saint of a lady if ever there was one,' remarked Warthog.

'She is the neighbour of the Lord Chief Justice. I did bury his wife some years ago,' said Morty knowingly.

'The jigsaw's complete,' I replied.

I invited them to join us.

'You must be joking, and give up all of this!' exclaimed Warthog, casting an arm to take in the expansive surroundings.

'Fair enough, we're off then,' I said. As we were about to drive away Warthog leaned into the car.

'What, you don't want to stay for dinner?' he asked, holding up a cage full of rats.

The Epilogue

The lamb, nestling in my arms, suckled hungrily from the bottle as I paced the kitchen floor. Rejected by its mother, I had found it crying on the dirt track outside the cottage. Giving a convincing impersonation of mother, I let out a loud 'Baaa,' hoping to encourage it inside – it worked. Poor little fucker, it looked so weak; was on its last legs with hunger and tiredness. No wonder it was now polishing off its second bottle of milk. This countryside lark being new, it left me feeling a bit out of my depth, but somewhere in my memory lurked a notion that what I was doing wasn't quite the right thing to help this little waif. Something about my body odour wiping out the mother and new-born's original bonding scent. On the other hand, when they get as weak as this little fella, the crows swoop, first plucking out the eyeballs, before devouring the rest of it. 'Hard choices, life's full of them, eh? The deed's done now, there's no turning back. I'm sure we'll figure something out, anyway you're alive and that's what matters,' I whispered, nuzzling my chin against the top of its head.

Outside the window our bull stood sniffing a cart full of newly stacked manure. He was a magnificent beast, his hide glistening in the sunlight, and he meant a great deal to all of us. Having survived slaughter at the hands of either Pig Thompson or C.P. Horn, the bull soon settled. Unlike him, the rest of us were still getting there; healing the deep wounds of the past would come with the passing of time. (It was hard to shake it all off; even now I still expect the door to burst open and see Gorky or Fat Head. The thought of it is enough to send shivers up a corpse.) In the field beyond I could see the others returning from the rabbit shoot. 'Wait till the triplets see you. I bet you'll win their hearts,' I said, teasing the bottle from between the lips of the lamb.

Mrs McCoy came rushing through the back door carrying a huge pot of soup. 'I'd better get this on or there'll be hell to pay,' she muttered, slamming the pot on to the cooker. Seeing the lamb, she came over. 'What a wee beauty,' she said stroking its head. 'I've got just the thing for her. Now, where did I put it . . . ah, the front room.' She scurried off. A few minutes later I heard her cry from next door. 'Hey . . . what do you want, who let you in?'

'The door, it was open. I'm a Jehovah's Witness going to a meeting in Gorton village. My car broke down near your driveway. Can I use your phone to call the garage?' replied a muffled, though familiar, voice that instinctively struck fear into my heart. It all happened so quickly that I was momentarily paralysed.

'You shouldn't just walk into people's houses uninvited,' said Mrs McCoy.

'Sorry, but I did knock and nobody replied . . . the door was open. But don't worry I'm not here to doorstop you,' he said, attempting a joke. That voice, I knew it so well, but shock and confusion obscured immediate identification.

'If your Jehovah's as scarce as Jesus it'll make no difference to me. In here then,' she said, pushing open the kitchen door. It was none other than the dreaded Fat Head. Stunned, I let the lamb and bottle drop to the floor. Landing at my feet, the animal stood petrified, crying amongst shards of glass, shit flowing from it, like me in relation to Fat Head and all that he represented.

A banshee scream pierced the air. 'Make a move and I'll fucking blow you to bits, you fat bastard.' It was The Widow walking determinedly towards him, a shotgun pointed at his head. 'Get on your knees you big lump of shit,' she ordered, her face white with hatred. Fat Head did as he was told, his corpulent body trembling like a jelly.

'Please don't, please . . .' he whimpered.

Placing the barrel against his forehead, she pressed his head backwards. 'I've always dreamt of this moment,' she spat.

The first thought that struck me was how odd he looked out of uniform.

'Where are the others, fuckface?' urged The Widow.

'My car . . . it broke down . . . I was on my way to a meeting. I'm a Jehovah's Witness . . . I didn't know,' he pleaded.

'You, a Jehovah's Witness, you fat lump of shit . . .'

Interrupting her, I turned to Sligo and Lockjaw. 'Get out there quick, check the place over.' They quickly disappeared only to return to say that his car had in fact broken down. 'Get it out of sight,' I ordered them. 'Right, fat arse, get moving,' I shouted to our captive. The Widow, taking the gun from his forehead, revealed two circled imprints where the barrel had been. All of us, the triplets included, shepherded him across the yard into the dairy. The huge vault-like milk cooler was the obvious place to secure him. With childlike enthusiasm I grabbed his shoulders, pushing him forcefully into the darkness, before slamming the heavy door shut, drawing the bolt to lock it. The others broke into spontaneous applause.

Then a sombre mood descended upon us. It was now

obvious that Fat Head had indeed accidentally stumbled upon us. The fact was that he had, somehow, contaminated the freshness of the place as we knew it. The Institution had again reached into our souls, almost as though it was reminding us that there was no escaping from it.

'Kill him,' said Lockjaw coldly.

'Easier said than done, me boy,' replied Sligo.

'Why is that?' asked The Widow.

'Could you kill someone?' I asked Lockjaw.

'Him and the others I could. It'd be like squashing a fly. I want my revenge.'

'What else can we do?' asked The Widow.

'Duff him up and dump him,' suggested Sligo.

'The first thing he'd do is bring the cops back here,' replied The Widow.

'I don't want to go back to The Institution, I couldn't handle it,' whispered Sligo fearfully.

'Nor I,' said Lockjaw, 'but I still want revenge for my brother.'

Nearby Mrs McCoy and her three young triplets sat at the kitchen fire oblivious to the desperate nature of our conversation. Here we had one of our hate figures, someone who had reduced our lives to abject misery and now, ironically, he was our prisoner. All the things that he and his pals had done to us, we could now do to him. The torturer was held by those whom he had tortured.

Lost in my thoughts I became aware of the clock ticking behind me. It reminded me of the one outside the sweat box and how it cracked Salacious Sam. I stood at the kitchen window looking into the yard at the triplets chasing each other. The sounds of crows cawing, cattle mewing and other farmyard noises had been music to our ears since coming here just over a year ago. The youngsters, using sticks, began to flick cow-pats at each other, a source of endless amusement for them. 'Oh fuck, why did he have to come here, of all places.' Having talked ourselves into a hole on the methods of disposing of him, we now found ourselves with not a lot to say. The Widow joined me in looking out of the window.

'Look at them, it's hard to believe that they jumped into their Ma's bed the first time they heard an owl hoot,' she said.

'Yeah, those wee tough-nuts from the city streets, now calling themselves the Cow-Pat Gang.' I looked at her face, the strain showing in her eyes. 'Why here, of all the fucking places he could've gone to?' I asked, shaking my head.

'What's for us, won't pass us,' said The Widow with a note of resignation.

'I often wonder if it's the bell tolling, summoning us back. It's as though we're not meant to live life any other way.'

'I know what you mean, it has been a bit too good to be true. The funny thing about here is that it's like being on holiday all the time.'

'Look at those kids, all of us for that matter. The colour in our cheeks, we've never looked healthier in our lives,' I said.

Putting my arm around her shoulder, I urged her towards the field.

'What are we gonna do, Hero?' she asked softly.

I shrugged, feeling guilty, part of me not wanting to see Fat Head walk away unscathed. 'We've achieved so much . . . everyone is so happy here.'

'I know, oh fuck!' she said.

It was time to sort this matter out once and for all. 'How long has he been here?'

The Widow looked at her watch. 'Three hours.' Turning

her around, I rushed her back to the main farmhouse. 'What are you gonna do?' she asked.

I assembled everyone in the front room as Lockjaw and Bonecrusher escorted Fat Head into our midst. He stood there shaking, his eyes red with tears, his pants soiled and smelly. 'Please, I didn't do anything,' he sobbed.

Walking to the fire, I slowly extracted the brass-handled poker, inspecting its white-hot point. 'Do you remember everybody here?' I asked. Looking down at the floor, he began to sob loudly. 'I said do you know people here?' He nodded his head in affirmative. 'Look at them, one by one.' He looked first at Sligo.

'It wasn't nice what you did, was it mister?' he said softly but with firm accusation in his voice.

'And me, do you remember me? Can you remember what you did, you and your big pal Gorky?' asked Bonecrusher.

'Look at him,' I shouted angrily as Fat Head tried to look away.

'And my brother, did he deserve to be killed in that way?' said Lockjaw, lifting the shotgun.

'Please, please, don't hurt me. I know it was wrong but Gorky, him and Snider . . . they were in charge . . . honest, I wouldn't have done it, but only for them.' He sank to his knees.

At that point the door burst open and Morty and Ruth entered. I put a finger to my lips signalling them to say nothing. 'Lookit him, there he is, the man responsible for heaping so much misery on us. See him as he truly is. Compare the bastard to what we have here, is it worth giving all of this up for that?' I asked, pointing to the shaking heap on the floor. Up until that point, all of them believed we were going to kill him. Their faces at first looked puzzled but suddenly, as though seeing everything anew, they looked at him differently, the anger and fury evaporating. 'There is more good in that cart full of manure out there than in this heap of shit on our carpet. Whatever him and the others did to us, we are not them and never want to be . . . and never could be,' I stated confidently. 'We are free, and this is ours, and we're not letting them take it from us.'

'What'll we do with him then?' asked Bonecrusher.

'Morty, why don't you hitch the bull up to that cart of manure, we need to escort this piece of shit off our property.'

And what a triumph it was, watching him have to climb atop. We followed them to the end of the driveway and watched him walk down the road, a picture of abject misery.

'Maybe we should build a high fence round this place,' advised Morty.

'Why should we do that, it'd be like a prison?' said Bonecrusher.

'No, far from it. It wouldn't be to keep people from escaping but to stop riffraff like him from breaking in,' Morty replied with a knowing wink.

I decided not to build a fence as Morty had suggested, because most of my life had been spent dreaming about pulling barriers down. Although past circumstances had taught me this, it was ironic that we all learnt our biggest lesson in life from our enemy – Fat Head. In deciding to let him go, we had begun the process of freeing ourselves from our past. The scars resulting from what happened to us in The Institution will take time to heal, of that there is no doubt. But, it's as though some guiding spirit, or whatever you want to call it, has said enough is enough, and exerted some justice into our lives. In the end, we chose not to behave like our tormentors and although that wasn't easy, with time having passed we now sigh with relief that we did. Whilst Fat Head returns to the hell he has created in The Institution, we begin anew in the paradise we are now creating. This has taught us that the ultimate revenge lies in making the positive decision.